Wealth
through
Leisure

D1492820

Wealth through Leisure

The Recumbent Journals of Nick Twisp II

Book XIV

Youth in Mar Vista

C.D. Payne

Front cover photo by Richard Sagrego on Upsplash.
Back cover photo by Sergei Wing on Upsplash.

"The neurotic: he is happiest when several people are in love with him, or love him. The more the better; it is like money in the bank." – Patricia Highsmith

A NOTE ON THE SERIES:
Youth in Revolt contains Books 1, 2, and 3
Revolting Youth is Book 4
Young and Revolting is Book 5
Revoltingly Young is Book 6
Son of Youth in Revolt is Book 7
Revolt at the Beach is Book 8
Licensed To Revolt is Book 9
Revolting Obsessions is Book 10
Revolting Relations is Book 11
Revolting Times is Book 12
Revolting Narcissists is Book 13
Wealth through Leisure is Book 14
Four Summers in L.A. contains Books 8-11
Cut to the Twisp contains text deleted from the post-1994 U.S. and U.K. editions of *Youth in Revolt,* plus additional short pieces.

Many thanks to my agent Jon Klane and to Till Hack for his editorial assistance.

Principal characters

The Twisps

Nick Twisp II: Our narrator. Divorced from Lucia (Luco) DeFalcc

Nick Twisp: Father of Scott Twisp and Nick Twisp II. Also father (
Nerea Lurrieta by Sheeni Saunders. Divorced from Ada Olson. M
resa (Treez) Zweez. Father of her son Teejay and daughter Edy.

Scott Twisp: Son of Nick Twisp and Ada Olson. Brother of Nick II
Chloe Ptucha. Father of Renth Twisp.

Jake Twisp: Nick's younger brother. Originally named Noel Wescc
to Lillian Twisp.

Joan Twisp: Nick's older sister.

Tyler Twisp: Joan's son and Nick's nephew. Billionaire sports team

Uma Twisp: Psychologist and wife of Tyler Twisp.

Frank C. Wyatt: Half-brother of Nick Twisp II. Son of Molly Wyatt. I
Seka Horvath. Father of Nick Twisp Wyatt.

The Saunders

Sheeni Saunders: Nick's first girlfriend (deceased).

Paul Saunders: Sheeni's older brother. Father of Veeva Saunders.

Connie Saunders: Paul's first wife and mother of Veeva Saunders.

Veeva Saunders: Sheeni's niece and long-time friend of Jake and Tyle
Divorced from Desmond Upton who writes under the name Miles Nc

Other characters

Trent Preston: Former boyfriend of Sheeni Saunders. Married to Apurv
Father (with Violet Barnes) of Azura Preston.

Azura (Zee) Preston: Daughter of Trent Preston. Divorced from Scott T

Amalda (Almy) Preston: Granddaughter of Trent Preston.

Pete Zweez: Juggler and brother of Teresa Zweez. Married to Azura Pre:

Valerie (Cal) and Harvey Haseltine: Sibling friends of Nick II.

Tiara Diamond: Actress and wife of Harvey Haseltine.

Cooper Tucker: Blind actor, married to Jackie Perlson.

Dior Perlson: Sister of Jackie Tucker.

Lauren Bedrossian: Daughter of Mary Moran and TV show producer.

Maya Chan: Actress and friend of Almy Preston.

Charlotte Caxton: Daughter of Nick Twisp's former tenant.

Brenda Blatt: Movie producer and business partner of Chloe Ptucha.

Ninian Skopa: City fire inspector and boyfriend of Valerie Haseltine.

Esmee Carstann: Friend of Valerie Haseltine.

Lefty: Boyhood pal of Nick and his current cook/housekeeper.

Fuzzy DeFalco: Boyhood pal of Nick Twisp. Father of Lucia DeFalco.

Montel E. Sherman: Stepbrother of Nick Twisp II.

Roland Pacalac: TV and film director.

Principal characters

The Twisps

Nick Twisp II: Our narrator. Divorced from Lucia (Luco) DeFalco.

Nick Twisp: Father of Scott Twisp and Nick Twisp II. Also father of Miren and Nerea Lurrieta by Sheeni Saunders. Divorced from Ada Olson. Married to Teresa (Treez) Zweez. Father of her son Teejay and daughter Edy.

Scott Twisp: Son of Nick Twisp and Ada Olson. Brother of Nick II. Married to Chloe Ptucha. Father of Renth Twisp.

Jake Twisp: Nick's younger brother. Originally named Noel Wescott. Married to Lillian Twisp.

Joan Twisp: Nick's older sister.

Tyler Twisp: Joan's son and Nick's nephew. Billionaire sports team owner.

Uma Twisp: Psychologist and wife of Tyler Twisp.

Frank C. Wyatt: Half-brother of Nick Twisp II. Son of Molly Wyatt. Married to Seka Horvath. Father of Nick Twisp Wyatt.

The Saunders

Sheeni Saunders: Nick's first girlfriend (deceased).

Paul Saunders: Sheeni's older brother. Father of Veeva Saunders.

Connie Saunders: Paul's first wife and mother of Veeva Saunders.

Veeva Saunders: Sheeni's niece and long-time friend of Jake and Tyler Twisp. Divorced from Desmond Upton who writes under the name Miles North.

Other characters

Trent Preston: Former boyfriend of Sheeni Saunders. Married to Apurva Joshi. Father (with Violet Barnes) of Azura Preston.

Azura (Zee) Preston: Daughter of Trent Preston. Divorced from Scott Twisp.

Amalda (Almy) Preston: Granddaughter of Trent Preston.

Pete Zweez: Juggler and brother of Teresa Zweez. Married to Azura Preston.

Valerie (Cal) and Harvey Haseltine: Sibling friends of Nick II.

Tiara Diamond: Actress and wife of Harvey Haseltine.

Cooper Tucker: Blind actor, married to Jackie Perlson.

Dior Perlson: Sister of Jackie Tucker.

Lauren Bedrossian: Daughter of Mary Moran and TV show producer.

Maya Chan: Actress and friend of Almy Preston.

Charlotte Caxton: Daughter of Nick Twisp's former tenant.

Brenda Blatt: Movie producer and business partner of Chloe Ptucha.

Ninian Skopa: City fire inspector and boyfriend of Valerie Haseltine.

Esmee Carstann: Friend of Valerie Haseltine.

Lefty: Boyhood pal of Nick and his current cook/housekeeper.

Fuzzy DeFalco: Boyhood pal of Nick Twisp. Father of Lucia DeFalco.

Montel E. Sherman: Stepbrother of Nick Twisp II.

Roland Pacalac: TV and film director.

MAY

MONDAY, May 23 – I'm back. Actually I got back last week, but was too jet-lagged to function. In traveling from U.K. to Los Angeles one hurtles across *eight* time zones. Very enfeebling to the human brain.

So where am I? Back (temporarily I hope) in my dad's in-law unit in Santa Monica. This time paying actual cash rent ($850 per month). Meanwhile down the block my ex-wife is cohabitating with her loving BF Cliff Swandon in his rented shackette. While across the street our former home is now occupied by Sligger and Richmond Shapcott.

Sligger's a professional skateboarder and she's a nurse. I'd certainly want to be married to someone in the medical profession if I did that for a living. Unfortunately, they're parking *both* of their cars plus his van out on the street. I'm told their single-car garage is crammed with his valuable collection of rare skateboards.

So far they don't seem to hate us for selling them our vastly overpriced midget house. But if I come out some morning and find all my tires slashed, I'll know who to confront.

We got multiple offers and our house sold right away. No inspections, no contingencies. After all the fees and commissions, my share came to about $316,000. Too bad a chunk of that got swept away in capital gains taxes.

Buying that house from Connie Saunders was the one smart thing I've done in my life. Marrying Lucia DeFalco was less brainy, but it seemed like a good idea at the time. Last year she decided I was a raging narcissist who was making her life hell in a hamster wheel. We did our own no-fuss quickie divorce as I was leaving for England.

Since I've been back, we have waved to each other twice on the street, but haven't stopped to chat. I'm fine if that remains the extent of our intercourse. Naturally, she's still bosom pals with Treez, Dad's latest (and mostly best) wife.

Speaking of which, Treez had her third (and final, Dad sincerely hopes) baby in February. They named her Marilyn after the kid's grandmother, who died of Covid in January. She was vaccinated, but the bug still got her. No, I didn't make it back for the funeral. I liked Treez's mother, but our shooting schedule had gotten totally messed up from the Omicron variant, so I had to stay put in Leeds. More on that as it dribbles out.

I can now legally hang out in bars. Yeah, I turned 21 in England; the cast of our show ("Over the Monastery Wall") threw a party for me. Too bad I never developed a taste for alcohol, especially beer (yuck). Hanging out with Brits, I was impressed by the speed with which the human body can distill immense quantities of beer into piss. I'm thinking the English may drink to distract themselves from the weather.

So what's happening with my short brother Teejay's TV series? Good question. It's in the can, but so far doesn't have a date for streaming. No, I haven't seen any of it. The word is some suits at the network are not thrilled with the edits. Dad is worried that too many cooks will be spoiling the broth. Apparently, it's been proposed to add some animated sequences imagining what's going on in little Teejay's precocious three-year-old brain. Kind of a scary thought, if you ask me.

Did I mention famed thriller author Desmond Orton beat the arson rap? The judge ruled that Dior Perlson's recording of his post-coital pillow-talk confession was inadmissible. He deemed it an "inappropriate use of police resources." So there went the prosecutor's case. Desmond would have walked free except for that forged passport he surrendered to the court. For that ill-judged caper he's now serving an 18-month sentence at the Federal pen in Lompoc. I'm hoping he doesn't have me snuffed when he gets out.

Speaking of lawbreakers, those knee-perforating gals Betty Kogstad and Lois Anikeevo are still on the lam. Teejay is hoping that someday soon they'll return to the scene of the crime and invite him out to lunch. No, I haven't heard from Charlotte Caxton, whose robber-baron dad was the target of their revenge assault. Her hippie bro' Dean got convicted on assorted charges and is now a guest of the state up at Chowchilla. He's still not saying where his lady accomplices are holed up.

Can't write anymore. Time to go sit on the beach and reabsorb the L.A. experience.

TUESDAY, May 24 – My friend Valerie "Cal" Haseltine finally phoned me back. I'd been leaving messages for her all week.

"I'm studying for exams, Nickie," she said. "I can't talk long."

"Since when do you have to study, dear?"

Cal is finishing up in film studies at UCLA.

"Since always, you moron. It's a feature of academic life, and something you college dropouts famously shirk. How was England?"

"Eventful. If we can get together, I'll tell you about it."

"This week is a disaster. Phone me sometime and we'll make plans."

Damn. I don't think that girl was pining away for me while I was gone. Over in England, I'd been reading up a bit on narcissists. They are said to lack "object constancy." In other words, for them out of sight means out of mind. Me, all I do is dwell on ex-girlfriends and/or my ex-wife. Object constancy is something I could do without!

I've been looking at apartments for rent, as living on the same block as my ex-wife is an acute source of ongoing heartache. Plus, I'm back in the place that was our original love nest. Lots of memories here I'd rather not obsess over. Not to mention that dwelling under the same roof as Dad's family makes me a prime target for babysitting duty. But try finding something on the west side for under $3,000 a month that's bigger than a rabbit hutch. I already lived in a midget house. Why should I now squeeze into a midget studio apartment?

WEDNESDAY, May 25 – I finished binge-watching the last season of "The Death of Guilt." I could have watched it in England, but I didn't feel like torturing myself. Call me biased, but I'd say it suffered from the absence of flamboyant high-schooler Bronson Flange. Where was the comic relief? Hell, where was confused and ever-clueless Jade Ming? Instead, viewers got elfin Pierce Wallensky being evil and scheming episode after episode. How is that fun or even interesting?

Nor was it pleasant to watch Pierce tormenting Whitey Fisher in the warehouse full of kabob skewers while Masked Girl tried desperately to switch off the lights (so Whitey, played by blind Cooper Tucker, could stand an even chance). But Pierce had strapped a tactical flashlight to his leg, so that was that. At least it was semi-satisfying in the season finale when Badrick Palmer (my stepbrother Montel) chased Pierce up the spinning carnival ride where he slipped and was ground to bits in the great gnashing gears. That scene must have cost Mr. Bedrossian a bundle to film. Just finding a stunt man as tiny as Pierce must have been a challenge.

So why was Masked Girl always masked? It turns out when she was four she pushed her identical twin sister off the playground jungle gym. So every time she looked in a mirror she saw her dead sister staring back at her. To keep from going insane, she had to obscure her face behind a mask. Fortunately, Whitey's traumatic death (and Badrick Palmer's sultry kisses) snapped her out of that syndrome. The mask was removed to reveal—not some disfigured and hideous visage—but lovely and talented Valerie Haseltine. Hollywood medicine (psychology division) had triumphed again!

THURSDAY, May 26 – Treez had to take the baby in for a checkup, so I got stuck babysitting Teejay and Edy. For this slave duty I'm compensated a measly $15 an hour, which is subtracted from my rent. How is that not medieval servitude?

The tots were having their mid-morning snack when I arrived. Lefty the cook/housekeeper was lying low elsewhere in the house. The vacuum was switched on, but I didn't hear it moving.

"Where's your dad?" I asked, not all that interested.

"In Las Vegas trying to get a job," said Teejay. "He doesn't realize he's unemployable."

"He still has a following," I pointed out. "He used to be big. It's the lounge acts today that have gotten small. How are you enjoying your new baby sister?"

"Babies get *alllll* the attention," whined Teejay. "It's not fair!"

"It's just an indulgence," agreed Edy. "Nobody needs three kids these days. Think of our poor planet!"

Edy is two going on 16.

"Have you spotted any interesting birds lately?" I asked, changing the subject.

"Hardly," she scoffed. "L.A. urban birds are so boring. I wish our ocean wasn't so cold."

"I don't get the connection," I said.

"If it was warmer, we might get a hurricane that could

blow in some interesting birds. When I'm 18, I'm moving to Canada. For good. Daddy says it's fine with him."

"Yeah," said Teejay, "and you can take stinky Marilyn with you!"

"So what do you hear about Lucia DeFalco?" I asked.

If I'm stuck babysitting, I could at least probe for information on my ex-wife.

"She's very happy at UCLA," said Edy. "She's the new star of the Psychology Department."

"That's nice to hear," I lied. "I hope she remembers her transferring to UCLA was my idea."

"I think she likes Cliff way more than she liked you," observed Teejay.

"That's mean, Teejay," said Edy. "Even if everyone knows it's true. It's not Nick's fault he's a loser with girls."

I debated that point with them, but didn't get very far. At least I filled up on kiddy health snacks, so I was able to skip lunch.

FRIDAY, May 27 – Cal phoned to invite me out for coffee. I guess she's not totally devoid of object constancy. We met at our usual place in Venice. We ordered, sat at our preferred table on the patio, and removed our masks. I planted a juicy wet one on her lips.

"I'm sure those lips have been in some disgusting places since we last met," said Cal. "Guess what, Nickie?"

"You aced all your exams?"

"Why do I feel we've had this conversation before?"

"So did you graduate?"

"I still need a few more hours. I didn't take full course loads in the fall because of the show."

Cal said the reason given for Masked Girl being masked was better than the other 47 alternatives the writers had cooked up. Quite a few of those lacked credibility.

"So how are those English girls?" she asked. "As ripe and willing as they say?"

"They're mostly masked up because of Covid. Not to mention generally elsewhere because we were holed up in the monastery trying to duck Omicron. My life was like something out of *Tom Brown's School Days*."

"I doubt that, Nick. I'm sure there were chicks in the production staff, wardrobe department, catering service, cleaning staff, and gardening crew. I knew it! I detected a slight emanation at the mention of catering. A *frisson* you could not disguise. What was her name?"

"Janice. And I only did her because everyone else was. I didn't want to her to think I was a snob. And who are you seeing these days? How did that poverty-plagued T.A. work out?"

"He turned out to be something of a sexist pig. I'm now resolved to avoid all swaggering and intellectually pretentious smokers."

"Glad to hear it. So what do you hear from your old boyfriend Ninian Skopa?"

"Nothing. He got a job in Boulder and dragged his skanky wife Dior with him. She transferred to the University of Colorado."

"That's great news. They both seemed morbidly and inappropriately obsessed with putting me behind bars."

"I'm not at all sure their motivations were inappropriate, Nickie dear."

"I for one hope I've seen the last of them. Did you check out the links I sent you to the reviews of my show?"

"I did. It sounds not untedious for a show about earnest but confused 1980s Catholic seminarians. And you got some decent mentions. Though I expect you're being selective in what reviews you choose to share. So when can I see it?"

"Nobody's picked it up in the U.S. yet, dear. It may not be every programming exec's cup of tea. I'm trying to get them to send me some DVDs, but they're wary about piracy."

"No doubt people are jonesing for a bootleg of that, Nickie dear. I'm sure it's at the top of *every* video pirate's want list."

"The English can be very sarcastic too, darling. You'd fit right in over there."

"I expect I would," she agreed, picking at my oil-filled muffin.

We compared notes and discovered we were both stuck in dreary BAJville (Between Acting Jobs).

She sighed, I sighed.

"A certain overrated Juilliard student is doing a picture at Fox this summer," said Cal, making a face. "I expect you'll be stalking her day and night."

"Not hardly. Almy Preston is entirely off my radar these days."

"Hah! That will be the day."

"Are you coming back for a tour of my apartment, dear?" I asked hopefully.

"Do you have any furniture?"

"Not much. Luco kept most of it."

"What are you doing for a bed?"

"A futon from IKEA. Brand new last week. Barely broken in."

"It will have to stay that way, Nickie. I'm kind of busy today."

Damn. As corrosive to the soul as celibacy is in your teen years, it's even more gnawing to your vitals in your twenties.

SATURDAY, May 28 – As I was returning by foot from the donut shop this morning, someone rolled up beside me. It was famed pro skateboarder Sligger Shapcott.

"My wife Richie thinks it's very commendable," he said.

"What is?"

"That you're fine living on the same block as your ex-wife and her boyfriend. She thinks that's extremely mature of you."

"One does try to be adult about these things," I lied. "How's your mini-mansion working out?"

"Great. Everyone comments on the incredible number of electrical outlets we have."

"Yeah, we upgraded the wiring quite a bit."

"And the back yard is like the jungle cruise at Disneyland. Of course, the rooms are rather cramped. Did you know my wife has a sister who likes you?"

"Really? What does she do?"

"She's getting her masters in psychology at USC. But she's super nice and even prettier than Richie. We could have you both over for a barbecue sometime."

"Uh, I'm kind of seeing someone now. But thanks for thinking of me. I appreciate it."

No way was I getting anywhere near another psychology major.

Someone yelled, "No skateboarding!"

We turned to look. It was Mrs. Pethigg, the old lady from down the block walking her gimpy Pekinese. Sligger zoomed off the curb and did some semi-amazing maneuvers in the street.

"Show off!" she yelled. "Grow up! Try getting a real job!"

Sligger laughed, leaped into the air, did a split, and landed neatly on his board as Cliff and my ex-wife jogged by.

Yeah, I waved. They sort of waved back.

Damn, I've got to move. And soon!

SUNDAY, May 29 – Potluck lunch at Dad's place today. My contribution was a jumbo bag of potato chips. (Bachelors generally don't cook.) It was a full house with the Scott Twisps, the Frank C. Wyatts, the Jake Twisps, the Ryder Ohlmanns (my half-sister Miren's family), the Pete Zweezes, and even creaky old Aunt Joanie. The Tyler Twisps also were invited, but were engaged elsewhere today. Just as well because the crush of humanity was rather overwhelming. Not to mention the din from the screaming kids.

I asked Dad if he had any news from Las Vegas.

"Things are livelier than the last time I was there."

"Did you get a gig?"

"I wasn't really looking, Nick. I was just visiting friends."

As if, but I let that pass.

"I hear you're all heading back to Nova Scotia this summer," I said.

"Only for two weeks this time. It's mostly so Edy can visit her friend Marie. We're traveling across the continent to a foreign country so a toddler can have some play dates."

"And your wife loves it there," I pointed out.

"Yeah, there's that too."

I scooted away to dodge Aunt Joanie, who had indicated a desire to discuss the failure of my marriage. I ran into Aunt Lillian (Jake's wife).

"Hi, Nick," she said. "There's a girl in my weaving class who admires your work."

"That's nice," I said, neutrally.

"By girl, I don't mean someone who's 42 and fat. She's a very pretty girl around your age with an amazing color sense."

"OK," I replied, still neutrally.

"I'm thinking you could take her out for coffee sometime. No pressure. Shall I text you her phone number?"

"Uh, yeah, sure. I guess so."

"Her name's Jordyn."

"This person is a female?"

"Yes, she spells her name with a "Y.""

"We sold our house to a gal named Richmond."

"People are being very creative with names these days,

Nick. They're not confined any more within those narrow gender strictures."

Right, but I've yet to meet a guy named Kathy. Or Edna.

Later, I was digging into a piece of Lefty's blackberry pie when Nick Twisp Wyatt scooted over on Edy's plastic tricycle. The short dude is nearly two and has acquired some language.

"Daddy says you're Nick Twisp," he remarked, staring up at me. He was modeling the remains of his lunch on his face.

"Yeah, kid. Bad news: you're an imposter."

"What's that?"

"An imitation. Not the real thing. Sorry."

"I am so too real. You're just a big fat butt head."

The junior lowlife rammed his front wheel into my leg. His dad came over and steered him back toward the open door to the atrium. Frank returned and shook my hand.

"I hear you're doing some production designs for Sony," I said.

"They're tryin' me out, Nick. Lauren Bedrossian was nice enough to recommend me."

"Keep me posted if they need any actors."

"I'm keepin' my ear to the ground, Nick. Always. Too bad we didn't hear about your house bein' for sale. We mighta been interested."

"Your house in Chatsworth is much bigger and nicer."

"Yeah," he conceded, "but it's in Chatsworth. Here we'd a been right across the street from the little guy's grandpa."

He said that like that would have been a good thing.

Lillian did text me Jordyn's number. Here's the thing: I have about a one-in-ten chance of being attracted to her. And she has about nine chances in ten of being repulsed by me. If you do the math, the probability of a "coffee date" leading to anything worthwhile is extremely low. So why even bother?

On the other hand, celibacy sucks.

MONDAY, May 30, Memorial Day – Still annoyed that Cal hadn't joined me on my futon, I phoned to get her opinion on coffee dates with Jordyn the Weaver.

"What does this alleged chick look like?" she asked.

"Aunt Lillian said she's very pretty."

"That's bad, Nickie. That just means your aunt neglected to put the qualifier 'not' in front of 'very pretty.' Had she said she was gorgeous that might have indicated that she was not gruesomely plain or actively ugly."

"Yeah, such descriptions can never be relied upon. Now if a guy said she was very pretty that might mean something."

"Quite true, Nickie. Plus, your dream date is engaged in the world's most boring activity. You can look it up in *The Guinness Book of World Records*. Most Boring Activity Ever Created by Humans: weaving on a loom. Endless tossing of a thread bobbin back and forth. The mind reels as the weave advances millimeter by excruciating millimeter."

"You could save me from this fate by coming over today for an apartment tour."

"I can't, Nickie. I kind of have a boyfriend now."

"Damn! I suspected as much. Who is this twit?"

"You're not going to like it."

"Oh, my God! You're actually going out with that shrimp Pierce Wallensky!"

"I'm not quite that desperate. Besides, I think Pierce went back to New York. If you must know, I'm dating my financial advisor."

"You've got a financial advisor now? Why? Is he 46 and bald?"

"Hardly. Liam is 28 and extremely gorgeous."

"He's old! Way, way old! Plus, I'm sure he's planning to swindle you out of your last penny."

"His name is Liam C. Collier and he works for a very reputable firm. You can Google him, if you like."

"Jesus, Cal, how much were the Bedrossians paying you?"

"More than they were paying you, thank God."

"I believe it. So what's this Liam creep doing with your money?"

"I don't know. Investing it in sound, uh, investments, I'm sure."

"He's probably got you in something risky like soybean futures. You'll be sorry when a truck pulls up in front of your house and you have to take delivery of 10,000 bushels of overripe soybeans."

"Go date your weaver, Nick. You two might hit it off. Then perhaps someday soon the four of us can go on a double date." *Click.*

She hung up on me.

I Googled the twit. Yeah, very handsome guy. B.A. from Princeton. Ivy League hair and smile. Enjoys golf and sailing. Former member of the U.S. Olympic ski team.

Fuck!

I knew I should have stayed put in England. In time I might have developed a fondness for icy rain and warm beer.

How ironic that on Memorial Day I have to bury my beloved sex life with Cal.

TUESDAY, May 31 – Producer Brenda Blatt's personal assistant Don (last name unknown) phoned this morning. They're showing a rough cut of my Christmas movie Saturday morning in a theater in downtown Santa Monica. I said I would be there.

"You have to get there promptly at nine a.m.," he insisted. "We're only renting the theater for two hours."

"Not a problem. I'm a very punctual person."

"You can bring a guest or two if you want," he added.

"OK. I'll think about it."

It took a while, but I manned up and phoned Jordyn the Weaver. Someone answered in a room where small children were singing lustily. She identified herself as Jordyn; I got it all over in a hurry. She was free Saturday morning, so we'll be meeting at the theater. Then we'll spend 90 minutes together in the dark. If the date turns out to be a disaster, I figure we can shake hands and go our separate ways. No harm done. No lingering trauma.

How does she sound? Nice. Not mannish at all. The children were not hers. She explained that she was at her summer job (teaching at a Montessori school). Do little kids weave? That sounds like something that could descend into chaos fast.

The painters showed up again today. The Shapcotts are painting the exterior of our former shackette. Dark blue with gloss black trim accented with vivid yellow pinstriping. The garage door is deep purple. Kind of like a color scheme borrowed from a skateboard. I think the effect is way more striking than the boring colors chosen by my ex-wife. You can't help wondering if the Shapcotts' sex life is as exciting as their lifestyle.

If Jordyn doesn't work out, perhaps I should take a second look at Richie Shapcott's sister. Or not.

JUNE

WEDNESDAY, June 1 – According to my journal, on this date six years ago I was being punished for having called slim and lovely Veeva Saunders a "big fat cow." Rather rude since we were living on Veeva's charity in her in-law unit. I had just met Cal and her friend Esmee Carstann, who decided to have some fun by getting me to do strange things under hypnosis. I was thinking about that this morning when Cal called.

"How's the apartment hunt going?" she asked.

"Not well, dear. Shall we find one together and split the rent?"

"I think that might annoy darling Liam. Besides, I like sponging off my parents. Why don't you rent Veeva's front house? It's just sitting there empty."

"Desmond would never agree. He's probably lounging in his prison cell right now cooking up ways to have me snuffed."

"Desmond is out of the picture. Those two got divorced. He got the Bel-Air house and she got the Venice property. I heard all the details from Harvey."

"That house is super swank, Cal. I doubt I could afford the rent."

"Veeva might give you a deal. She's being bizarrely generous with my brother and his so-called wife."

"Tiara Diamond *is* Harvey's wife, Cal. They show every sign of loving each other. They make a lovely couple. You should bury the hatchet and be nice to your sister-in-law."

"Grabbing the starring role in your lousy Christmas movie was the last straw. The only place I want to bury a hatchet is in her skull."

"As I recall, you were not enthusiastic about our holiday film endeavors."

"Your fat pal Brenda could have at least considered me. So call Veeva and put it to her."

"I'm not sure I'd want to sit in my posh rented house and watch you come and go on your hot dates with Liam C. Collier, busy golfer, skier, and sailor."

"Oh, so you Googled him. Awfully impressive, isn't he? The guy's so cute and truly amazing in bed."

"I could do without the phone torture, darling. Thanks for calling."

Nevertheless, desperate to move, I phoned Veeva. She was still holed up on her 27-acre Covid-free ranch outside San Luis Obispo.

"I wasn't thinking of renting the place, Nick," she said. "I might give my kids some time at the beach this summer. We're all vaccinated now."

"Oh, well, it was just a thought."

"I'm sorry your marriage didn't work out, Nick."

"Thanks. And I'm sorry about yours too."

"Desmond told me it was your idea to blow up that man's house."

"I know. That's the story he likes to tell."

"His credibility is pretty low with me. But you did exhibit those Twisp tendencies to go to extremes."

"I was just adjusting to life with my new dad. It took me a while to settle down."

"I'll think about what to do with that house. Maybe we can work something out."

"OK. There's no pressure. I'm fine where I'm living for now."

A lie, but it seemed like the polite thing to say.

THURSDAY, June 2 – I'd Google Jordyn the Weaver to get a preview of my date, but Lillian didn't tell me her last name. I Googled "Jordyn Montessori teacher," but didn't come up with anything useful. So it's to be a groping-in-the-dark, pre-Internet kind of blind date. Rather scary. I'm glad it's still a couple days away.

I did more apartment-searching on Craigslist. How do people afford these rents? Nasty thought: will financial uncertainties compel me to take on a roommate? Do I want to share my living quarters with some smelly, intrusive, and possibly obnoxious stranger?

I know what old-school Nick would do. He'd deal with the Luco/Cliff proximity problem by burning down their house. Or he'd talk some idiot into doing it for him.

FRIDAY, June 3 – My mother phoned from Indiana today. She said my stepbrother Montel has joined a theater company in Indianapolis for the summer. Guess we won't be seeing that dude until he graduates next year. He's a star in the Drama Department at Indiana U.

My mother reminded me that old Aunt Grace died from Covid last winter. Actually, she was my late stepfather Leonard S. Davidson's aunt, so I guess that makes her my great-aunt. I skipped her funeral too.

"Anyway, Nick, I heard from her lawyer. He was asking me for your phone number. Shall I give it to him?"

"I guess so. What does he want?"

"She may have left you something in her will."

"Shouldn't she have left it to you? You were married to the guy."

"I expect she blamed me for contributing to his death."

Mom was driving. She survived the accident, but Leonard exited at high speed through the windshield. Perhaps in his next life he'll be buckling his seat belt.

As I recall Aunt Grace was some kind of nurse. Perhaps she left me her white shoes, her white cap, and her blood-pressure kit.

SATURDAY, June 4 – Movie preview day!

I was loitering nervously on Third Street at 8:51 when this very pretty girl walked up to me. She smiled and held out her hand.

"Hi, Nick. I'm Jordyn Michaels."

My clammy hand met hers. "Hi, Jordyn. Why do you look familiar?"

"Well, we did go to high school together. We graduated the same year. But Santa Monica High is a big school. There were lots of girls more distracting than me."

"I remember now. You used to get your photo in the school paper."

"I was the pitcher on the girls' softball team. We kicked major butt."

She appeared to be fit, but not muscle-bound. Very rosy complexion. Brown hair and eyes. Not petite, not tall. Not voluptuous, just normal. She smelled good too.

Then everyone arrived, including the Scott Twisps and Harvey and Tiara. I muttered some introductions as we entered the theater.

Brenda introduced the film: "OK, gang, I know it's June, but imagine it's December, snow is falling outside on the Santa Monica Promenade, and you're in the mood for an enchanting holiday film. But you'll have to make do with our crazy little movie. If anyone can think of a better title than 'Crime Father Christmas,' we'd be eternally grateful. Do fill out and turn in your comment cards. We love constructive criticism! Not really, but you know the drill."

The story didn't diverge that much from the outline that I cooked up last summer with Charlotte Caxton. I already knew that my brother Scott was in it as the second brother. He played the nurse who lived in Hawaii. The dude who stole my part was some wannabe actor named Noah Szreter. Kind of a low-budget Ryan Gosling clone. Not all that much older than me, but perhaps more bristly when unshaven. I noticed Harvey was squirming a bit when Noah was on screen simulating sex with Harvey's severely undraped wife. Pretty spicy for a Christmas movie. It sure gave me a boner, but then I'd spent the last nine months in a Catholic seminary.

We applauded at the end and filled out our cards. I congratulated Tiara and was obliged to shake Noah's clammy hand. The dude had not shaved for this special event. I kissed both Brenda and Chloe, then we were all outside again in the brilliant non-December sunshine. We were invited to lunch by several parties, but decided to head off by ourselves. How many people do you need tagging along on a first blind date?

We strolled toward a Thai restaurant on Wilshire. I asked Jordyn what she thought of the movie.

"I don't think the story was very realistic, but it held my interest. The fellow playing Jack seemed like a bit of a dork."

"I expect Mr. Szreter was all their budget could afford."

"And I'm not sure we needed to see quite so much of Tiara Diamond's chest, but you may disagree."

"Speaking frankly, I was not offended."

"Guys tend not to be. She's even more beautiful in person. She's almost as gorgeous as her husband. What does he do?"

"Harvey's in college and clerking for the summer at the Haseltine Pet Shop on Lincoln Boulevard."

"I may have to buy some goldfish soon."

"Buying even one would make his day."

"So, Nick, what do you think of my lipstick?"

I inspected her invitingly kissable lips. "Looks good to me."

"I don't normally wear much makeup, but I got this for you. It's the Gunslinger brand."

"Always the correct choice, Jordyn. What color is it?"

"The shade is called Teasing the Vice Squad. I'm not sure what they mean by that."

The color, a muted red, nicely accented her skin's rosy glow.

We beat the lunchtime rush at the restaurant. After we ordered, the conversation resumed.

"I get it," I said. "Your last name is Michaels so your parents named you Jordyn."

"They were hoping for a tall, basketball-playing boy, but got me instead. I remember when you showed up in our school. You were this strange boy trying to be invisible, and then you starred in a real movie. Nobody could figure you out."

"We Twisps don't thrive in institutional settings. That's why I went on to drop out of UCLA."

"How far did you get?"

"Part of one semester."

For some reason she found that amusing. I asked her what she'd been doing since graduation.

"I got my A.A. at Santa Monica J.C. In the fall I'll be working on my teaching credential at Biola."

"Where's that?"

"Everybody asks me that. It's a college a bit to the north of Knotts Berry Farm."

"Sounds like a nightmare drive unless you leave for campus at 3 a.m. on a Sunday."

"Yeah, that's why I'm doing the dorm thing there in September. I'm aspiring to be a grade-school art teacher, assuming any school system is still funding art classes when I graduate."

Our food arrived and we dug in. She did not have objectionable table manners. She did not grip her fork in her fist or chew with her mouth open. No green basil curry spilled down her blouse.

"Lillian Twisp told me you got divorced. I expect you're on the rebound now."

"Yeah, I'm kind of a hot mess. How about you?"

"Not me. My friends say I'm too sensible ever to fall in love. So you had an acting job in England. How was that?"

"Very deflating to the ego. Those Brits really know their stuff. You can be chatting with this ordinary bloke, and then when the director calls 'action,' he transforms himself into a frighteningly stern Catholic priest upbraiding you for your latest transgression. It's like they have a magic switch they can just turn on. It appears to be universal. There are no bad actors in England, except for us visiting Americans."

"I thought you were great as Bronson Flange. I was disappointed when I heard you weren't in the final season."

"Jade Ming left, so ol' Bronson got declared redundant."

"I loved his outfits."

"Yeah, fashion was more his thing than mine, as may be obvious."

"Right, Nick, I gathered that."

We chatted on long after we had finished our food. Eventually, the dirty looks from waiting customers prompted us to go. I insisted on paying the bill. As we were leaving Jordyn gave me a present: two linen napkins that she had woven herself. On one she had embroidered the initials N.T.II. Stitched on the other one were the initials B.F.

"These are great, Jordyn," I said. "Very artistically done."

"Just for the record that's not machine embroidery."

"I'm touched that you were so thoughtful. Thank you."

"And thanks for lunch, Nick. And the movie. Well, I for one hope to see you again."

"And I hope to see you too. I'll call you soon."

We had parked in different directions, so we parted in front of the restaurant.

Wow, a blind date that wasn't a disaster. I did find a parking ticket on my car, but at least it wasn't towed away.

SUNDAY, June 5 – Cal phoned as I was breakfasting with Dad and his crew. I took my coffee and phone out to the atrium.

"I just had breakfast with my parents, Harvey, and you know who."

"You mean Liam slept over?"

"No, I was referring to Harvey's repulsive wife. She said you went to yesterday's screening with a very attractive girl."

"That would be Jordyn the Weaver. Your theory about girls described as 'very pretty' got seriously disproved."

"So do you like this alleged beauty?"

"We seem to have hit it off. She had purchased a tube of Gunslinger lipstick just for our date."

"Then I can see she's a hopeless case. Harvey's annoyed at Tiara for disrobing excessively in that movie."

"It was nothing you couldn't see on any beach in France."

"How was the sag factor?"

"I couldn't tell. She was lying on her back with a guy on top of her. Sort of a position favored by you and Liam."

"I'll thank you to leave Liam out of this. So are you seeing your weaver again?"

"I hope so. She didn't appear to be totally repulsed by me."

"She was probably feigning interest to spare your feelings."

"I sincerely doubt that. Anyway, I need someone to distract me from the all heartache you're dishing out."

"You shouldn't have gone away for so long."

"You had no time to see me anyway."

"What's this trollop's full name?"

"Jordyn Michaels. She'll be a student this fall at Biola College."

"Where the hell is that?"

"Apparently it's to the north of Knotts Berry Farm."

"Damn, Nickie. She's even more hopeless than I feared. Oh, did I tell you I got a letter from Desmond?"

"From Lompoc Prison? What did he say?"

"He's lost 72 pounds. He spends four hours a day pumping iron with his fellow inmates. His gout disappeared and he's got abs of rippling steel."

"Damn, Cal! He's piling on the muscles so he can strangle me with his bare hands!"

"No doubt. If you marry that weaver, you'll leave behind a skinny corpse, a pretty young widow, and a few meager possessions. You should wait at least a week before you call her back. You don't want to appear too needy."

"Dating advice from you, dear, I don't really crave."

I expect Cal will be Googling Jordyn. I didn't tell Cal about the hand-woven and embroidered napkins. I'm sure that would have sent her completely over the edge.

Not taking Cal's advice, I phoned Jordyn after lunch. We made a date to go to the beach tomorrow after she gets off work.

Having nothing better to do, I Googled Ms. Michaels. Not much of a presence on social media. She's into making stuff: candles, ceramic vases, woven shawls, embroidered lamp shades, etc. Apparently, she went on a ski trip last winter with some guy named Addison. I am therefore assuming she's not a virgin, which is something of a relief.

MONDAY, June 6 – My phone rang this morning. I didn't recognize the area code, but I answered it anyway. An elderly-sounding dude identified himself as Arthur K. Murchison, attorney for the late Miss Grace Anne Davidson.

"OK," I replied. "What's up?"

"We are processing your late relative's will. You are named as a beneficiary. Your presence here is required. We can procure a ticket for you. You will fly to Chicago and my assistant will pick you up at the airport."

"Sorry, I only fly first class," I joked.

"That is not a problem, Mr. Davidson. From what airport do you wish to depart?"

"I'm closest to LAX. And I changed my name to Twisp. Why can't we handle this over the phone?"

"That is not possible. Can you travel here tomorrow?"

"Tomorrow, huh? I guess I could. If I have to."

"Good. My assistant Timothy will call back with the details of your flight time and seat assignment."

"Uh, OK. You're sure this is necessary?"

"Unfortunately, yes, Mr. Davidson. I look forward to meeting you tomorrow."

As I recall, my great-aunt lived in some suburb south of Chicago. Orland Park, I think it was. We used to go visit her once in a while during Christmas vacations. My step dad was always tense because he hated driving in snow. His greatest fear was freezing to death on some snowed-in interstate. He did die on a freeway, but it was on a warm summer day.

That Timothy dude phoned a bit later. I told him if the ticket was in the name of Nick Davidson, I had no I.D. that would get me on a plane. He assured me that he had made the reservation in my actual name. I also suggested he call and find out if I was on any Do Not Fly lists. I had no trouble at London airport, but you never know. He called back to say I was not banned from flying in the U.S. That was good news. I guess the Santa Monica police gave up on trying to wreck my life.

I got a haircut in preparation for my second date with Jordyn. I didn't want her to think I harbored any latent hippie tendencies. I also shaved, as unshaven I will never in any way resemble Ryan Gosling.

I picked her up at her school. She looked just as fine as

before, although she was now skipping the lipstick. We got a pizza and ate it on the beach. I told her about my upcoming trip to Chicago.

"My aunt had a big brick house on a fairly fancy street," I said. "It's possible she left it to me. That may be why they want me there."

"How could she afford a big house on a nurse's salary?" asked Jordyn.

"I think her parents left it to her. As I recall, her dad owned a bowling alley. That's why she was a bit hard of hearing."

"Could you elaborate on that?"

"It was back before they had automatic pin-setting machines. If a pinboy failed to show or they got extra busy, her dad called her to help out. The clatter of all those rocketing pins damaged her hearing."

"Wow, that sounds like child abuse."

"It was a different time. I don't think they knew about hearing protection back then. Her house, if you moved it to Beverly Hills, would be worth $7 to $8 million easy. Back east it probably would sell for less than you could buy a one-bedroom condo here."

"I know, Nick. Prices are getting insane."

"I remember the way that house smelled: like face powder and furniture polish. It never varied. My aunt gave me the single worst Christmas gift I've ever received."

"What was that?"

"A boxed set of seven clip-on bow ties. One for each day of the week. In bold colors and ugly patterns. I had to wear one the entire time we were there. My step dad was always sucking up to her for some reason."

Jordyn laughed. "I can't remember my worst gift. I mostly received craft supplies, which I love."

"You'll have to meet my half-brother Frank. He's artistic too. He made all the masks for Masked Girl."

"That's impressive. You Twisps are so talented."

"His last name is Wyatt. He got discovered accidentally."

"How's that?"

So I had to tell her the story of how Frank and I came to be. It's a long story and kept us occupied for quite some time.

TUESDAY, June 7 – Travel day. They did buy me a first-class ticket. Really, it's the only way to fly—assuming your private jet is unavailable. My plane left at 6:30 in the morning and we landed at 12:27 p.m. (you lose two hours flying in that direction). I found Timothy as specified in the cavernous baggage area. He was holding a sign that read: "Nick Davidson."

OK, that used to be my name, but why does it sound so alien now?

We hiked a long way to a distant parking deck, the humidity fighting us every step. Timothy was driving an old mint-green Cadillac. I recognized the car. It was my great-aunt's. Inside was the same sea of shiny mint-green vinyl. The dash was green and so was the carpet. They don't make 'em like that anymore.

"What year is this heap?" I asked.

"It's a 1976 Fleetwood Brougham," he replied. "Only 51,000 original miles. It runs like a top. Even the A/C still works. Would you like to drive it?"

"No thanks. Assaulting the planet is not my thing."

Timothy was a chubby bald dude in his fifties. On the drive south he told me all about Orland Park. One of its residents had won Season One of "The Apprentice," Donald Trump's TV show. The town also had produced some notable athletes and pro wrestlers. Also a couple of actors I had vaguely heard of.

"We got you a suite at the Hilton," said Timothy as we entered town. "Mr. Murchison thought you could rest up there and then we can meet for dinner in the restaurant. They do a good prime rib."

"OK," I said. "So who's picking up the room tab?"

"It's already paid for, Mr. Davidson. Don't you worry."

Easy for him to say. Lawyers have a way of sending you hefty bills after the fact.

The suite was OK. The sign on the back of the door said the tariff was $827 a night, but nobody actually pays that much. I took a shower, then fell asleep on the giant bed. The nap worked as a distraction from my having missed lunch.

I was feeling quite peckish when I met up with my two hosts in the murky restaurant. Mr. Murchison may have been younger than my great-aunt, but not by much. He and Timothy went for the prime rib, I ordered pork chops. Hey, wasn't Chicago supposed to be the Hog Capital of the World?

The portions were massive and the food was not bad. I dug in with gusto. Eventually, Mr. Murchison began his spiel.

"As you may know you are the late Miss Davidson's only living relative. Therefore, she has provided for you in her trust, of which I am the trustee."

"I believe she owned a house," I pointed out hopefully.

"That property and its contents have been left to the Orland Park Women's Club," he replied, smiling. "Miss Davidson served as the club's president for several terms."

"Oh," I said, disappointed.

"However," he continued, "Miss Davidson did leave you her fine vintage automobile. It has been gone over by the local Cadillac dealer. They changed the fluids and installed four new tires. I'm assured it is in perfectly sound condition for making the journey back to California."

So that was her legacy to me. An old Cadillac!

"Here's the thing, Mr. Murchison," I said, slicing viciously into my pork chop. "In California any car from the year 1976 or newer has to be smogged every two years. It's tough for old cars to pass the smog test. Had it been a *1975* Cadillac, I might have been interested. This car missed the smog cutoff by one year. Frankly, I don't need the grief."

"That's unfortunate," he replied. "Your great-aunt was quite clear that she wanted you to take possession of her car. She felt sure that you would appreciate it."

"Sorry, not interested."

"Of course, the luxury sedan is not the extent of her bequest to you. She also left you considerable investments in stocks and other assets, some of which have been liquidated to pay estate taxes."

Perking up at this news, I ordered two desserts.

"Could you be more specific as to the dollar amount?" I asked.

"Timothy, what was the value of her remaining holdings as of this morning?" asked Murchison.

Timothy extracted a sheet of paper from his sport coat. "I added it all up as of 10:27 a.m. Central Time. Of course, the market was still open at that time. This is more of a snapshot value."

"Read the number, Timothy," commanded Murchison.

Timothy took a swig of his beer and cleared his throat. "OK, today's market value of the accumulated Davidson accounts is $129,687,312.47. You're up about $37,000 give or take since yesterday."

I stared at him in stunned disbelief. Then the doubt set it.

"What!" I exclaimed. "Is this some kind of joke!?"

"Certainly not," said Mr. Murchison, offended. "I would never joke about such matters. Your great-aunt was a very wealthy—and I might add—generous woman."

"But she was a nurse," I pointed out. "How did she get so rich?"

"Miss Davidson was a *surgical* nurse," Murchison replied. "She rose to the very top of her profession. She assisted when I had my gall bladder removed. That was years ago, of course. She owned her own home and paid no mortgage. She never married, so had no husband to cause unnecessary expense. Investment research was her primary, if not her sole avocation. Being in the health profession, she took special interest in health and medical companies. I believe she got in on the ground floor when many of those innovative new firms went public. She made very few investment mistakes and reaped the rewards of many long years of effort. I only wish I had followed her advice that she had so willingly offered."

"You're telling me I'm now a multi-millionaire?" I asked, flabbergasted.

"Your great-aunt's generosity is conditional on one small point," he elaborated.

"I have to keep the Cadillac?" I asked. Yeah, I could make that sacrifice.

"You must change your legal name back to Davidson. You must cease being Nicholas Twisp II."

"But that's how I'm known as an actor. Can I retain Twisp as my professional name and make Davidson my legal name?"

"I'm sorry, no," said Murchison. "Your aunt was quite firm on that point. I'm afraid she very much disliked the name Twisp. Nor was she a fan of your impersonation of, who was it?"

"Bronson Flange," prompted Timothy.

"Right, Bronson Flange. His eccentricities she found most objectionable. She especially deplored those lipstick commercials. She'd been thinking of altering her will when Covid-19 cut short her life."

"Right, well that was a shame," I said. "And if I don't change my name?"

"Then your great-aunt's fortune will go to the local and national charities specified in her will."

"Not a problem," I hastily assured him. "I never much liked the name Twisp anyway."

My two desserts arrived. Sized for Midwestern appetites and loaded with carbs. Something of an anti-climax, but I shoveled them in.

Dad isn't going to like my ditching his illustrious name. It could have been worse. Aunt Grace might have required that I wear a clip-on bow tie every day for the rest of my life.

I was too excited, jet-lagged, and full of dinner to sleep. So I phoned Jordyn. She was at her sewing machine and making a dress for one of her Montessori kids.

"Did you get the house?" she asked.

"No, but I got her cherry 1976 Cadillac and some stocks. I'm driving it back tomorrow."

"You want a car that old?"

"Not really, but she was kind of insistent in her will. I figure I can keep it for a few months and then donate it to some charity."

"Where are you now?"

"In my hotel room. It's not bad. It would be more fun if you were here too."

"I don't usually hang out in hotel rooms with men I barely know."

"Glad to hear it."

"So I guess I won't be seeing you for a while."

"Or ever if the car breaks down on some lonely deserted road."

"I'm hoping that doesn't happen. Are there any single women in your hotel bugging you for an autograph?"

"Not so far, but I might get lucky."

"Have a safe trip back, Nick. I'll be missing you."

"Same here, dear."

I watched some TV and then went to bed. Damn, I was ahead $37,000 since yesterday and hadn't even known it. I could get used to this income bracket.

I'm thinking I'm going to keep this jackpot windfall under my hat. I see no reason to go blabbing around that my circumstances have changed.

Hell, I may wake up tomorrow and find out it's all been a big mistake. Or a Bernie Madoff-type scam.

WEDNESDAY, June 8 – The hotel offered a complimentary breakfast "buffet," but I went in the restaurant and ordered a real breakfast. While waiting for my food, I phoned Dad and told him I was driving a dead relative's car back from Illinois. He had a lot of questions, but I said I was in a hurry and rang off.

Later, while picking bacon out of my teeth and waiting for my check, my phone rang. It was Cal inviting me out for coffee. I told her I was sitting in a hotel restaurant in Orland Park, Illinois.

"Oh, my God!" she exclaimed. "You're on your honeymoon! With that weaver with the manly name!"

"Not hardly, dear. My late aunt left me her 1976 Cadillac. I'm driving home in it today."

"Are you lying, Nickie? You never told me you had an aunt."

"The topic never came up, dear. I'm sure you have some aunts and uncles we've never discussed."

"In fact, I don't. *Not one.* All of my ancestors were only children, which makes my parents' decision to have *two* children even more inexplicable. Not to mention reprehensible."

"You should give your brother a break, darling. He's a worthwhile person."

"Harvey says the 1970s were the absolute nadir for American cars. So why are you bothering with that old junker? Are you that hard up for money? Didn't you get a chunk of cash for selling your peewee house?"

"My finances are OK, darling. The Caddy's not a junker. It's a low-miles Bicentennial classic."

"Are you driving back on Route 66 while listening to Nat King Cole ballads on your 8-track tape player?"

"No, I think that highway's mostly been replaced by interstates. I'll see you in a couple of days. Think about dumping Liam while I'm gone."

"Not likely, buddy!"

As arranged, I was out in front of the hotel with my bag when Timothy pulled up in the Caddy. Behind him was Murchison driving a silver Lexus. Timothy handed me two sets of keys and the title.

"I filled her up for you, Nick," he said. "This old gal prefers high-test."

Right, but she'll be getting regular gas. My cars make do with tough love.

Murchison parked his car and walked over. He said "good morning" and handed me a thick envelope.

"I found this in your great-aunt's wall safe," he said. "I don't think she intended it to go to the women's club. It's some cash you can use for travel expenses."

"Gee, thanks, Mr. Murchison."

"Don't thank me, thank your thrifty great-aunt. Do you know any lawyers?"

"This girl I'm seeing, her father's a lawyer. He works in the rights department at Universal."

"Universal what?" asked Murchison.

"Universal Studios. They make movies."

"Not to put pressure on you, Nick, but the sooner I see proof that a petition for changing your name has been filed with the California court, the sooner I can turn over the estate to you."

"Oh, I have to do that first, huh?"

"I'm afraid so. I also suggest you get a financial advisor and tax accountant as soon as possible. You'll need to get a handle on your financial affairs."

"Oh, OK."

Suddenly, my life was feeling very complicated.

The old guys shook my hand and wished me "safe travels." I tossed my bag in the car, adjusted the power seat, waved good-bye and was on my way. I drove about a half mile and pulled over. I needed to switch on my phone's GPS app to get directions to the interstate. I also checked out the envelope, which was stuffed nicely with Benjamins and fifties.

I switched on the radio. It worked, as did the clock in the dash. It was 10:37 a.m. Central Time. I was single, white, 21, rich, and piloting a powerful (sort of) luxury sedan. Before me lay the open highway and the vast expanse of America. I was heading to southern California, land of sunshine, beaches, and movie stars. Hell, I was sort of a movie star myself.

Except for the absence of a stunning babe in the passenger seat, life at that moment had never tasted sweeter.

I had a late lunch in Springfield, birthplace of Abraham Lincoln. My Caddy was making Dad's Town Car look like a Prius. While passing a truck, you can watch the fuel needle zip toward EMPTY. At least the pillow-like seats are comfortable and the ride as smooth as my ex-wife's ass.

One thing driving on boring interstates gives you is time to think. First, I was feeling guilty about not going to see my mother. But the last time I checked Terre Haute, Indiana is in the *opposite* direction from California. Then I was thinking about the monster fee my Toyota Matrix was racking up in the parking deck at LAX. Then I reminded myself I'm rich. Soon I may have to upgrade from those humble but reliable wheels.

Then I spent some time thinking about what Jordyn had

said. I was not trying to be invisible in high school, I was just the new kid. By the time I showed up the pecking order had been set, the cliques had been formed. Where was I supposed to fit in? I was not a jock, brain, druggie, surfer, or nerd. I wasn't into cars, motorcycles, or skateboards. I had no interest in joining the school newspaper or yearbook staff. The Chess Club offered no appeal. I wasn't hanging with the cool black kids or Chicano kids.

OK, somebody with a different personality might have had an easier time of it. But that first year at Santa Monica High I don't recall a single person going out of their way to be friendly to me—including Ms. Jordyn Michaels. The only kids who said "hi" were the ones whose lockers adjoined mine. I wasn't trying to be invisible, I just was.

After lunch I stopped at a mall and bought some socks, underwear, and decent sunglasses. I had underpacked for this trip, since I expected to be flying back today. I decided I was done forever with cheap sunglasses scored from beach vendors in Venice. My next pair I'll be purchasing in an exclusive shop in B.H. Should I ever come face-to-face with Brad Pitt, I expect he'll be casting envious glances at my shades.

THURSDAY, June 9 – Rain today. How gauche. In California we have no rain in June. Last night the desk clerk outside Kansas City was amazed when I showed up.

"My, God," she said. "Are you Bronson Flange?"

"No, but I played him on TV."

"Have you been crying?" she asked, concerned. "Is something wrong?"

I pointed to my red eyes. "Eyestrain from driving."

"You can call on me if you need anything, Mr. Twisp. Anything at all. I get off at nine."

"Uh, thanks. I think I'll be fine."

At least there was one person in Missouri who found me attractive.

She gave me their "best room," which I doubt differed much from their other rooms. The bed was comfortable and I slept nearly ten hours.

After breakfast I filled up my green gas hog. The fellow on the other side of the pump commented, "Nice Caddy. What year is it?"

"1976," I replied.

"Not passing many gas stations are you?"

"I stop at every other one I see," I replied.

Yeah, the guy laughed.

I was eating lunch in Wichita when Aunt Lillian called.

"I saw Jordyn last night in weaving class," she said. "She told me you're driving back from Chicago in an old Cadillac."

"I'm traveling in style and comfort. I just finished a Chinese lunch in Wichita, birthplace of Dennis the Menace and Pizza Hut."

"I'm glad you called Jordyn, Nick. She's a very talented and sweet girl. I hope you'll be nice to her."

"Contrary to what everyone thinks, Aunt Lillian, I was nice to my wife. She was the one who had trouble with monogamy."

"All too often the incompatibilities don't show up until after you're married, Nick. I think it's best to take things slow."

"I totally agree. I learned my lesson, Aunt Lillian. Slow and steady is the way to go."

"And one girl at a time. That helps keep things on an even keel."

"Right. That's a good idea too."

Aunt Lillian likely has been comparing notes with Treez. They think I'm the playboy of the western world, callously discarding chicks left and right.

I also got a text from Teejay. He's totally pissed I didn't invite him along on my trip.

Later, I was returning from the men's room at a rest stop when a gal walked up to me and asked if I wanted "a date." Where was she proposing to do it? In the back seat of my car? I told her I was transporting a refrigerated transplant kidney and had to be in Amarillo a.s.a.p. I don't think she believed me.

I stopped for the night in a vintage motel on Route 66 in Tucumcari, New Mexico. I checked out my eyeballs in the mirror over the little sink. Like two cherries on top of a sundae. I don't see how truckers rack up all those miles without suffering terminal eyestrain.

When I came back from dinner, I thought of calling Jordyn, but dialed Cal instead. She sounded semi-pleased to hear from me. I described the town and my hotel room.

"Sounds enchanting, Nickie. Have you asked the grizzled desk clerk where a lonely guy could get some action?"

"Not yet. I thought I'd try you first for phone sex."

"Just strip down to your thong and go hang out by the pool."

"You have me confused with your pal Desmond."

"I'm sure he looks better naked now than you do. I love jailhouse tattoos on bulging muscles. Harvey wants to know if you've checked the oil in your car."

"No, but that's a good idea. I'll do it when I gas up tomorrow. Did I tell you I'm changing my name?"

"To what? George Clooney Jr. in a desperate attempt to jump-start your career?"

"I'm going back to Nick Davidson."

"What on earth for? You realize you'll have to change your driver's license, your passport, your credit cards, your bank account, et cetera. Plus, no casting agent in Hollywood will have a clue who you are."

"I know, dear. But I never warmed up to the name Twisp."

"True. It's the most risible name on the planet. I wouldn't

give that name to my hamster. But everyone thinks of you as a Twisp, dear. Is your bossy weaver making you do it? Does she not wish to be Mrs. Twisp?"

"Not at all. I'm just ready for a change."

"Well, I suppose it's easier changing your name than your sex. Good luck with that plan!"

She had to go as Liam was due to arrive.

I switched on the TV and lay back on the modestly sized bed. The sagging mattress vibrates when you drop a quarter in the slot. Probably activated experimentally during countless sexual acts over the decades. The vibrations added nary a tingle while I was going at it by hand. I still think of my ex-wife or Cal during solo acts. I keep them in reserve as a distraction from that Preston girl I used to know. As I recall, she was my companion on my last road trip (excluding that ill-advised honeymoon trip to Vegas).

FRIDAY, June 10 – My Caddy's massive engine had burned not a drop of oil. I'm getting to like this car. I just have to remind myself at the gas pump that I am now a wealthy person. It pings a bit on hills from its new diet of low-octane gas. I may have to splurge on a higher grade.

Traveling through the stark landscape of New Mexico, I thought about the last Christmas we spent in Orland Park with Aunt Grace. I was 13. She gave me a chemistry set. Kind of useless because it was one of those revised kits that didn't let you make anything fun like stink bombs or nitroglycerine. A lifelong love of science it failed to instill in me.

As I contemplated my test tubes and safe, non-toxic chemicals, Aunt Grace looked on approvingly and said I was the "one last hope of the Davidsons." Like what kid wants that laid on him?

So I'm wondering: did Aunt Grace ever find out I wasn't genetically a Davidson? The fact that she left me all her money sort of implies that she was in the dark. I could see her nephew Leonard keeping it a secret from her to stay on her good side. And my mother had no incentive to tell her the truth. Nor was I blabbing it to Murchison this week.

Then I started wondering if this whole thing was a scam. But why would a scammer buy you a first-class airline ticket, put you up in a hotel, spring for dinner, then give you a vintage car and a big wad of cash? Where's the payoff for them in that deal? No, if anyone was running a scam here, it was me. I was a Twisp pretending to be a Davidson.

Then I started thinking about Jordyn. I hadn't called her in a few days. She's probably wondering where I am. But let's face it. Isn't she too nice of a person to be hooking up with a Twisp? Isn't that why Aunt Lillian was warning me not to hurt her?

Attraction is weird. I only seem to be attracted to girls who cause me pain. Even Avery Weston, my original crush in Terre Haute, later showed up in L.A. wanting to get together. Except she had dragged along her boyfriend. Her plan: the three of us would go to Disneyland and watch Nick squirm. Jesus, who needs that?

Then I switched to thinking about Cal. She mostly treats me like one step up from dirt, yet I love hanging with her. She's the one person I wanted to talk to last night. I bet if I told her I was inheriting a fortune, she'd be willing to marry me. There's the secret to long-term happiness: marry a girl who's immensely attracted to your money. What a disaster that would be.

Perhaps I'm over-thinking all this. My stepbrother Montel says I do that. "Stinkin' thinkin'" he calls it. I'm sure he would advise me to put the moves on Jordyn and just see where it goes.

Stopping for lunch in Albuquerque, I bought some drops in a drugstore for my beleaguered eyes. I parked in the shade of a building, dripped in the drops, and phoned Jordyn. It was nap time at her school, so she could chat briefly.

"I remember nap time," I said. "That's where I first learned to sleep with cute girls."

"And no doubt you've experienced a lot of that since then."

"Not that much actually."

"Uh-huh. How's your car running?"

"Great. She's purring like a kitten. A very thirsty kitten."

"You could do the planet a favor and trade it in on a Tesla."

"I don't think they offer Teslas in mint-green with matching vinyl interior."

"Is it mint-green or sea-foam green?"

"You're the artist. You can tell me when you see it."

"Any estimate when you'll be arriving?"

"I don't like to put the whammy on things by making bold predictions."

"Oh, superstitious, huh?"

"Very. Feel like meeting up in Vegas this weekend?"

"Sorry. I have a softball game tomorrow."

"Your college has a team?"

"No, I play in a mixed-sex adult league."

"That sounds kind of racy."

"Right. We swing, Nick, but only at baseballs."

SATURDAY, June 11 – I bunked last night at the same Indian casino that Mom and I stayed in on our historic trip west all those years ago. This time I was assigned a room on the sixth floor. Still the same view across endless tracks of Arizona wasteland. Very alien to me back then, but now I'm accustomed to parched western landscapes.

I had a déjà vu steak downstairs in the Golden Eagle Room. I asked the waitress to recommend a cocktail for someone who hates the taste of alcohol. She brought me a margarita. Not bad. Perhaps I was a Mexican alcoholic in a previous life. I thought of taking a swim in their indoor pool, but a sign said it was closed because of Covid.

Since gambling in casinos is for tourists and suckers, I went back to my room and hit the sack.

This morning my eyes seemed a bit less inflamed. Those drops may be helping. No hangover from my one margarita. I may turn into a boozer after all. Then I drove across the state of Arizona to Bullhead City, a sun-baked touristy town on the Colorado River. Thank God my aging A/C is still blowing cold air. Otherwise, I would have passed out from the heat and gone flying off into a canyon in a mint-green ball of flame.

I saw no point to detouring up to Vegas to relive enchanting memories of my honeymoon there. If Dad hadn't bought that bargain, slide-prone house I never would have met Lucia DeFalco. Hell, I might have been honeymooning in Vegas with someone far more suitable!

I checked into a low-slung motel overlooking the river. Across the broad but shallow river lies the state of California, home to about 40 million people (including me). I made sure to fill up my tank on this side, since they really gouge you for gas in California.

Saturday night in a swingin' river town devoted to giving tourists a good time. I had a pizza delivered to my room, lay on the bed with a wet wash rag over my eyes, and fell asleep.

SUNDAY, June 12 – I got up early and hit the road. Only about 300 miles left to go. I put the pedal to the metal and didn't stop until I got to Barstow. That's the scrawny desert town Dad was always threatening to move us to for its low cost of living. Could be, but my breakfast with tip came to $22.

The gods of traffic were smiling today. I exited I-10 in Santa Monica at 1:47 p.m. No place to park on our clogged street except in front of Cliff Swandon's house. His girl-friend came out to eyeball me and my car.

"Did you buy that thing?" she asked.

"I inherited it from my late aunt," I replied. "See, it has Illinois plates."

"You drove it from Illinois?"

"I did. Runs like a top. Very easy on gas too."

"I bet. You intend to keep it?"

"I will if it can pass its smog test."

"Well, try not to park it in front of our house."

"Right."

Wow, hostility on the hoof. My ex-wife is now sounding like Mrs. Pethigg, the old lady with the Pekinese.

I hauled in my stuff, then phoned Jordyn. I asked if she was free for dinner.

"I made some soup, Nick. I could bring the pot over to your place."

"Sounds good. And bring the soup too."

A cheap joke, but she laughed.

The soup was more like a tasty stew. She'd also brought a salad. A welcome change from road food. She checked out my crib as I scrounged for silverware.

"This place has potential," she commented.

"Don't worry. I'm planning on moving soon."

"I live with my parents, Nick. I'd invite you over, but you'd have to run the gauntlet of my mother."

"My dad's family is just on the other side of that wall. Fortunately, this place has decent soundproofing. I have two plates, two forks, and two spoons, but no bowls."

"We'll put the soup pot between us on the sofa and eat out of it communal style as they do in some cultures."

We did that. Awkward and primitive, but that's bachelor life for you.

"I saw your car down the street, Nick. I think it began as a sea-foam green, then faded to a mint-green. I'm surprised it's not rusting out like most cars back east."

"My Aunt Grace took pride in her car."

"And it shows. How did it do on gas?"

"Not bad. On flat terrain I was getting a solid 12-13. In the mountains I was getting a respectable eight."

"Oh, dear. And what would you consider disrespectable?"

"Five would cause me to question its morals."

While we ate, we discussed my trip, her softball game, and my bloodshot eyes. I assured her I was not hooked on drugs or having an emotional breakdown.

"Speaking of that, Nick, my mother thinks I should ask you about your divorce."

So I told her about Luco delving into psychology, its consequences for me, and her adventures with other guys.

"So are you a narcissist, Nick?" she asked.

"I read up on it some in England. If you ask me, my ex-wife ticks more of the boxes than I do. But I'm no expert. If you notice any tendencies in that direction, please let me know."

"It's hard to tell, Nick. Narcissists can be very charming and seductive when you first get to know them. Then later they turn into monsters."

"You've had first-hand experience of that?"

"Not me, but one of my friends from school did."

I told Jordyn about changing my name. Like the rest of the world, she thinks it's a dumb idea. I'm not mentioning the actual reason behind the change. She thinks I should write a letter to my dad explaining my reasons because otherwise she thinks he'll be "deeply hurt and offended."

It's true that it will be something of a massive "don't exist" message for the guy. I'm stuck in a giant squeeze play between two relatives: one dead and one alive.

Jordyn volunteered to read over my letter before I send it. Probably a good idea.

We agreed that we were taking it slow, but some minor nuzzling ensued on the sofa in lieu of dessert.

MONDAY, June 13 – I phoned Phil, my entertainment lawyer, and asked if he could do a name change for me. He laughed.

"I heard of an actor a few years back who changed his name to John Barrymore IV. Casting agents still ignored him. Stick with Twisp, Nick. That's how people know you in this town."

"I don't feel comfortable with that name, Phil. It's like people born one sex, but sense they really belong in the opposite sex."

"Jesus, Nick, are you having gender issues too? Maybe you should talk to a therapist."

"I was just making an analogy, Phil."

"If you're serious about changing your name, Nick, you could do it yourself. The form is available online. You file your petition with the court and post a notice in a newspaper for four weeks. If nobody comes forward to object, the court usually grants it automatically. Or, there are businesses that will handle the whole thing for a couple hundred bucks plus costs."

"Where do I find them?"

"On the Web, where else?"

He also gave me the names of several tax accountants that his clients use. No, I didn't mention that soon I will be roasting alive in inheritance hell.

I found a company in West L.A. that handles name changes. I phoned them, and gave them my information and credit-card number. The gal said they would get the ball rolling today. She also said she missed seeing those fun Gunslinger lipstick commercials. I said I missed receiving those fun residuals.

Then I took an Uber car to the airport to retrieve my Matrix. The stupendous parking charge made a further dent in the travel cash scored from Murchison.

When I returned, I went next door and got grilled by the assembled Twisps about my trip. They all trooped down to inspect my new wheels, which Dad said I would be "an idiot to keep." The guy's just jealous. I expect as a kid back in 1976 (and dressed in Bicentennial red, white, and blue) he would have given his left nut to own such a prestigious car.

Treez had some news. Old Mrs. Pethigg from down the block called the cops on the Shapcotts for painting their house "illegal colors." The cop who answered the call assured her that the bold color scheme, while "unusual," was in violation of no city codes.

I hope in 50 years I'm not a cranky old guy dragging around an ancient mutt, muttering to myself, and annoying the neighbors.

Later I got a call from a number I didn't recognize. Living dangerously, I answered it anyway. It was that heart-stomping girl Almy Preston.

"Hi, Almy," I said. "Whose phone did you borrow to call me this time?"

"My grandfather's housekeeper's. Has Stuart Dunham contacted you?"

An ugly name from the distant past.

"You mean that lumpy Kansas creep who knocked up your best friend and was forced to marry her?"

"He and Sue Ellen Pingleton are now divorced. She has custody of their kid. Now he's here and stalking me. He says he wants me back."

"You do make a strong impression on a fellow, darling. I sort of want you back as well."

"I'm serious, Nick. If Stuart contacts you, don't tell him where I am!"

"Not to worry, dear. I won't tell him that you're staying at your grandfather's place up in Bel-Air."

"How did you know that?"

"You just told me, Almy. I'm not retarded. What is your movie about?"

"I play a 1950s aspiring actress who's raped by a big-time star and struggles to deal with it in the context of those times."

"Who's playing the inappropriately horny star?"

"Clive McGregor."

"He should be good. All English actors are great."

"He's actually Scottish."

"Same difference."

"My grandfather is really worried, Nick. He hired a bodyguard to protect me."

"Didn't Patty Hearst marry her bodyguard?"

"I probably won't be doing that, Nick. Mr. Clancy is a 250-pound retired L.A. cop."

"And is Everest guarding you as well?"

Vile and loathsome Everest Weeden is her piano-playing BF.

"Everest is teaching this summer at a music camp in up-state New York. *Not* that that is any of your business."

Possibly not, but it was welcome news anyway.

"I was sorry to hear your marriage didn't work out," she added.

"It was fine for two years and then sort of blew up over-night. Not my fault though. Want to get together some-time?"

"I'm pretty busy, Nick. I just called to warn you about Stuart."

"Right. If he shows up here, I'll tell him to grow up and leave you alone. If he gives me a hard time, I'll deck him."

"Don't be a hero, Nick. Stuart is a much bigger guy than you."

As I recall, Harvey pounded Stuart's flabby ass without even working up a sweat. And ripped a gold earring right out of his lobe. That had to smart. Should I hire Harvey to serve as my bodyguard this summer? Protecting me 24/7 couldn't be as boring as clerking in a pet store.

Hearing from Almy is a bit like an alcoholic being served a large and delicious margarita. It ain't conducive to continued sobriety.

TUESDAY, June 14. I worked on my lousy, stinking letter to Dad. The first of four name-change legal notices comes out on Thursday in a weekly paper in Glendale. Apparently, it offers the cheapest rates. Not something Dad reads, but some busybody might see it and alert him. Here's what I came up with.

Dear Dad,

Let me begin by saying how much I appreciate the help you've given me over the years. I'm so happy we met up finally and I joined the Twisp family. I feel blessed to belong to this large and growing family.

As an actor, however, I feel a bit lost among all these Twisps in the business. There's you, Scott and his wife, Uncle Jake, and now little Teejay. Therefore, I have decided to change my name back to Nick Davidson.

I realize this may come as a shock to you, but I assure you I am taking this step only for professional reasons. I hope you do not feel in any way that this is a rebuff to you. I assure you that is not my intention.

I shall always be Nick Twisp II in my heart, but I hope to achieve greater success as an actor as Nick Davidson.

I hope you understand.

Best wishes,

Nick

It took me most of the day to grind out those five para-
graphs. I emailed the proposed text to Jordyn for comments. She phoned ten minutes later.

"It seems fine, Nick, but you don't mention anywhere
that you love your dad."

Oh, right. Were people supposed to love their fathers?
At times I found my father less annoying than usual, but
that state seems fairly remote from the L-word.

"Do you love your dad, Jordyn?" I asked.

"Of course, I do. Don't you love your dad?"

"Uhmmm, sort of. I guess, maybe."

"You sound awfully tentative, Nick."

"I first met him when I was 15, Jordyn. I think I missed
out on those years where the bonding process takes
place."

"I hope not, Nick. Loving your parents is important for
developing positive mental health."

"Right. But what if your parents aren't that lovable?"

"Is that true for you?"

"I don't know. I only had the parents I was stuck with. I
lack a reference to compare them to."

"I think you may need to work on some things, Nick,
besides changing your name."

"Oh, you think so?"

"It appears that way to me, Nick."

Damn.

After we rang off, I changed "Best wishes" to "Your loving son." Beyond that I am not willing to go.

WEDNESDAY, June 15 – I knocked on Dad's front door
this morning and handed the envelope to his wife. Then I
beat it out of there. I also switched off my phone's ringer to
enhance my inaccessibility.

I drove my vintage car to Venice, where I was meeting
up with Cal for coffee. Parking this beast in the city can be

a challenge. Not as hard as wooing Almy Preston, but close. Fortunately, I was able to overhang into the space occupied by Cal's Miata.

"Driving a car this immense screams that you're compensating for a micro-penis," she commented.

"I don't think my Aunt Grace had a penis at all," I replied, locking my mint-green door. "I think it just means you were a person in the 1970s who appreciated style and luxury."

"How could a nurse afford a car this outlandish?"

"She was a *surgical* nurse, dear. She kept a tip jar in the operating room. I'm buying today. Order anything you want."

"Uh-oh, his car has gone to his head," she replied. "He thinks he's Elon Musk."

Cal stuck with her usual low-fat soy latte. I told her I had filed my petition with the court to change my name. And at Jordyn's urging had written a letter to my dad explaining my reasons.

"So you're still seeing that pesky weaver?"

"Yeah, pretty much."

"You have something in common with an artsy girl going to Knotts Berry U?"

"A lot," I lied. "So what do you have in common with Liam besides an excessive interest in money?"

"Successful relations have been built on far less than that, Nickie."

"Let's see, darling, you don't golf or ski and have no interest in sailing."

"I could see myself lounging topless on the deck of a sailboat," she replied, picking at my muffin.

"Sure. As long as it doesn't leave the marina."

"That is a given, of course."

Cal has a morbid fear of drowning like her idol Natalie W.

"Feel free to lounge topless on the hood of my car, dear. You can't get wet in that venue."

"In your dreams, buddy."

I checked my phone. I had received this text from Dad: "Good luck w/ yr plan." I showed it to Cal.

"What do you think, dear? Is he sincere or is it sarcasm?"

"Knowing your father, I'd say it reeks of brutal sarcasm."

"Yeah, I think I'm in trouble with that guy."

I also had messages from Treez and Teejay, which I was in no hurry to review. Driving back, I spotted a house for sale in Brenda Blatt's neighborhood. I pulled over and called the number on the sign. The gal who answered said the house had received eight bids over the asking price and was now in escrow.

"Damn," I said. "That's too bad."

"You're looking for a house to buy?" she asked hopefully.

"Yes, I am. The sooner the better."

"Are you working with an agent?"

"Only you so far."

"Good. I can show you some properties. What are you looking for?"

"I don't know. A driveway with a garage. The house should be decent. An ocean view would be nice. And not on a busy street."

"May I ask your price range?"

"The sky's the limit."

"Then you'll want to look north of Montana Avenue."

"No, I like Mar Vista."

"Would you be willing to inch into Venice or Culver City?"

"Maybe. If I have to. I'd rather not though."

"So you're a man who likes Mar Vista. I can see why. It's an up-and-coming area."

"I sort of like the way it is now."

She took down my name and number.

"Are you Nick Twisp the actor?" she asked.

"Yeah, but I'm changing my name to Davidson."

"Can I ask why?"

Even random real estate agents think my name change is a dumb idea.

"Too many Twisps in that field. What's your name?"

"Ginny Koven."

"OK, Ginny. You are officially my agent. Now go find me a house."

"Any interest in condos?"

"Certainly not."

OK, grass mowing sucks, but I figure I can hire a gardener for that. My plan is to buy a modest house and tell everyone I'm renting it. No one needs to know I've inherited a massive pile.

Ginny phoned back as I was reparking my boat in front of Cliff Swandon's house.

"There's a house that's coming on the market tomorrow on Ocean View Avenue. The house may be too modest for you. It's two bedroom, two bath in 1,422 square feet built in 1957. But it's been nicely redone."

"Sounds perfect. Is there a garage?"

"There's a two-car garage in back and still room for a pool on the fairly deep lot. They're asking one point eight."

"When can I see it?" I asked.

"I could pick you up in 20 minutes, if you're free now."

"Let's do it."

Ginny was a nicely packaged gal in her mid-thirties. If we were stranded alone together on a remote island, I expect there would be a Twisp in the oven fairly soon. But a diamond ring on her left hand was telegraphing her current unavailability.

The house was a one-story stucco number with single-pane aluminum windows and a low hip roof. They had painted the old kitchen cabinets white and replaced the counters and appliances. The bathrooms had the original 1950s pink and yellow tile. A view of the ocean from the master bedroom. The floors in the living room and dining room were narrow oak boards that had been refinished. Not a profusion of electric outlets. Either the sellers were extremely neat with no "stuff" or the place had been staged for the sale.

Because the lot sloped slightly, there was a lower-level utility room with newish furnace and water heater, plus hookups for a washer and dryer. No musty smells, but I suspected Luco would give the place a pass.

"What should I offer?" I asked.

She thought it over. "With only two bedrooms that should cut down interest from families."

"Plus, you're over the border, so you're not getting desirable Santa Monica schools."

"That's right, Nick. I think if you offered two point two, you'd have a good chance of getting it. But it might not appraise that high for securing financing."

"I don't need no stinkin' financing."

"Good. Sellers love all-cash offers. Do you wish to make your offer contingent on a termite report? The sellers haven't provided one."

"Nah, termites are slow eaters. Let's write up the offer."

We filled out the forms, and I wrote a check for $20,000 as the required "good faith" gesture.

"Are you willing to go higher than two point two if the bidding gets hectic?" asked Ginny.

"For this dump? Sure, why not."

THURSDAY, June 16 – Treez invited me over for breakfast with "the family." Yeah, Dad was there and not looking much at me. It didn't appear that my letter had done much to appease the dude despite my having laid the L-word on him. Lefty had baked warm and loving cinnamon rolls to ease the conversation into the topic at hand.

"I talked this over with Tyler and your uncle Jake," said Treez.

"Right," I replied. "And they both think it's a really dumb idea."

"I got in trouble for changing my name in Canada," said Teejay. "But I was doing it every day. I really like the name Chadwick J. Twisp, but Daddy said no way."

"Chadwick is a stupid name," commented Edy.

"Frank C. Wyatt has a different name, Dad," I pointed out. "But you still like him. He's still your son."

Dad deigned to look at me. "I'm not taking this personally, Nick," he lied. "I just think changing your name at this point will be a needless setback to your career."

"I'm only 21, Dad. It's not like I've been in the business for decades. Look at Robin Wright. She changed her name when she married Sean Penn."

"So she did," said Dad. "And how did that work out for her?"

"She's still working. She's still famous. As I said, I'm a Twisp through and through, but I want to be known by a different name. I want to have my own identity apart from all the other Twisps."

"I'm not stopping you, Nick," said Dad. "You've obviously thought this through."

"And perhaps being a Davidson will help him get past his divorce," said Treez. "And that business with Desmond Orton."

"Yeah," agreed Dad. "And all his other assorted crimes and misdemeanors."

Jesus, my own family thinks I'm a felonious hoodlum. Thanks a pantsful, gang. I expect Dad will be rewriting his will. Good thing I no longer need to worry about that.

When I got back to my hovel, I phoned Murchison. Fortunately, he hadn't changed his number or blown town. I told him I had filed a petition to change my name, and the first of four legal notices was being published today.

"Very good, Nick. Please mail me copies of the petition and newspaper notice as soon as you can."

I also told him I had made an offer on a house and might need a large cash infusion soon.

"I expect the escrow will be for at least 30 days, Nick," he said. "You should have access to your funds before escrow concludes."

All good news. I'd hate to be on the hook for millions with no way to pay it. That would be a real Twispian predicament, but I was evolving beyond such disasters (I hope).

After lunch, I rode my bike back to Mar Vista to look over my prospective neighborhood. Some McMansions had gone up here and there, but most of the houses were still the modest bungalows built for the working class back in the 1950s. These days only rich folks could afford to live so close to the ocean. Joe Lunch Bucket and his buddies—unless they bought decades ago—mostly had moved on. All those manufacturing jobs on the west side had moved away too. I doubt many places change as fast as L.A.

Living on Ocean View Avenue in Mar Vista. A promising prospect, but isn't that address a bit redundant?

Uncle Jake phoned as I was nuking my dinner.

"I saw the letter you wrote to your dad," he said.

"Yeah, so I heard."

"Obviously you have some other reason for changing your name."

In his younger days Jake had toured the world with the Ken Kern Singers. So he had a better grasp on the realities of life. The one anomaly was his fixation on Tyler's wife Uma (Jake's first love back in high school). But that just proves he's a Twisp.

"Uh, that's right," I admitted.

"And this reason you're not disclosing?"

"I don't plan to, no."

"So there's no point to my stating my opinion on your proposed name change?"

"Not really."

"And you're not in any kind of legal jeopardy are you?"

"Not at all."

"All right. Davidson is an OK name. There was that bland singer named Davidson, but he's mostly been forgotten. I'll tell your dad to get off your back. And you don't have to go out with that girl just because my wife is trying to play cupid."

"I know. But I kind of like her."

"So everything's fine with you? No problems or troubles?"

"Nothing major, Uncle Jake. Life is fine these days."

"Remember, I'm here if you need anything, Mr. Davidson."

"Thanks, Mr. Twisp. I appreciate it."

FRIDAY, June 17 – I had a scary dream last night. Murchison and Timothy were lugging in giant bags stuffed with Benjamins. I was rolling in the green stuff. Then Murchison said there was one last thing to do before he turned over the cash. I had to pass a DNA test proving I was Leonard Davidson's son. Aunt Grace had insisted on it.

So in my dream Timothy was a licensed DNA tester and had brought along his apparatus. I started sweating bullets and grabbing at the bags that were just out of reach. Timothy approached with a scalpel and said just to be absolutely certain he needed a one-inch square sliced out of my hide. Alarmed, I was backing away when I jolted awake.

Fuck! Talk about anxiety dreams. I don't see why people need to be tortured by their own subconscious. What's the point of that? I had no say in what horny dude engendered me. And what difference does it make now? At this point neither Leonard nor his aunt is giving much thought to my ancestry. Those two are deceased. Nor is Aunt Grace racking up any expenses in her present location. So why shouldn't I make use of her money?

Ginny Koven phoned early. A total of four bids came in yesterday, and a couple more are expected today. The listing agent reported that the sellers (a gay couple) were impressed that Bronson Flange is interested in their house. So that may give me a leg up when they make their decision.

"When are they deciding?" I asked.

"We hope by the end of today, Nick. Remember, if you don't get the house, it's not the end of the world. After all, this is the first place you looked at. Something better might come along soon."

Right. That's what they say about love, but it doesn't seem to work that way for me. I just grab the first girl and hang on tight until she peels herself away from me. Then I roast in rebound hell.

Speaking of which, I phoned Trent Preston's housekeeper and asked to speak to Almy. Eventually, she came on the line.

"Did you see Stuart?" she asked, breathlessly.

"Is he still driving a yellow Camaro?"

"No, according to Mr. Clancy he's lurking about in a big Ram pickup."

"Oh, then I guess I haven't seen him. What's happening with Maya Chan these days?"

I asked that to keep the conversation going. My interest in Maya rates slightly below nil.

"I don't know, Nick. She was in New York, so I invited her to my engagement party. She didn't show and I haven't talked to her since."

"So you're engaged? I'd heard rumors to that effect, but naturally I dismissed them."

"And why is that?"

"Aren't you awfully young to be getting married?"

"Asks the man who got married at age 19."

"Well, you might learn from my mistakes. Or, you could marry me instead. I've had some experience at it."

"Nick, I feel I know you very well. And I feel I know Everest very well. In every category I can think of I prefer him to you. The choice between you two could not be easier."

Wow, that was harsh. Nevertheless, I pressed on.

"Er, right. Of course, you haven't seen me lately. I have matured considerably in the past few years."

"I'm sure that's very good news for your next girlfriend. I have to go. I'm due at the studio. Please don't call me again unless it relates to Stuart. Good-bye."

Everest may be in tight with her at the moment, but it seems like he's making the same mistake Stuart did. He's off loitering in a distant state while Almy is here in this city with me. Well, not exactly *with* me. More like avoiding me like the plague. But proximity does have its advantages.

As arranged, I picked up Jordyn at her parents' house after she got off work. They live in the high-rent district north of Montana. Her dad was away at his office, but I got introduced to her mother, who studied my face intently.

"If you're wearing makeup, it's very subtle," she commented at last.

"I told you, Mom," said Jordyn. "Nick doesn't wear makeup."

"That was a character I played on TV," I pointed out.

All MOGs (mothers of girlfriends) hate me, so I was accustomed to the abuse.

"So what did that Chinese girl see in you?" asked Mrs. Michaels.

"We were, uh, confused. That was the point. We were in the show for comic relief."

"Comic relief, huh? Well, the jokes were going right past me. So what's up with you and Valerie Haseltine?"

"Not much, Mrs. Michaels. We go out for coffee sometimes. That's all. She has a boyfriend."

"I heard that Valerie Haseltine broke up your marriage."

"Not true, Mrs. Michaels. That was a fabrication by social media trolls."

"The people I talk to have a very low opinion of Ms. Haseltine and her morals."

"I find her character to be exemplary," I lied.

"And how many girls are you going out with now?" she asked.

"Only your daughter. I'm fine with monogamy. It was my ex-wife who had trouble with it."

"Are you working now?" she asked.

"I'm between projects at the moment," I admitted.

"I've been around film people all my life, Nick. My husband is an executive at Universal. Speaking frankly, I don't think you have the looks or talent to make it in the business."

"Uh, right, but I've done fairly well so far."

Eventually, the interrogation concluded and we escaped. We drove off in my freshly washed Matrix.

"That was my mother, Nick," said Jordyn. "You can let me off at the corner if you're done with me."

"I've met worse. How come you weren't sticking up for me?"

"My mother always has a certain number of questions lined up. It's best just to let her ask them."

"Does she grill all your boyfriends like that?"

"Pretty much. You're the first guy I've gone out with

who's divorced. That makes her extra wary. You're lucky she wasn't pulling out your fingernails with pliers."

"Perhaps she's leaving that to your dad."

"You'll have to meet him one of these days. He brings a sharp legal mind to the exchange."

"I can't wait."

Famished from herding screaming kids all day, Jordyn wanted to dine early. We went to a Mexican place she likes in West L.A. After we ordered, I told her about my family's reaction to my proposed name change.

"Writing the letter was a good idea," I said. "I think I would have had a much rougher time without it."

"Sometimes it helps to spell things out in black and white. So when do I start calling you Nick Davidson?"

"I guess in about a month—assuming no troll comes forward to object."

"You mean like the president of the Nick Twisp II Fan Club?"

"I think fan clubs in general have died out. Too bad. I could use the adulation."

"That's sounding a bit narcissistic, Nick."

"Don't knock unconditional love from strangers. Sometimes it's all you can get."

My phone buzzed on the table; I checked the screen. A call from Ginny Koven.

"Uh, excuse me, dear. I need to answer this."

I hurried out to the parking lot.

"You're in escrow, Nick," said Ginny. "The sellers have accepted your offer. In 30 days—barring unforeseen complications—the house will be yours."

"Wow, that's great," I said, somewhat stunned. "So I don't have to raise my bid?"

"Not at all. The sellers are enthusiastic about turning over their cherished home to an actor they admire."

Yeah, and pocketing $2.2 million in the deal. I'd be enthusiastic too.

I thanked Ginny for the welcome news and returned to our booth. The food had arrived in my absence.

"Important call?" inquired Jordyn, digging in.

"I may have a bead on a house for rent in Mar Vista."

"That's ambitious. How much is the rent, like $10,000 a month?"

"No, this place is affordable. Of course, that's why tons of people are interested."

I refused to spill further details so as not to jinx the deal.

After dinner we drove up into the hills of Bel-Air to watch the sun go down. We parked by the lot where my dad's former house slid down the hill and got replaced by three fake fir trees and an electrical shack. We admired the view while being irradiated by powerful cell phone transmissions.

Some rich person was building a second story on the mansion at the end of the road. Much swankier than Dad's house, it was formerly owned by that now-deceased reclusive actress. I told Jordyn about her spooky minion showing up at my noisy party to request we turn down the music.

"Do you give a lot of parties, Nick?" she asked.

"That was my one and only. We were trying to fix up Cooper Tucker with a nicer girlfriend."

"And did you?"

"Two days later they got married and are still together. They have a son named Marant, whose name you are required to pronounce the French way."

"There's a Marant in my Montessori class. It's an up and coming name among affluent west-siders. But our Marant is a little girl."

"Jesus, we're descending into gender chaos."

"So how do you feel about kids, Nick?"

Instantly alert, I recognized a trick question when I heard one. I gave it some thought.

"One or two might be doable. Ten I feel would be excessive."

"I agree," she laughed.

We necked a bit, although we would have been more comfortable in the Caddy. I asked Jordyn if she wanted to go back to my place and make a night of it, but she declined.

Oh right, we were taking it slow.

I took her back to her house. No, I didn't invite myself in to meet her dad.

SATURDAY, June 18 – My second day in escrow. It still seemed like a positive step. No cold feet yet. In less than a month I could be parking my cars in my own garage!

Returning from a donut run, I spotted the dusty pickup truck before I saw its owner. Stuart Duncan stepped out from behind a parked van. He was flabbier than before, about as disheveled, and smelled even worse. One earlobe was scarred and ragged from having that earring yanked out years ago by Harvey.

"You're the guy who stole my girl!" he growled, advancing menacingly. No steel pipe, baseball bat, or tire iron. The big bully intended to pummel me with his bare fists.

I backed away. "I haven't seen Almy in three years, Stuart. Don't try anything you'll regret!"

"You turned her against me!"

"It wasn't me! It was Cooper Tucker!"

Sure, blame it on the blind guy. Not exactly my most heroic moment ever.

"Liar!" bellowed Stuart. "You wrecked us!"

He swung, I ducked, and a neighbor rushed out from his garishly painted house.

"My God," said Stuart, halting in his tracks. "You look just like Sligger Shapcott."

"I am Sligger Shapcott," said Sligger. "What's going on here?"

"You're like the greatest skateboarder ever," said Stuart, awe-struck. "The best in the world! I wanted to be you when I was a kid."

"How many bones did you break?" asked Sligger.

"Three! I was in a cast most of the seventh grade! One leg is shorter now! I have to wear a prosthetic in my shoe!"

Yet somehow Almy once fell in love with this cripple?

"Sounds like you were making a serious effort," Sligger replied. "It takes commitment. Do you have a dispute with Nick here?"

"I want to kill him, Sligger. He stole my girl!"

"The person you want to talk to, Stuart," I interjected, "is a fellow named Everest Weeden. For your information he happens to be engaged to Almy."

"Like engaged to be married?" asked Stuart, stunned.

"Exactly," I confirmed.

"So where is this dude?" he demanded, flexing his massive paws.

"All I know is he's teaching at a music camp in upstate New York. He's a pianist. I'm sure you could find him if you Googled his name."

"Damn, Nick, I don't have gas and eats money to get there."

"Not a problem, Stuart. I have some cash up in my apartment. Let me go get it. I'll be right back. Don't go away."

"OK, Nick. And write down how the asshole spells his fucking name."

I retrieved Murchison's envelope from my sock basket (I have no dresser) and stuffed in a supplementary wad of Benjamins from my personal stash. I didn't want Stuart to run out of funds before he reached his target, whose name I wrote out carefully on the envelope.

The chunky but smelly dude accepted the envelope eagerly.

"Thanks, Nick. You're a pal. Sligger here vouched for you, which is good enough for me."

The big guy hugged us both, then roared off in his truck.

"Are you going to phone this Everest person and warn him?" asked Sligger.

"I wasn't planning on it."

"You still love the girl, huh?"

"Yeah, I guess I do."

Soon I may be scoring higher than Everest in at least one category—assuming ol' Stuart rearranges his face.

SUNDAY, June 19, Father's Day – Dad pounded on my door this morning. He wasn't enraged that I'd forgotten to get him a card. He was dragging me to brunch at Cousin Tyler's. Dad likes to suck up to his billionaire nephew. He thinks all the family should show up.

Since Tyler only welcomes people who are vaccinated and boosted, we didn't have to mask up. His wife Uma had ditched her filtering snorkel too. But we still dined outside on the terrace and weren't allowed inside their mansion. So far Treez's mother is the only person in the Twisp circle who's died of Covid.

Taking a break from Dad on this special day, I sat at a table with Scott's family and the Frank C. Wyatts. The little imposter Nick Twisp kept flashing me dirty looks as he stuffed in his waffle. His older cousin Renth, once a scream-er, ate quietly. Renth's mother Chloe said all the streaming services are interested in "their" Christmas movie, but now they're getting nibbles from studios for a theatrical release. I will be so pissed if that movie turns into a monster hit, and all I got was a measly $33K for the vital story outline.

Frank C. Wyatt said after he graduates from Cal Arts next year they want to sell their Chatsworth house and buy in Culver City.

"I'd hold off on that," warned Scott.

"And why's that?" asked Seka (Frank's wife), who chafes at her confinement in distant burbs.

"The feds are raising interest rates to curb inflation," replied Scott. "That means housing prices will drop."

"Why's that?" I asked.

"Simple economics, Nick. The more people pay in mortgage interest, the less house they can afford."

"But demand always will be high on the west side," I pointed out.

"Not in overpriced areas like Culver City and Venice," said Scott.

"What about Mar Vista?" I asked.

"That's the most overpriced neighborhood of them all," he replied.

"Yeah," agreed Frank. "We're not even considering Mar Vista."

Damn!

Kind of embarrassing. Scott, Frank, and Miren brought cards and gifts for Dad. I was the only ungrateful bastard who'd forgotten all about it.

Later, as I was contemplating what to nuke for dinner, my phone rang. Another unknown number, yet I felt compelled to answer. It was some girl.

"Is this Nick Twisp?" she asked.

"Let me check my I.D. Yes, that's me."

She giggled.

"You don't know me, but I'm going to be your neighbor in Mar Vista. I'm friends with Gary and Keith, who are selling you their house. I sneaked your phone number off a real estate form they received."

"Uh, right."

"My name is Rodeo. Rodeo Birdsong."

"Rodeo like the street?" I asked.

"My parents met on Rodeo Drive. They're both shopaholics."

"Right. And what do you do, Rodeo?"

"I'll be a senior this fall at UCLA. I'm a theater major. So naturally I was thrilled to hear I'll be living right next door to you."

"Right. You live there with your parents?"

"Hardly. They live in Palm Springs and Geneva."

"Geneva, Ohio?"

"No, the one in Switzerland. They're there now escaping the desert heat. They bought my little house as an investment while I'm going to college."

"Yeah, parents do that these days. How come they didn't buy you a house in Westwood?"

"Have you checked the prices there lately? So I saw you riding your bike around the neighborhood yesterday and just had to call. I'm thinking we should get together."

"OK, want to come here for a drink?"

"Sure. I could be there in 15 minutes."

"You know where I live?"

"Your address was on the real-estate form."

Rodeo arrived promptly. Surprising pretty for a girl calling up strange men. Nice figure and large dark eyes reminiscent of Almy's. Sort of a long, oval face. She shook my hand and looked around.

"Don't tell me," she said, "your decorator was going for the lean and hungry look."

"I'm camping here temporarily. What would you like to drink?"

"What have you got?"

"Uh, how about tea or coffee?"

"Coffee sounds good. Are you a regular at AA meetings?"

"No, I'm just not a boozer. I had a margarita last week that wasn't bad."

"You'll have to invest in a blender someday. Or you can come over and borrow mine."

That line she uttered with a most inviting twinkle. It surprised the hell out of me, but 20 minutes later we were stripped naked and rolling around on my futon.

We did it three times. As we paused after the second go, she said, "Can I ask you a question, Nick?"

"Yes, I'm vaccinated and boosted."

"That's nice. So am I competing here with Valerie Haseltine?"

"No, she has a boyfriend."

"Oh, I hadn't heard that. Is he an actor?"

"Financial advisor."

"That sounds boring."

"You have extremely lovely breasts, Rodeo."

"If only I had realized in junior high school that I was developing them just for you," she replied, tugging me gently again toward her divine fulcrum.

"God, I needed that," she said, after we concluded.

"Yeah, me too."

"I hope you noticed I'm vaginally orgasmic. Not all girls can say that."

"Frankly, dear, your talents are amazing."

"You're no slouch yourself. Young guys can get it up fast, but usually don't have such good control. How do you delay orgasm?"

"I think about my negative reviews."

"Bronson Flange didn't get many of those. Everyone loved him."

"Well, Jade Ming was on the fence."

"I would have dumped that girl for good after she socked you in the stomach."

"Did you enjoy my post-assault soliloquy?"

"Like Richard Burton in glamorous makeup. A guy in my acting class performed that speech for laughs, but he wasn't nearly as good."

I phoned out for Chinese, and we had a get-acquainted meal. She had a confession to make.

"I lied to you, Nick. Rodeo Birdsong is my persona for madcap adventures. She's inspired by Holly Golightly. My real name is Carli Eryngilli."

"What is that, Italian?"

"Half Italian and half Hungarian. But don't worry, I'm definitely all Hungarian in my heart."

"That's a relief. I'm sort of burned out on Italians."

"So what are you, Nick?"

"A mongrel mix of low-grade nationalities."

She leaned over and kissed me. "I'm sure you're an improbable combination of flavors."

"Yeah, all the shit-hole countries in the world came together and said let's brew up some Twisps."

"It works for me, Nick. So what other girls are you seeing?"

I 'fessed up about Jordyn, the weaver. I told her we had been taking it slow.

"You mean as in no sex?" she asked, incredulous.

"Not so far," I admitted.

"But how could she possibly keep her hands off you? I mean, really?"

"She's being cautious because I'm divorced."

"I wouldn't be cautious even if you *were* still married! Now I see why you were so eager to jump me."

"I hope this is not going to turn into one of those #metoo incidents, Carli dear."

"Only if you start screaming that I raped you. Of course, things could get awkward if you dump me and we're living right next door."

"We can build a tall spite fence between the properties and ignore each other. I'm used to that. My ex-wife is living right down the block with her new boyfriend."

"No wonder you're so desperate to move. Gary was

skeptical on their asking price. He told Keith they'd never even get one point five. You just blew past the other bidders."

Not great news, but I reminded myself that I'm still rich. Best of all, I appear to have a sex life again.

But here's the question: Did I have sex with Rodeo/Carli just to get back at Jordyn for what her nasty mother said to me?

MONDAY, June 20 – Sipping my coffee in Venice this morning, I berated Cal for not taking me on our annual shopping trip for Father's Day cards.

"I shopped with Liam this year, Nick. Not as much fun, I admit, because he actually likes his dad. Ignoring my suggestions, he bought something sloppily sentimental. If some kid of mine ever handed me a card like that, I'd slap his face."

"That sounds like another major strike against Liam, darling."

"My portfolio of stocks was up nine percent last month. There's something to be said for a decent, well-adjusted guy who's good at his job. Not to mention in bed."

"I totally forgot what day Sunday was, Cal. I had no card for my dad!"

"I expect the reading of his will may be an even sadder occasion for you. Have you had sex yet with your kinky weaver?"

I told her about the sudden appearance yesterday of Rodeo/Carli and all that ensued."

"So how did you meet this trollop?"

"I may be renting a house in Mar Vista next to hers. She's a senior in Theater Arts at your exalted university."

"And what is this slut's name?"

"Carli Eryngilli. She's very nice."

Cal looked her up on her phone.

"I think I've seen this girl on campus. I think she hangs out in men's rooms taking on all comers."

"She does no such thing. You're just jealous."

"Her acting credits couldn't be skimpier. That's why she's sucking up to you. Or should I say, sucking you off?"

"Don't be catty, darling."

"So are you ditching your weaver?"

"I don't know. What do you think?"

"Invite both of them over for a threesome. Then you can compare and contrast."

I decided Cal was not the person to ask for romantic advice. I told her I was thinking of hiring a publicist.

"And why would you do that, Nickie?"

"Why else? To get my name out there. To get producers thinking about me."

"Here's the thing, Nick. Publicists only succeed if they have something to publicize. What are you doing that's noteworthy besides driving around in an old Cadillac and being seduced by groupies?"

"Carli is not a groupie."

"Then she should stop acting like one!"

As if Cal had ever been that hard to get (except with me).

Since the name-change company wasn't sending me the stuff I needed, I drove to Glendale and bought three copies of the weekly newspaper. Then I went to the office in West L.A. and got copies of my name-change petition. Then I hurried to the post office to mail the stuff to Murchison by overnight mail.

While having a late lunch at the diner on Pico, I got a call from Treez. She said considering the difficulties I had last week with my dad, a card yesterday would have been a welcome "gesture of reconciliation."

"I know, Treez. I just forgot. I've had a lot to do and

didn't think to look at a calendar. And I don't have a wife now to remind me."

"You might want to drop by and apologize."

"Good idea. I'll do that today."

"Come to dinner. We haven't had you over since you got back."

"OK, sounds good."

All the stores I went to already had ditched their Father's Day cards. Those guys just don't rate. So I bought a generic blank card and wrote a semi-sappy message. No gift though. Like most Twisps, Dad's virtually impossible to please.

I did my abject groveling thing with Dad and sat down to dinner. He had some news. Teejay's Depression-era series commences streaming on July 5.

"Isn't it a bad sign that they're dumping it in the schedule in summer?" I asked. "Why don't they wait until fall?"

"People watch TV all year round now, Nick," he replied. "The summer doldrums season is a thing of the past."

"And what are they calling this turkey, I mean show?" I asked.

"It's titled 'The Beauty and her Little Genius,'" announced Teejay, proudly. "I play the genius."

"We're all too painfully aware of that," commented Edy.

That short girl shows signs of evolving into a Twisp. Her brother may be the star, but it sounds like they're giving top billing to the beauty: Almy Preston.

I used to do that too until she ripped out my heart and stomped on it.

TUESDAY, June 21 – Murchison phoned. He got my stuff. He said he was releasing an account to me presently worth "$17 million and change." He asked me if I'd found a tax accountant.

"I have some names, but I haven't called them yet. I've been busy."

"I'd do it right away, Nick. You will own lots of dividend-paying stocks. You'll need to pay the feds quarterly as you may do now. You don't want to get behind."

Being rich can be a real nuisance. I called the first guy on the list, Grangert Vanoxit. His secretary said he wasn't taking on any new clients. I said I was inheriting $129 million. She said, "Please hold while I transfer your call."

So I talked to the dude. He's interested. I have an appointment to have lunch with him on Friday. Why we need to break bread together I do not know. I'm still waiting for Zach, my elusive talent agent, to take me to lunch. Not to mention to find me some work.

I thought about which girl to call. Jordyn was a nice artistic person with a hostile and insulting mother. Our sexual compatibility was unknown. Carli was a sexy, budding actor with rich parents now in Switzerland. Their level of hostility toward me was unknown. Jordyn seemed to be well-adjusted and emotionally mature. One could make a strong case that Carli had been "love-bombing" me as narcissists often do.

I mulled it over and called Carli. She invited me over to her place. I felt I should go, as it was the neighborly thing to do. I stopped at a drugstore on the way to stock up on condoms. We had burned through my aging, pre-Lucia DeFalco stash. (My wife had been on the pill.) I tucked three in my pocket and hid the rest in my Toyota's glove box.

Since Carli owned a mid-century house, she had done up the interior in a spare, mid-century modern style. After kissing me enthusiastically, she said, "What do you think, Nick? Is it too much my mother's taste?"

"It's nice, Carli. Very period-correct. All you need is an I LIKE IKE button pinned to your blouse and Bobby Darin crooning on the hi-fi."

"I hope you're not allergic to cats," she said.

"You have a cat?"

"No, but Gary and Keith's cat Heidi visits frequently. I'd love to have a dog or two, but I'm away too much."

That could be a good sign. Narcissists, being singularly into themselves, are not usually big on pets. That reminds me: I should think about getting a pet someday.

The conversation resumed in her Danish modern bed after a strenuous workout.

"I appreciate your using a condom, Nick," she said. "A former boyfriend said it was like he was phoning in the act from Pacoima."

"This whiner is out of the picture?"

"Very much so. As the song says, I only have eyes for you."

"You're very, uh, affectionate, Carli, considering we hardly know each other. That could scare off some guys."

"It's not fake either, Nick. I've been stuck on you since I saw your first movie. But I haven't been stalking you. Honest!"

"What in my first movie appealed to you?"

"Your nude shower scene with the old lady. Your endearing embarrassment melted my heart forever."

I guess Dad's showcasing my bare ass worked out for me in the long run. From what I'd seen of Carli's lily-white body (which was a lot) she appeared to be devoid of tattoos. I commended her for that and said tattoos on chicks make me nauseous.

"Not to worry, Nick. Needles freak me out."

I asked her where Gary and Keith were relocating to.

"They bought an old Carnegie library in a small town in Indiana."

"And what are they going to do with that?"

"Fix it up and live in it. You're paying them so much for their house they're thinking they may not have to get jobs ever again."

I guess that's good news for them. I pointed out to Carli that I was from Indiana.

"I know, Nick. I think that is so great."

"And why's that, dear?"

"I love that you're not some jaded, stuck-up, laid-back California jerk."

"And where are you from originally?"

"California. Where else? I grew up in Van Nuys."

A Valley girl like Luco. Possibly a bad omen.

I asked Carli what she was doing this summer.

"Trying to get acting parts, like 500,000 other girls in L.A."

"There are lots of summer theater programs for college students," I pointed out. "Did you apply to any of them?"

"Most of them are shut down because of Covid, Nick. That bug just about wrecked my entire college experience. It's like it totally targeted our generation!"

I agreed. All those Boomers, who were dying like flies, had overstayed their welcome anyway.

WEDNESDAY, June 22 – I didn't sleep over at Carli's. She said she was too gnarly in the morning to be seen by people she liked. Don't ask me how she's planning to accommodate some future husband.

Ginny Koven phoned as I was washing my breakfast spoon. She said the title report had come in on the house and everything looked fine. I told her I was getting feedback that I had offered too much.

"Don't worry, Nick," she replied. "A bit of buyer's remorse is normal at this stage. I can assure you that you won't find many houses in a great west-side neighborhood with an ocean view for such a modest price. And remember, your lot has room for a pool."

Right. As opposed to actually having a pool. Instead it has grass that some pricey gardener will be mowing. Pools attract hot chicks sunning themselves topless. No one is jonesing to come over and hang out half-naked on your grass.

Then Jordyn phoned and apologized again for her mother.

"I know you think I should have stood up for you, Nick, but it really is best just to let my mother rant. She said what she needed to say, so now she should be fine. How about coming over tonight for dinner? I'll cook."

"Cook for whom?" I asked warily.

"Well, for you and my parents. They live here too."

I considered the offer.

"Here's an idea, Jordyn. How about suggesting that they go out for dinner? Tell them to save their restaurant receipt, and I'll reimburse them for the charge."

"I think they would feel highly insulted, Nick."

"OK, how about bringing the food over here like you did before?"

"The meal I'm planning isn't all that portable."

"I like simple meals, Jordyn. How about making a pot of chili and a pan of corn bread? I'll run out and buy some bowls so we won't have to eat like Communists."

"It sounds like you're not all that enthusiastic about seeing me."

"I'd like to see you, Jordyn, but if you only come as a package deal with your parents, I'd rather not."

Long silence on the phone. Eventually, she said, "OK, Nick. I'll talk to you sometime." Then she hung up.

Probably just as well. In September she'll be off to college, and it will be a long drive in heavy traffic to La Mirada to see her. What could we do in that burg after we've explored Knotts Berry Farm? And do Biola dorms welcome overnight guests? Not likely. Plus, I feel I'm too old for intercourse in a bunk bed with assorted giggling roommates on the scene.

I wonder if she'll be demanding back her hand-woven and embroidered napkins?

THURSDAY, June 23 – I got a package in the mail to-day from Murchison with all the info on my $17 million account. He included a note saying he would be releasing the rest of the accounts as soon as the court approves my name change.

After I pay for my house, I'll still have nearly $15 million on hand, plus much more on the way. If this is all a scam, it's got to be the most convoluted one on record.

It must be my lucky day. My aged Caddy passed its smog test. The technician said I was close to the borderline on NOx, whatever that is. He recommended I think about get-ting my radiator re-cored. I've decided not to clutter my brain with such trivialities, since that car crossed the blaz-ing hot deserts of Arizona without overheating.

According to a Web search, the highest retail value of my car is a mere $2,750. So there's not much point to load-ing it up with expensive new parts.

Then I spent nearly three hours at the DMV doing the title transfer. The clerk didn't like that the car was a gift, the person giving it to me was deceased, the signature on the Illinois title was by her lawyer, and I was changing my name from the one on my driver's license. What a nightmare!

FRIDAY, June 24 – Lunch today in Century City with my new tax accountant Grangert Vanoxit. Yeah, I hired the dude. How many tax accountants can you interview before you go insane? He had seen none of my movies or our TV show. In fact, the only Twisp he had heard of was Cousin Tyler.

Grangert said changing my name while simultaneously buying a house and inheriting "a significant fortune" was a dumb idea. I replied I wasn't getting the money unless I legally changed my name. He said inserting such a cov-enant in a trust was "most unusual and more than a bit overbearing." I said, "Yeah, that's a good description of my great-aunt."

I told him I wanted my windfall to be kept secret. I said I needed an accountant who was discreet.

"And why is that, Nick?" he asked, crunching into his salad.

"Because if people know you have money, they start acting weird. I just want to look like a regular struggling actor."

"An actor who's paying $2.2 million in cash for a house," he pointed out.

"I'll be telling people I'm renting the house. No one needs to know my business. Besides, the house I'm buying doesn't look all that expensive. In Indiana you could buy it for under $100K."

"True, Nick, but you won't be shoveling much snow in Mar Vista."

"Right, or dodging tornados."

Eventually, we got around to fees. Grangert said he would be billing me at the rate of $412 an hour. I said that seemed kind of high. He said you didn't want to scrimp on your accounting services. He said he was "highly regarded" in his field and would be saving me many times over his "modest fee" by minimizing my tax exposure. I said OK, but I'd rather not spend time up in Lompoc for tax fraud. He stressed that he was extremely well-versed in all applicable laws, both federal and state.

When the check arrived, Grangert did a fast calculation in his head and put down exactly his share. Plunking down my share, I asked if he would be billing me for this consultation.

"Some of my colleagues might, Nick, but I like to start a business relationship as friends. Are you married or engaged?"

"Recently divorced," I replied.

Grangert swiped through some photos on his phone, then showed me the screen. "This is my daughter Kinsley. She's a student at USC."

Blond girl with vast beaming smile. Good teeth. Fortunately, not looking much like her father.

"Very pretty girl," I said, neutrally. "What is she studying?"

"She's finishing up in the film school. She aspires to be a director. I could tell her about you and give her your phone number if you like."

"OK, but you need to stay mum about the $129 million."

"Of course, Nick. That's a given."

At this point I may be desperate enough to audition for Kinsley's next student film.

Grangert must find me worthy of squiring his daughter. That's a switch. I expect my being in the funds may have helped.

Later I got a surprise phone call from Jordyn's mother.

"Hi, Nick," she said. "It appears I may have offended you in some way."

"You said I didn't have the looks or talent to succeed in Hollywood."

"So who am I? The film critic for the *New York Times*? The president of the Screen Actors Guild? Barry Diller's favorite nephew? Not hardly. Don't be so touchy! So my daughter told me your plan. It's fine with us!"

"Er, what plan is that?"

"Tomorrow you come here at seven. You meet my husband Walt. Two minutes later we leave for a restaurant. You have a nice home-cooked meal alone with Jordyn. The old fogies are out of your hair."

"I can't tomorrow. I'm having dinner with a friend."

"And this friend is a male person?"

"No, she's not."

"OK, we're all flexible here. Call my daughter and schedule a time. Will you do that?"

"Uh, sure."

"If you're going to be an actor, Nick, you need to grow a thicker skin. Critics are paid to bash actors. That's their job. And I suspect you're someone who will be getting bashed frequently."

Somehow I didn't get around to phoning her daughter.

SATURDAY, June 25 – My buzzing phone jolted me awake absurdly early. It was flashing the number of Trent Preston's Mexican housekeeper.

"Buenas dias," I said, cheerfully.

"You are even more evil than I thought," said Almy.

"What did I do now?" I asked, trying to sound both innocent and aggrieved.

"You know what you did. Stuart Duncan has been arrested! He tried to attack Everest!"

"You mean he tried, but somehow was foiled?"

I imagined a dozen delicate but musical teenagers jumping on Stuart and wrestling him to the ground. Or menacing him with their oboes and flutes.

Almy continued with her rant. "As a child Everest was busy with dual after-school activities: piano lessons and karate lessons. He is more than capable of defending himself. Stuart was subdued and left heavily bruised. He told the cops you put him up to it."

"That's a lie!"

"He said you told him how to find Everest."

"I was trying to send him out of the state, darling. So he wouldn't be stalking you! I was thinking of your welfare! I merely told him that Everest was at a music camp back east. I may have mentioned Vermont or Delaware. He must have Googled Everest's name to find the actual location. Is it my fault your egotistical boyfriend likes to brag about his activities on social media?"

"Stuart said you gave him the money to make the trip!"

"I handed over some cash under duress. He was threatening me with physical violence. The big smelly lug wanted to kill me."

"And did you report that robbery and alleged assault to the police? Did you warn me of Stuart's intentions? No! You wanted him to find Everest! And do him injury!"

"That's just your interpretation, dear. Clearly, the actual facts are on my side. So how's your movie going?"

She hung up on me.

Why do large dumb guys think they can prevail in fights just by dint of their superior size? Why don't they work on their skills? Would it kill them to take a few martial arts classes? Why can't they make a serious effort to turn themselves into bone-crunching warriors?

Later, Carli phoned. "I'm thinking salmon for dinner tonight, Nick. How are you on fish?"

"I like fish."

"You like it, but you don't love it?"

"I love salmon, Carli. Salmon is fine. I would date a salmon if I were a fish."

My first use of the L-word with that girl.

"Gary and Keith just headed off to Indiana in a big truck. They're towing their car behind it."

"Did they take their cat?"

"Heidi's in her carrier in the cab. I kissed her goodbye. So sad! A five-day trip across the country with a nervous cat. Not my idea of fun. Gary said they're fine if you want to end escrow early."

"OK, I'll run it by my agent. I've transferred the funds to my bank account."

"Are you ready to perform?" she asked in her sultriest voice.

"I am so ready to perform, dear."

"Does the thought of writing that big, fat check get you excited?"

"I'd be more excited if I could leave off a zero or two at the end."

"Welcome to the 21st century, darling. I'll see you at seven. Don't be late—or early."

"Why shouldn't I be early?"

"No girl wishes to be seen before she's ready. Didn't your wife teach you that?"

"I don't think so."

"No wonder you got divorced."

I phoned Ginny Koven. She was pleased to hear the sellers had moved out. She said she would look into ending escrow early. Of course, the sooner the deal closes, the faster she gets her commission.

I arrived on time with a chilled bottle of sparkling wine. Carli broiled salmon on her gas grill. She served it with salad and parsnip fries blasted in her hot-air fryer. They were to actual French fries as celibacy is to intercourse. I made an effort to gag down my serving, but declined seconds.

Unlike my house, Carli's kitchen has a cute built-in booth, but we ate in the dining room on her Danish modern teak table. The dishes were by Heath Ceramics (not to be confused with Brenda Blatt's favorite candy bar). The "candles" were a vintage metal set glowing with butane flames. I commended her on the excellent cuisine.

"I think it's going to work out great, Nick."

"What is, dear?"

"Your living next door. We'll sleep in my bed and set the alarm for two a.m. Then you can stroll back to your house."

"Why don't we sleep in *my* house and you can do the return stroll?"

"We could do that, dear. Assuming you don't mind your best girl wandering around in the middle of the night in a crime-infested urban neighborhood."

"All right, I guess I can do the sleep walking. Will you look less gnarly at two a.m. than at nine a.m.?"

"Probably not. But at two a.m. the bedroom will be *dark*."

After dinner we went outside to introduce Carli to my new wheels.

"What year is this beast?" she asked.

"1976. Jimmy Carter was President and our parents were young."

"Ancient times, Nick. It looks like something from the seventies. Has anyone figured out why things went so bad in that decade?"

"I think it had something to do with Richard Nixon and the war in Vietnam. Cocaine got super popular back then too. Also psychedelics. Bras and draft cards were being burned. Some of the movies were pretty good."

"Better than the 1950s, that's for sure. Although I'm kind of stuck on Sandra Dee. You can get up to seven letters on a custom license plate. Have you checked if GAS HOG is available?"

"I expect someone has grabbed that."

"Or try GAS HOGG, with double Gs at the end.

"OK, I'll look into it."

"Or check out D-E-T-H S-T-R."

"I get it: DEATH STAR. I like that."

"You're only 21, Nick, but already you got your grandpa wheels. You're all set for old age. Your walker should fit nicely in the trunk."

Do all Caddy drivers face that kind of abuse?

"Which do you like best, dear? My Caddy or my Matrix?"

She made a face. "Let's just say I never thought I'd be dating a guy driving *either* of them."

Looks like Carli may not wish to be seen in my new car. Not entirely disillusioned, she dragged me off to her bedroom. I'd left my condoms in my Toyota, but she had a stash left over from whiney Mr. Pacoima.

SUNDAY, June 26 – Another mystery phone caller. It was some guy.

"You don't know me," he said, "but I'm Walter Michaels. I believe you're dating my daughter."

"OK," I said, noncommittally.

"I believe you have had some conversations with my wife. She's a nice person, but can seem a bit abrasive if you don't know her well. Anyway, it's been like World War III around here lately. You'd be doing me a big favor if you would call Jordyn and accept her invitation to dinner here. My wife and I will not be present when you arrive."

Damn, I'm ensnared in a family that's even more dysfunctional than us Twisps.

"Uh, sir, I'm dating someone else now."

"Oh, dear. I hope it's not because of anything my wife said."

"She didn't help matters."

"Oh dear. This could make things even worse. What would it take for you to reconsider?"

Wow, was the dude offering me a bribe?

"I've got to go, sir," I said. "I'm expecting an important call."

I hung up fast. How high do you suppose that guy was willing to go for me to resume dating his daughter? Back in my poverty days I might have considered it.

I went next door and mooched breakfast off the Twisps. I told Dad I was renting a house in Mar Vista and would be moving out very soon.

"You can afford exorbitant west-side rents?" he asked. "Aren't you currently earning zero dollars a week?"

"The rent was too good of a deal to pass up," I lied.

"Better than the deal you're getting here?" he demanded.

"I need to get away from my ex-wife," I explained.

"That's fine, Nick," said Treez. "We'll need your apartment anyway when Otilia gets here."

Otilia is their former nanny.

"I thought she went back to Guatemala to take care of her sick mother," I said.

"Her mother died," said Treez. "So she's coming back. And I sure can use her help."

"When is she arriving?" I asked.

"That depends on how fast she can sneak across our porous borders," said Dad, helping himself to another cinnamon roll.

"That Guat lady better not think she can boss me," said Teejay.

"Or me either," added Edy.

"You'll both love her," said their mother. "Otilia is a very fine person. She has very high standards."

Yeah, as I recall she didn't think much of Dad. Or me.

"Why can't I have Nick's apartment?" asked Teejay. "I got rent money. Otilia could sleep in the stinky baby's room."

"Three-year-olds do not live on their own in separate apartments," replied his mother.

"Who made up that rule?" he demanded.

"I did," said Treez. "So deal with it."

"You'll be sorry when I'm a giant TV star," warned Teejay.

"I expect I will be," she sighed.

My phone rang again. This time it was Carli. I took my coffee out to the atrium.

"Good morning, Carli," I said. "Are you gnarly?"

"I'm sure I must be. I haven't dared look in a mirror. So, Nick dear, who are you getting to decorate your house?"

"I was thinking nobody. I think they'll work out fine and their rates are very affordable."

"But, dearest, you have no furniture."

"I have my new futon."

"If that futon winds up anywhere except in your guest-room, it will be a crime against humanity. We can go shop for furnishings and accessories together."

Another warning sign. Narcissists tend to be major control freaks. It was time to put my foot down.

"No thanks, dear. I'm an adult. I can go to a furniture store and pick out what I need."

"Please, Nick, promise me you won't go near IKEA."

"Those Scandinavians have to make a living too, Carli. As I recall, most of your furniture came from Denmark."

"My pieces are vintage, Nick. There are decorators in West Hollywood who would kill for my sideboard."

"There are hairdressers in India who would kill for my futon."

"That's hardly comparable. And highly debatable. I hope the cars you drive aren't harbingers of your taste."

"I think a house should be comfortable for its occupants."

"Nick, if I see a recliner in your living room, I may have to reevaluate our relationship."

"Oh, OK. You can advise me on furniture shopping. But be warned, I'm not into girly styles. There's a limit to the number of throw pillows I'm willing to tolerate."

"Our first stop will be a paint store. Let's face it, Gary and Keith, although seemingly gay, picked some very boring neutrals."

"I don't mind the wall colors, Carli. I bid on that house because it was move-in ready."

"I thought it was the only one you looked at."

"Yeah, that too."

Later Jordyn the Weaver phoned. She apologized for my receiving harassment calls from both of her parents.

"I'm an only child, Nick," she said. "So they're used to running rough-shod over my life."

"I know how that can be, Jordyn. I was an only child until age 15. Now I have seven half-sisters and brothers."

"That's amazing, Nick."

"One half-sister I've never even met."

"How is that possible?"

"Nerea runs a circus in Argentina. It keeps her too busy to visit. I expect things will get better for you when to go away to college."

"I'm counting down the days. Only two months to go. If things don't work out with your new lady friend, I'd be happy to hear from you again."

"I'll keep that in mind, dear. Thanks for calling."

I hope I haven't made a mistake ditching that girl. She seemed nice and never once expressed a desire to control what furniture I bought.

MONDAY, June 27 – Ginny Koven phoned as I was piloting the Caddy toward Venice to meet Cal for coffee. She said we have an appointment at the title company tomorrow morning to sign the papers. I won't have to write a massive check. They will suck the purchase money and fees from my bank account by computer.

I reminded Ginny that the deed should be in my new name. She said since I'm going back to my original name, the title company wants to see a copy of my birth certificate. I said OK, I'd bring it with me.

Cal seemed more cheerful than she was last week. She's up for the starring role in a movie. They want her for a second callback tomorrow.

"What's the part?" I asked, trying not to sound envious.

"I play this compulsive shoplifter married to a rich older man. I've got very skillful sticky fingers. I'm so good and so bored I have to invent new challenges for myself, like stealing things in alphabetical order. So if I heist a diamond bracelet one day, the next day I have to steal an Edsel car."

"That could be tough. Those cars are few and far between these days. So is it a comedy?"

"Hardly, Nickie. It's a serious psychological drama. Sort of Luis Buñuel meets Alfred Hitchcock. That's why they need a sultry but chilly blonde. My husband grows concerned and sends me to this attractive shrink. We have an affair and the shrink starts swiping stuff too. He's swept up in my darkness. I'm thinking if I get the part, I may have to do some actual shoplifting to prepare."

"I wouldn't count on the nice warden letting you out of prison to work on your movie. Are there any parts for me?"

"Sorry, Nick, there are no juvenile roles in the script."

"Thanks a pantsful, dear. Who are you up against for the part?"

"The usual suspects. If Tiara gets it, I'll be strangling that girl with my bare hands. I so wish my brother would knock her up. That would take her out of commission for at least a year."

"It would also make you an aunt. I got the house in Mar Vista. I'm getting the keys tomorrow."

"And what's the rent on that dive?"

"I'd rather not say, but I got a very good deal."

"This is the place that's next door to your slutty groupie?"

"Carli's neither slutty nor a groupie. The house is on Ocean View Avenue."

"And do you have a moist but watery view?"

"I'll have one as long as no one builds a McMansion behind me. I took your advice and ditched the weaver."

"Good for you, Nick. Now ditch the groupie and all will be right in your world."

"Not happening, dear. I can't be living like a monk while you carry on licentiously with Liam. Where's a good place to buy furniture?"

"Considering the rent you must be paying, I suggest the Salvation Army. Or cruise Beverly Hills for discards on the street. The director of my movie is this Brit named Nigel Froster."

"Froster as in cake froster?" I asked.

"Froster is not nearly as silly as Twisp. He's done some wonderful work on English TV."

"All Brits are great, Cal."

"Well, Jack the Ripper may not have been so wonderful. And nobody much liked Oswald Mosley except Diana Mitford. And poor Prince Andrew's been getting some bad press lately. I expect you sympathize with him."

"Why's that?"

"As I recall, you were trying to molest me when I was underage."

"I was younger than you, dearest. Therefore, my attempts constituted normal and acceptable teenage lust."

"Teenage yes, normal perhaps, and acceptable certainly not."

"I did ultimately prevail, dear, proving that persistence pays. I hope you get the part in that movie."

"I hope you get over your groupie. And soon!"

As usual we parted with a kiss. Then I drove to Lowes and bought a washer and dryer. The pair will be delivered on Thursday. I hope Carli won't be pissed that I didn't consult her first on brand, style, and color.

I'm so looking forward to staying out of laundromats. I hate it when I'm folding my underwear and some grungy stranger says, "Hey, aren't you Bronson Flange?"

Later, as I was back home and packing up my meager possessions, I answered another mystery call. This time it was USC film student Kinsley Vanoxit (daughter of my new tax accountant). She apologized for her dad never having heard of me.

"Yeah, I'm trying to crawl up from obscurity," I admitted.

"I'm surprised he took you on as a client. He usually only works with very wealthy people."

"I'm not wealthy," I lied.

"I don't see how you could be. You made two Poverty

Row movies. Then you did a series for Ed Bedrossian. He's like Latin America: all the pesos flow to the top; not much filters down to the peons. And how much could Gunslinger have paid you for those awful commercials? I don't know anyone who buys their lipstick."

"You should hang out more with prostitutes. It's a very popular brand with that crew."

"So what are you doing now?"

"I just finished a multi-part series in England."

"And now you've got nothing?"

"I've got some irons in the fire," I lied.

"My father spoke highly of you. That, of course, is the kiss of death. Should we get together? I leave it completely up to you."

It's possible Kinsley is not a control freak. That could be a plus.

"I'm busy moving this week, Kinsley. Why don't I call you when I get settled in?"

"Where are you moving to? Bakersfield? Fresno?"

"A bit closer in. I'm renting a house in Mar Vista."

"Did you have a paper route when you were a kid and saved every nickel?"

"I'm rather thrifty. I look forward to meeting you."

"Don't worry, Nick. If we meet for coffee, we'll go dutch."

TUESDAY, June 28 – I'm now a second-time homeowner, this time without Lucia DeFalco hogging half the space, most of the closet, and all of the garage. I received two sets of keys and a bottle of (non-sparkling) wine from Ginny. I've decided to forgive her for causing me to overpay for my house. It helps that she's personable and attractive. As we were leaving the title company's office, she asked how I was fixed for furniture.

"I have one futon," I replied.

She handed me a business card. "My friend Jim deals in

consignments and quality estates. He has a big shop in the Valley in a former K-Mart store. His prices are reasonable and he specializes in post-divorce needs."

"I'll go there right now," I said.

"Good, Nick. I'll phone Jim to alert him that you're on your way."

Jim looked like he could have been Danny Devito's shorter cousin. Perhaps to compensate for his size, his store was immense. We sat in his cluttered office, and I described the house I had just bought and my needs, but said my girl-friend wanted some input.

"Is this chick going to be living there?" he asked.

"No, she lives right next door."

"OK, you get your furniture here today, then let her pick out your towels and linens. She can settle for that input. I take it you want the masculine bachelor pad look. No frills, trills, or floral prints."

"Quality stuff and tasteful," I said, "but not looking like my granny lives there. No fake woods or particle board."

"I wouldn't let that junk in my shop, Nick."

"And no recliner in the living room, but I need a com-fortable chair."

"I got a nice knock-off Eames chair for you. All the com-fort of a recliner without the Archie Bunker vibes."

We sat at his desk and made a long list of what I needed: sofa, end tables, lamps, area rugs, wall art, dining room fur-nishings, master bedroom needs, study/guestroom require-ments, kitchen table, wastebaskets, etc.

"You got any china, Nick?"

"I have no dishes to speak of. I just got divorced."

"So she left you with your comb and your toothbrush. You want service for eight or twelve?"

"I think eight should be plenty. I need some silverware too."

"You got it. You want a set of fine china that stores in the dining room and everyday china for use in the kitchen?"

"I guess so."

Jim added them to his list, plus a selection of glassware. "You need a flat-screen TV?"

"Do you have those?"

"You name it, I got it. What size you need?"

"I don't know. What size would you recommend?"

"Anything bigger than 56 inches makes you look like a TV addict."

"OK, let's do 56 inches, plus a DVD player."

"Are you a reader, Nick? You need a bookcase?"

"One bookcase should do me fine."

"You want a selection of hardcover books with that? Very helpful for impressing chicks with your finely honed intellect."

"No, I can supply those."

"You want glass doors on your bookcase?"

"OK, I hate dusty books."

"How about pots and pans and utensils for the kitchen?"

"Sounds good. Plus, I need a microwave and a toaster oven."

"No problem. I'll also put you down for a mop, bucket, and vacuum cleaner. You need a lawn mower?"

"No, my gardener will be lugging his."

"OK, but you'll need two garden hoses. One for front and one for back. Anything else, Nick? You need a bowling ball or a ping pong table? How about a croquet set?"

"No thanks, but the desk chair in the study needs to be super comfortable."

"I'll test-sit it personally before it goes on the truck. So how does your girlfriend feel about this new futon of yours?"

"She hates it."

"How much did you pay for it?"

"$1,100."

"They saw you coming on that deal. Any unsightly stains?"

"No, I'm careful. It's in pristine condition."

"OK, we'll take it in on trade and substitute a nice sofa bed for the guestroom. You specified a double bed for the master suite, but I think you'd be happier in the long run with a queen."

"Love fades, huh?"

"I don't know about love, but passion certainly does. The mattress and box springs, of course, will be new. You want firm, extra-firm, or pillow top?"

"What do you think?"

"A young guy like you, no back problems, I'd go pillow top. Chicks like to be comfortable. You want the full white-glove delivery?"

"What does that entail?"

"My guys deliver, arrange the furnishings according to *their* tastes, hang the art on the walls, and put away the dishes and other incidentals. It's best if you keep out of their way. And all chicks must be off the premises. That's our strict rule."

"Sounds fine."

"I'll be sending a three-man team, who will expect tips of at least $100 cash each. You down with that?"

"No problem."

Jim went to work on his adding machine. The total before tax came to $19,612.47. I asked him if he could do any better than that since I was an unemployed actor. He offered to eat half the sales tax. I agreed and wrote out the check.

"How soon can you deliver?" I asked.

"We'll be there tomorrow at 11 a.m. sharp. You be there too or you'll be subject to tremendously exorbitant extra charges. I'm not kidding."

"I'll be there. Don't you worry. So everything's going to be in matching styles and nicely coordinated?"

"Do I look like a clueless, color-blind Philistine?"

He did sort of, but I let that pass. I reminded myself that he'd been vouched for by Ginny Koven, a very nicely packaged gal.

That was much less of an ordeal than I'd been expecting. Even traffic driving back from the Valley wasn't too bad. I was tying my futon to the roof of my Caddy when my ex-wife returned from her summer carpentry job. She parked and strolled over.

"Moving somewhere, Nick?"

"I'm renting a house in Mar Vista."

"Sounds expensive. How big is it?"

"Fourteen-hundred square feet plus lower-level utility room."

"Wow, that's big. Way bigger than our house. You can afford that?"

"I wouldn't be doing it if I couldn't afford it."

"Your cousin Tyler offered to sell Cliff our house, but we need something bigger."

"Bigger gets pricey fast."

"I know. I'm sorry I got picky with you about parking your car."

"Not a problem, dear. All is forgotten."

WEDNESDAY, June 29 – I slept last night partly in my new house, having returned from next door at 2:01 a.m. I'm not sure how that arrangement is going to work out. It took me quite a while to get back to sleep.

Fortunately, Gary and Keith had left behind the window mini-blinds, so I wasn't flashing the neighbors. Nor was I stumbling around in the dark, since I'd had the utilities transferred to my name.

Carli was dubious about my one-stop shopping marathon, but agreed to reserve judgment. I told her if she showed up while the men were delivering, I'd have her arrested for trespassing.

"You'd really do that, Nick?" she asked, offended.

"With great reluctance, dear, but Jim was firm on that point: no females on the premises during delivery."

"He sounds like a total sexist pig. And you're entrusting your home decorating needs to that Neanderthal?"

"I am, dear, but we'll have fun shopping for linens and towels."

She might be having fun; I doubt I will be.

The truck arrived at 11:04 a.m. While the burly dudes hauled in the goods, I washed my Caddy in the driveway with my new (barely used) garden hose. Carli crouched behind her hedge and spied on the action. I sprayed over in her direction periodically to keep her confined to her yard. At 12:58 p.m. the men were done. I handed each two Benjamins and thanked them for their work.

"What year is your green Caddy?" asked the man in charge, pocketing his tip.

"It's a 1976," I replied. "The Jimmy Carter special."

"The height of the Malaise Era," he noted. "Not many of those clunkers left on the road."

After the truck roared off (hauling away my banished futon), Carli approached warily.

"Have you gone in to view the disaster?" she asked.

"Not yet, dear. Shall we go do the grand tour together?"

To create the proper ambiance, Jim's crew had left all the new lamps switched on. The giant TV was tuned to a sports channel. I could almost imagine a young Hugh Hefner kicking back in my stylish living room. Amenities included a taut but comfortable sofa, authentic Eames chair knock-off, coffee table with a selection of *GQ* magazines, matching end tables with lamps, low cabinet serving as a TV stand, framed vintage prints of champion race horses, and a decorative Persian rug tying it all together.

"What do you think?" I asked.

"It desperately needs some throw pillows. And too bad you didn't get a tall cabinet to hide that ugly TV."

The appetizing dining room featured an imposing rectangular table with eight chairs, a buffet, and a matching hutch. My dishes were tasteful Crestwood Platinum china by Noritake. The manly stainless pattern was Column by Gorham Silver. All neatly stowed in the buffet. The hutch was loaded with assorted glassware and stem ware. Doors in its lower section opened on a mirrored bar with slide-out counter and mirrored lift-off tray. Sure to be handy in my later alcoholic years.

"What kind of wood is this?" I asked, rubbing my hand over the gleaming table.

"It looks like rosewood," said Carli, impressed. "Probably not solid, just veneer."

Gracing the guestroom were an ample desk, matching credenza, bookcase with glass doors, and attractive sofa bed. Despite the compactness of the room, it didn't feel crowded. Mounted over the desk was a selection of framed vintage movie posters, including one from my accordion movie. If you looked closely, my name could be discerned in the tall but extremely squeezed type.

I tested the rolling desk chair. Super comfortable and adjustable in 27 places to conform to every body contour.

My bedroom was just as richly furnished, complete with walnut bed, night stands with lamps, bureau, and matching dresser with mirror, framed views of Tuscan hillsides on the walls, and flat woven rugs on either side of the bed. There was even a Chinese-style screen that milady could hide behind if she was feeling too gnarly to be seen.

Carli pulled out a drawer and examined its construction.

"All dovetailed joints," I pointed out.

"This one smells like some dead woman's cologne," she commented.

"Reusing quality, well-constructed furniture is friendly to the planet," I stressed.

Carli flopped down on my new mattress, still wrapped in its factory plastic. "I never heard of this brand," she said, "but it seems comfortable."

I lay beside her and gave her a kiss.

"I expect you'll be entertaining lots of girls in this room," she remarked.

"No doubt, dear. But you'll have the satisfaction of knowing you were my first."

"Wow, I am so lucky."

She unclinched and slunk across the room to check her appearance in the dresser mirror. No gnarliness was seen.

"You did OK, Nick. It's not horrible. It's at least a couple steps up from the total Motel 6 dystopian look. You could have done worse."

"I think it's great, Carli. Already, I feel like I've lived in this house for years."

"Your furniture does look like it's been here for decades."

Carli suggested I think about rearranging things. I disagreed.

"Everything seems ideally placed," I said. "Positioned exactly where it should be for maximum utility and serene enjoyment. Those pros really know what they're doing. I only wish I could hire them to take command of every other aspect of my life."

I phoned Jim and congratulated him on his taste, design expertise, and professional service. He thanked me and said positive reviews on Yelp are always welcome.

Carli was meeting some UCLA friends for dinner. Before she left she suggested I check the underside of all my new drawers.

"And why's that, dear?" I asked.

"Lots of people tape their escape money under there."

"I don't think they do that much anymore. Now they just make a quick stop at the ATM as they're blowing town."

I nuked my dinner in my new (used) microwave and ate at my new (used) kitchen table. Full domesticity had been achieved in less than a day.

THURSDAY, June 30 – The mattress was fine; I slept very well. Yesterday evening as I was relaxing in my faux Eames chair, a flea bit me on the ankle. Probably a little pal of Heidi's who missed the boat when the truck left for Indiana. So I had to vacuum the entire house.

There's a vital donut shop a short walk away on Venice Boulevard, but here's my dilemma: There's a *much better* one five blocks farther along. I did the long trek this morning, but it was a challenge on an empty stomach. I may have to do the L.A. compromise: skip the exercise and just drive to the preferred shop in my Caddy.

While waiting for Lowes' delivery truck, I decided to check the underside of my drawers. Taped under my top desk drawer was a yellowed envelope containing this note typed on an old-style typewriter.

To whom it may concern:

If you are reading this, I likely am deceased and my possessions have been sold for back rent and/or funeral expenses. So be it!

I came to Los Angeles from Iowa in 1953 with the intention of becoming an actor. I graduated from the same high school as Donna Reed, who was my inspiration.

Since then I have worked at almost every sort of job except acting. Many are called, but few are chosen. I know I would have been a decent actor had I been given a chance. Instead I had to labor at jobs I disliked to keep a roof over my head and food on the table.

If I sound bitter, it is because my choice of profession has stunted and embittered my life. I never married and have no children. I should not have embarked on a career where success depends on the whims of directors, producers, talent agents, casting agents, etc.

I realize now I should have stayed in Iowa and gone into my father's lumber business as he wished and expected. I could have married a local girl and had children with her. Instead, I wasted my life in a futile quest for what? Acclaim by a fickle public? A brief taste of fame? Imaginary wealth dangled just out of reach?

If you are reading this, I hope and pray you have chosen a wiser path in life than I did.

Sincerely yours,

Samuel F. Broughton

Gee, that was certainly a cheerful message from a dead guy. I wonder if he got nailed by Covid. I Googled his name and came up with nothing. Never making it on the Web anywhere is a serious case of dying in obscurity.

Can't write anymore. My new washer and dryer have arrived.

Later, after doing my laundry in the privacy of my own home, I rode my bike to a 99-cents store and bought a frame. I mounted Samuel F. Broughton's letter in the frame and hung it on the wall above my/his desk.

If fate chose to deliver that message to me, I figured I should honor it.

Of course, if I was really listening to the guy, I'd move to Iowa, go in the lumber business, and marry Avery Weston.

JULY

FRIDAY, July 1 – I went back home and mooched break-fast off the Twisps. My excuse was I needed to return the key to the apartment.

"We want to come see your new place," said Treez.

"Yeah, preferably before you're evicted for non-payment of rent," added Dad.

"I think I'll be fine for a while," I replied. "You're welcome to drop by anytime."

"Will you have a place for anyone to sit?" asked Dad.

"The house came fully furnished," I lied. "The setup is fairly comfortable."

"My TV show starts streaming in four days!" announced Teejay.

"I see they're promoting it heavily on the Web," I said. "I hope people don't get sick of seeing your face before it even airs."

"I'm sure they'd rather look at me than you," he retorted.

"I'm in it too," Edy reminded him.

"Bit parts," said Teejay. "You have a few bit parts. I'm the star!"

The kid was small, but his ego was huge.

I showed Dad a photo on my phone of Samuel F. Broughton's framed letter. He read it through.

"All extremely wise counsel," said Dad. "You should learn from this fellow's mistakes. I'm still willing to chip in for real-estate school for you."

"You went into show business," I pointed out. "It worked out for you. You're married and have eight children."

His youngest was slumbering in a sling on his chest.

"I worked at a skill that separated me from the crowd," he replied. "I succeeded primarily as a comic juggler, not an actor."

"Daddy wants to teach me juggling," commented Tee-jay, "but I don't want to wind up old and unemployed."

"I'm not unemployed, son," he replied. "I'm busy writing my memoirs, but my progress is hindered by the impositions on my time of my excess children."

Kind of a "don't exist" message for the younger set. Sensing the negative vibe, little Marilyn leaned over and urped down his shirt.

As a wannabe actor, Carli didn't think much of my framed letter. She thinks I should tear it up and dismiss it from my mind. Also she suggested I drag the author's desk outside and set it on fire. I declined. Nevertheless, she invited me over for lunch at her place. This time we sat at her cozy kitchen booth. I reminded her that when my friends and family show up, we were going with the story that I was renting the house.

"And why is that again, Nick?" she asked.

"Nobody needs to know I can afford to buy a house. I value my privacy."

"Most rich people like to brag about their wealth. Some Russian oligarchs buy giant yachts with indoor swimming pools. Showing off how rich you are is a status thing."

"I'm certainly not rich," I lied. "Speaking of which, what do your parents do?

"I told you, Nick, they shop. Last I heard my dad was pricing coffee plantations in Hawaii."

"OK, so how did they acquire all this money for shopping?"

"My dad's a chemist. He used to work for a big chemical company, but wanted to go out on his own. So whenever he met someone, like on the golf course, he would ask what they needed from the field of chemistry."

"You mean like a better way to get high?" I asked.

"He got a lot of responses like that. So one day this fellow he met at a Rotary lunch said what he needed was a better mold release."

"He had a mold problem?"

"Not that kind of mold. It turns out lots of things in this world are molded, you know in factories. And sometimes the castings don't want to release from the mold. So my dad got on it and invented a superior mold release. Now they sell millions of gallons of the stuff around the world, and my dad gets a royalty on every gallon sold."

Damn, I should have devoted more effort to that chemistry set Aunt Grace laid on me. I suppose it's too late now.

After lunch we drove to Beverly Hills in my Matrix (easier to park) and spent $9,000+ on bed sheets, blankets, comforters, down pillows, throw pillows, towels, dish towels, napkins, etc. This ordeal by fire was way too exhausting for me to describe here.

SATURDAY, July 2 – When I returned at 2:01 a.m., I was shocked to see that sprinklers were spraying all over my yard. After breakfast I went out and switched off the timer. I see no reason I should run up my water bill just to encourage the grass to grow. That reminds me, I need to find a gardener. Or would it be cheaper in the long run to have the entire lot paved over?

Several neighbors came over this morning to introduce themselves. I can't tell them I'm renting because Gary and Keith had been bragging that the buyer was a "famous actor." The neighbors seemed confused when I introduced myself as Nick Davidson. But I see no reason why my life should be an open book to any and all Mar Vistians. I don't pry into their affairs.

Having put away all my stuff, I thought about what I

should do next in life. So I phoned USC film student Kinsley Vanoxit.

"I thought you were busy moving this week," she said.

"I'm all moved and unpacked. Want to meet somewhere for coffee?"

"I'm kind of fully caffeinated for the day. Want to come here and hang by the pool?"

"Where's here?"

"My parents' house in Holmby Hills."

Jesus, my tax accountant lives in Holmby Hills. I told Kinsley I could be there in 45 minutes.

"Do you offer valet parking?" I asked.

"Hardly, Nick. Our house is the crummiest one on Brooklawn Drive."

Their house (not crummy) was a short drive up the hill from Walt Disney's former home. Very posh neighborhood, but you can't see much from the street as everyone is secluded behind high walls and/or hedges. It's a look I may need to replicate in Mar Vista.

I punched in the code provided by Kinsley, the motorized gate swung open, I parked, and I found my way down to the fabulous pool. Kinsley, looking tanned, relaxed, and rich, had buttoned a man's shirt over her bikini. She was seated at a chaise and working on her MacBook Air.

"My God," she said, not rising. "It's Nick Twisp in the flesh."

"Well, mostly clothed," I replied, giving her an awkward air hug where she sat. "And soon to be Nick Davidson."

"At least you're not changing your first name. That would be too confusing. There's a fridge in the pool house, Nick. Go grab yourself a drink."

I selected sparkling apple juice and sat back in the chaise next to Kinsley. I took a swig and looked around.

"I could get used to this lifestyle," I said, "but probably won't."

"My mother's family invested in Douglas Aircraft back when it was a tiny little company."

"Very smart of them. My family was investing in flophouses."

"You come from a line of slumlords?"

"No, my grandfather was a bum on skid row. He lived in flophouses. So what are you working on?"

"Story outline for our student film. You want to be in it?"

"Are you paying SAG minimum?"

"Dream on, dude."

"What's it about?"

"Good question. I wish I knew."

"Yeah, story outlines are tough. Stick to a Christmas theme. It worked for me."

"I heard about that project."

"I saw the rough cut a few weeks ago. I have to admit, I liked it."

"I hear Christmas movies are the easiest to get distributed."

"That was my thinking too."

"Too bad no one at USC would dare make a Christmas film."

"Why not, Kinsley?"

"The ridicule would kill you."

"Peer pressure is an ugly thing. I'm thinking of giving up acting."

"Really? And why's that, Nick?"

"Too much grief and disappointment. Why should I sit around waiting for the phone to ring? Why should I be subjected to the whims of directors, producers, talent agents, and casting agents?"

"I know what you mean. It's very competitive."

"I have a new neighbor who wants to be an actor. But

I know she'll have a hard time. She's attractive, but she missed out on being beautiful."

"Missed out how?"

"Her face is a bit too long. It strikes you right away. The proportions are slightly off. This is making her sensitive about her looks."

"So how well do you know this new neighbor?"

"Oh, we've chatted a few times. She's a student at UCLA."

"Ask her if she wants to be in my movie. So what would you do if you give up acting?"

"I'm thinking now I'd rather be a producer. You know, be the big dude in charge. Rake in all those profits."

"You're a detail-oriented person who can play the hustle game and deal with constant demands, setbacks, and conflicts in a business rife with sharks and shysters?"

"Uhmmm . . . I was thinking I could delegate most of that to underlings. I'd be in charge of making actors crawl."

"I'm not getting street-smart hustler vibes off you, Nick. I'd stick with acting. You're a proven success in that field."

Why are girls never able to discern my inner shark?

Although I had worn my bathing trunks under my clothes, neither of us actually got in the pool. We chatted until the time was approaching for her parents to return from their golf outing. Kinsley invited me to stay for dinner, but for some reason I felt the need to bail. Too much concentrated affluence?

Since I'm now wealthy, I may have to work on being relaxed and comfortable around rich folks. Right now they mostly give me the willies.

SUNDAY, July 3 – The Twisps arrived in force at breakfast time. Fortunately, Lefty had provided them with a picnic basket stuffed with lavish brunch items. They checked out my house while I put on the coffee.

"I didn't think landlords rented out furnished houses anymore," said Dad, returning to the kitchen. "Is this a sublet?"

"No, I can stay as long as I like."

"And you're not going to tell me how much you're paying?" he asked.

"Let's just say it's a real bargain," I replied.

"It's nicer than Cliff's house," said Teejay. "And bigger too. Lucia's going to be sorry she dumped you."

"That's not a very polite thing to say," cautioned his mother.

"Hey, she did dump him," Teejay replied. "And I didn't mention the sexual betrayal. My TV show starts in two days!"

"Wow, there's some news we can use," I said.

"What's down these stairs?" asked Edy, opening the door to the lower level.

"A utility room," I said. "I wouldn't go down there unless you like big hairy spiders."

Edy quickly shut the door.

We ate in the dining room on my good china. Mouths were wiped on my new cloth napkins that cost $32 each.

Dad had lugged along his Sunday paper, but hadn't unfolded it. He did so and let out a muffled shriek. There was a review of Teejay's (and Almy's) new series. On the front page. On the front page of the newspaper, not the entertainment section. The headline said it all: "Extraordinary child actor triumphs in Depression-era series."

Damn.

Not at all a pleasant way to begin your Sunday.

Bad timing too.

Here was my little brother at last putting us Twisps on the showbiz map right as I was changing my name to Davidson. Thanks a pantsful, Aunt Grace.

Cal phoned. I excused myself and took the call outside on my still-green grass.

"Nickie, did you see the review?" she exclaimed.

"We just discovered it."

"Your ex-girlfriend is going to be insufferable!"

"My little brother already is. They're over here now. You want to come join us? We're brunching on Lefty's gourmet items."

"I couldn't handle that many Twisps at once, Nick. Instead of going out for coffee tomorrow, why don't I come to your place?"

"Sure, OK. Shall we make it our usual time?"

"Sounds good, assuming you'll have all the chicks and groupies cleared out by then."

"I'll do my best. See you tomorrow, darling."

I returned to the house to endure more Teejay bragging. That kid sure likes to exult in his own glory. To change the subject, I inquired what was up with Otilia, the once and future nanny.

"She's made it to Puerto Peñasco," said Dad.

"Where's that?" I asked.

"It's a town on the Gulf of California. American tourists drive there in their RVs to get their teeth worked on. There's a dentist there who will give you a big discount if you make the return trip with a passenger in the bathroom of your RV. Apparently, those vehicles are not often searched at the border."

"So who pays the dentist?" I asked.

"In this case it's the patsy hiring the nanny," said Dad.

Later, against my better judgment, I bought a paper and read the full review. At the very end, discussing Amalda Preston's burgeoning career, the reviewed noted, "Now engaged to a fellow Juilliard student, Ms. Preston was once romantically linked with Teejay Twisp's older brother Nick Twisp II, who has had something of an acting career."

Yes, that certainly made my day.

MONDAY, July 4, Independence Day – Last year on this day I was married and attending a barbecue with Luco and Charlotte Caxton at the Frank C. Wyatts' in Chatsworth. Now I'm divorced, unemployed but not hard up, and haven't heard from Charlotte in nearly a year.

Cal was only 10 minutes late. I had procured everything to make her standard decaf low-fat soy latte—including a bulky espresso machine, which now gleamed on my kitchen counter. When I answered her knock, she asked me to point out the house of my "groupie neighbor."

"It's that one," I said.

"Oh, right next door, Nickie. I'm sure that's immensely convenient for you."

"It can be at times," I admitted.

I gave her a house tour; she oohed and aahed appropriately. In my study she leaned in close to examine the framed letter. I explained how I had come to find it.

"I can see why the fellow never made it as an actor," commented Cal. "He's much, much, much too morose. Inspired by Donna Reed. How pathetic can you get?"

"Hey, I like Donna Reed. What have you got against her?"

"Donna Reed was nothing but a poor man's Paulette Goddard. I'd rather have the original than the imitation. So why are you showcasing Mr. Broughton's maudlin self-recriminations on your wall?"

"He's my new guru."

"I see. So you now are receiving career counseling from beyond the grave. That is so sick."

While I struggled in the kitchen with the Italian technology, Cal poked around in the far corners of my house. Eventually, I got my new machine to produce a cup of espresso and to steam Cal's soy milk.

"I finally figured it out," she said, returning to the kitchen and accepting my offered cup.

"OK, darling, what have you figured out?"

"That dead relative of yours left you more than that relic Cadillac. She somehow left you a big enough legacy for you to sign a one-year lease on this overpriced rental."

"That certainly qualifies as a theory, dear. Care for a muffin?"

Cal peered doubtfully into the offered pink box.

"Keep these away from an open flame, Nickie. They contain enough oil to burn down the entire west side."

We retired to my sunny dining room with our breakfast treats.

"Have you called Almy Preston to congratulate her on the review?" asked Cal.

"She's not really welcoming my calls these days. I can tell you that Teejay is being inundated with requests for interviews. I expect Almy is too. What's happening with your shoplifting movie?"

"The idiots are still trying to decide on casting. Meanwhile, I'm going quietly insane. Liam isn't helping either."

"Why? What's up with Liam?"

"He's gone and bought a sailboat."

"Probably with funds he embezzled from you!"

"I think not. But now he wants to go sailing every weekend."

"And you're leaving port with him?"

"Certainly not. You know how I feel about that. Plus, you'll recall I was raped in a sailboat."

"I know. That was terrible, darling. Liam is being very insensitive."

As we all recall, in retribution for that assault Harvey (with my assistance) brought the rapist to the ultimate threshold of human pain endurance. You don't really want to cross Harvey.

"So Liam is off on his boat all weekend while you're left cooling your heels alone?" I asked.

"Exactly. Plus, there are all these wannabe sailor girls hanging around Marina del Rey hankering to 'crew' on boats."

"And Liam is extremely good-looking," I pointed out. "He's probably getting quite a few eager volunteers."

Cal sipped her latte and sighed. "From now on I'm only going out with guys into solitary land activities like stamp collecting."

We heard a tap on my back door. I ignored it. They rapped again.

"Someone's knocking on your door, Nickie."

"I think that was a woodpecker on a pole," I lied.

"You should answer the door, Nick. They are being most insistent."

The back door caller was Carli; I did not invite her in.

"Hi, Nick. Did you buy a new car? There's a blue Miata parked in your driveway."

"It's not my car, Carli. I'm having coffee with a friend. This really isn't a good time—"

I stopped when Cal strolled into the kitchen. Carli peered around the door.

"Aren't you going to introduce me, Nick?" Carli asked.

"Uh, Carli, this is Valerie Haseltine. Cal, this is my neighbor Carli Eryngilli."

"Hello," said Cal, not warmly.

"Nice to meet you, Ms. Haseltine. I've admired your work."

"Thank you," said Cal. "You live around here somewhere?"

"Next door, as it happens," she replied.

Eventually, that chilly exchange terminated and we two returned to our coffees.

"Now the shoe is on the other foot," observed Cal.

"How so, darling?"

"It is *you*, Nickie dear, who is being spied upon."

"Yeah, this could get awkward."

"Your groupie would look better if she gained about 40 pounds."

"Dare I ask why you say that?"

"Then her face might get wide enough to balance out its length. She looks like Popeye's girlfriend. What's her name?"

"Uh, Olive Oyl?"

"Right. Your groupie looks like Olive Oyl."

In fact, Carli looks nothing like that cartoon character, but I let it pass. I can only hope such overt animosity shows that Cal still cares for me.

Unlike on our previous house tours, this time Cal did not stay to sample the delights of my bedroom.

Later I drove alone to Encino for a Twisp-thronged July 4th cookout at the Scott Twisps. My brother had heard about my new digs, and is eager to see them.

His wife's business partner Brenda Blatt was lounging beside the pool in a peppy summer outfit. I sat down next to her.

"Hi, Nick," she said, "I hear you're now a fellow Mar Vistian."

"Yes, I've now moved into the world's greatest neighborhood."

"Mar Vista got swallowed by Los Angeles in 1927, Nick. We needed their water."

"So how did Santa Monica and Culver City avoid that fate?"

"Santa Monica got its water from springs in the Santa Monica Mountains. I think they still do to some extent. I don't know about Culver City. Perhaps M.G.M. kept their extras busy between setups digging wells. I'll have my assistant Don look into it."

"So, Brenda, how are you fixed for interns?"

"What?" she asked, startled.

"I want to learn to be a movie producer. Do you need any interns?"

"We have an intern for the summer, Nick. Sorry."

"How about when they leave in the fall?"

"You want to answer phones, copy scripts, file correspondence, pick up lunch orders at the deli, and take abuse from me? All for zero pay?"

"Yeah, that's the idea."

"Nick, I think you're well past the intern stage in your career."

"OK, how about I buy into your business? How much would I have to invest to become your partner?"

Brenda gave it some thought.

"Nick, you show up at our office with $10 million and we'll give you some serious consideration."

I told her I would think about it.

TUESDAY, July 5 – Streaming day for Teejay's series. Yeah, I plan to watch it tonight. The self-torture may firm up my commitment to abandoning acting as a career.

Since I was still pissed at Carli for spying, I phoned Kinsley and asked if she wanted to watch the show on my big 56-inch TV.

"That's not really that big of a screen by modern standards," she replied.

"Oh, are you only interested in guys with super-big screens?"

"Don't jump to conclusions, Nick. What time do you want the body in the chair?"

"How about eight p.m.? What sort of snacks are you into?"

"Popcorn suits me fine. I don't do beer or sodas. Is ice tea out of the question for you?"

"I can do that. Black, green, or herbal?"

"Whatever you got. I'm not picky."

I gave her my address and told her to feel free to park in my driveway.

After thinking it over, I decided Brenda wasn't serious about the $10 million offer. I think she just came up with that figure to discourage me from pursuing the topic. I'm sure she'd be amazed to know I actually have $10 million. It still astounds me daily.

Carli knocked on my door again. This time she was at my front door and bearing a gift-wrapped box.

"Hi, Nick," she said. "I got you a house-warming gift."

I invited her in and unwrapped my gift. It was a hot-air fryer.

"Now you can make your own oil-free parsnip fries," she said brightly, adding, "I'm sorry about butting in on you and Valerie. I guess she spent the night, huh?"

"No, she stopped by to see my house and have coffee. I don't appreciate your spying on me."

"I wasn't spying, Nick. Honest, I thought you bought a new car. I thought you traded in your crummy old Matrix."

"There'll be another car in the driveway tonight, dear. And I won't have bought that one either."

"Fine, Nick. I'm not trying to interfere with your busy life. Enjoy your hot-air fryer!"

She departed pretty much in a huff. I may need to let things cool off with that girl. She did get me thinking about my Matrix. Is it time to move up from my reliable but austere car? The lack of padding in its seat and my butt did not make for comfortable long-distance driving. My Cadillac, though swaddling me in luxury, was a constant challenge to park.

The Haseltine Pet Store is much closer to me now. I walked there to check in with my buddy Harvey. As usual, he was awaiting customers behind the counter.

"Harvey," I said, "I was talking to Brenda Blatt yesterday. She thinks you should give up on engineering and become an actor like your wife. She's willing to sign you to a life-time contract."

"I may do that if I undergo a sudden and profound dim-inution of my I.Q. We're having a sale today on gerbils."

"I try to maintain a lifestyle free of small rodents. I'm thinking of trading in my Matrix. You know about these things, what car should I get?"

"What are your automotive needs?"

"I need something that's comfortable, easy to park, reli-able, and a magnet to chicks."

"You want foreign or domestic?"

"Nothing German. Those people are trying to take re-venge for World War defeats by keeping Americans con-stantly in the repair shop."

"How about a Tesla?"

"Range anxiety I don't need. I have enough worries al-ready."

Harvey suggested I look into a Honda Accord hybrid.

"I already have a grandpa car, Harvey. I don't need two of them."

"My sister told me about your ancient Caddy. That thing pass smog?"

"Barely. I'm sure the Smog Board would love to see it compacted to a small cube in a crusher. Or driven off the nearest cliff."

Eventually, we concluded that the car I needed was a Ford Mustang. Of course! Why hadn't I thought of that be-fore?

Kinsley was right on time. Now that I saw her upright, I realized she was on the short side. Fortunately, I like pe-tite girls. My popcorn was freshly popped; the tea was iced oolong.

"How long have you lived here, Nick?" she asked, look-ing around. "I thought you just moved."

"I did, but I make myself at home fast. It's a rental. So

are you going to watch the story unfold like a normal viewer? Or just concentrate on the director's technique?"

"Nick, if you walk into a custom tailor shop wearing a suit from JC Penney, you can bet the tailors will be checking the details of your threads. But I'm optimistic. Roland Pacalac has a reputation for achieving great things from skimpy material. His first film 'Store Rage' is studied in film schools around the world."

"He was the DP on my dad's movie, the one I starred in."

"Right. Well, we can all have our career setbacks."

What did she mean by that?

Kinsley grabbed the knockoff Eames chair, consigning me to the sofa. We streamed the first two episodes. Rather painful to watch dear Almy suffer through the Depression. The screenwriters piled on the hardships with a trowel. They even had them freezing with no heat in the middle of summer.

At one point Kinsley asked, "Does your little brother have eye trouble or is he doing a bad impression of Robert Mitchum?"

"It's the latter, Kinsley. Very astute of you to notice."

To build viewer interest and word of mouth, the network is limiting streaming to two episodes a week.

"What's your verdict?" I asked, as the credits rolled.

"I'm impressed, Nick. The story is fairly standard stuff, but your brother is just mind-bogglingly precocious. He steals every scene."

"Yeah, he has an ego to match in real life."

"I thought Almy Preston was quite effective as well. I suppose she was channeling all the pain you put her through."

"The pain-dishing was mutual, take my word for it. What can I get you?"

"I better go, Nick. This has been fun."

"Want to meet here next week, same time, same station?"

"Sure, Nick. I think I'm free. I'll let you know ahead of time if I'm not."

"It's a plan, dear. Say hi to your dad from me."

"Right. Will do."

She escaped without being grabbed by me. Probably just as well.

WEDNESDAY, July 6 – Teejay's show was all over the news today. Apparently, the first two episodes racked up the largest viewing audience in the history of streaming. Everyone connected with the show (except me) must be immensely pleased.

Then Cal phoned with some news. She got the part in the shoplifting movie.

"Congratulations, dear," I said, grudgingly. "How soon do you start?"

"They want me for makeup and wardrobe tests as soon as my agent finalizes the deal."

"Where will you be filming—Georgia, Toronto, or Vancouver?"

"None of the above. Right here in L.A. They want us in our homes at night to minimize Covid spread."

"That's progressive. I'm sure you'll be great. Do you know who else is in the cast?"

"They're not saying. I hope I'm working with major stars."

"Yeah, don't we all."

Then Connie Saunders called. She had been talking to Dad about my name change and house rental.

"Is everything all right with you, Nick?" she asked, sounding concerned.

"Couldn't be better. I'm sorry I missed you when I picked up my car from your garage. Your housekeeper said you were in Las Vegas."

"I was dipping my toe in casino gambling."

"How did you do?"

"Not excessively depleted. It was fun and educational. Your dad is worried that you're going off the deep end from your divorce."

"Nope. I'm fine. Not troubled in my personal life. Not in need of drastic helicopter parenting."

"How are your poker skills?"

"As great as ever, I'm sure."

We made a date for tomorrow at her place. She needs a victim to practice on. I wonder how long it would take for her to win my entire inherited pile? Fortunately, she doesn't try to collect on her winnings from me.

I went on the Web to find a car. It turns out new Mustangs are in short supply because of the computer chip shortage. I found a dealer in the Valley with a Mustang Eco-Boost in Velocity Blue. That's the one with the turbo four-banger. Since I don't expect to be drag-racing crazed teens on urban streets, I prefer Ford's less gas-thirsty model.

The salesman said to come right away and bring the pink slip for my Matrix. Through some miracle I located it in my new desk. The dealer offered me only $3,000 trade-in for my car and wasn't willing to negotiate on the Mustang's list price. He said he was doing me a favor selling it for the sticker price. These days, it's a seller's market for cars as well as houses. So we made the deal, and I wrote out another fat check.

The salesman took a selfie with me standing next to my new car. I told him I would be most grateful if that photo never wound up on social media.

"Nick, this is a very prestigious car," he assured me. "It's the perfect wheels for a major TV star such as yourself."

Not entirely true and we both knew it, but I let it pass. I felt a bit sad leaving behind my Matrix, which was my very first car. It served me well for many years. Too bad I never had occasion to do it on the diagonal in the back. Nor do I expect to be trying that in my Mustang.

My new car is much more comfortable and powerful than my Toyota. It also has lots of new safety features, such as scoping out cars lurking in your blind spot. The salesman recommended I watch online videos explaining how to use the infotainment screen and its controls. Not as complicated as flying a 747, but close.

THURSDAY, July 7 – Watched Almy and Teejay being interviewed on TV last night. Both very personable and articulate. No mention of my name.

Drove my Mustang to the better donut shop today. Came out to find a big seagull splatter on my hood. You'd think those birds could do a more thorough job of digesting their fish. I was washing it off back home when Carli emerged.

"I'm not going to ask whose car that is, Nick," she said. "I know it's none of my business."

"It's my car, dear. I traded in my old Matrix."

"A Mustang, huh? Aren't those a bit redneck and blue-collar?"

"I'm working on changing my image. I'm going for the full unemployed lowlife look. But it will take me a while to grow my mullet and get addicted to meth."

"Are you telling people that your car is only rented?"

I gave it some thought.

"No, I'm saying that it's leased."

"And is it leased?"

"No. I bought it."

"Will you be giving me a ride in it?"

"We'll take it on our next date."

"Oh, we're having one of those?"

"Soon, dear. I'll be in touch."

That must have been good news. She gave me a hug and a kiss.

I showed up at Connie Saunders's Bel-Air mansion with a surprise hostess gift: a brand new hot-air fryer in the original box. Connie seemed intrigued by the concept and said she would turn it over to her cook for experimentation.

Connie also had a surprise for me: a house guest in the person of Charlotte Caxton, who gave me my second hug and kiss (on the cheek) of the morning. Looks like that girl has worked through any lingering resentment over my (very) peripheral involvement in her father's violent knee-capping.

Both Connie and Charlotte strolled out to look over my new car.

"Did you blow all the profits from your house sale on this flashy car?" asked Connie.

"Not at all, Connie dear. I played a lot of poker with the cast of my English TV show."

"And you won?" asked Charlotte, incredulous.

"English actors must be the worst poker players in the world!" exclaimed Connie.

As usual, I ignored the abuse.

"How's your dad doing?" I asked Charlotte.

"He's walking OK with his cane. He's aged about ten years though."

"Tell Nick what he said about the attack," prompted Connie.

"He says shooting him in one knee would have been making a valid economic point. But he regards shooting him in *both* knees as excessively sadistic and cruel."

"You know what I heard, Charlotte?" I said. "I heard that the cops are never going to find Betty Kogstad or Lois Anikeevo. The rumor is that your dad hired thugs to track them down. Those ladies have now gone the way of Jimmy Hoffa."

"Not true, Nick. My dad would never do anything like that."

"I hope not. Is Hunter here with you?"

Hunter McCaffrey is her studly boyfriend from Cleveland.

"Hunter is not here, Nick. He had a change of heart. He decided he didn't want to be an actor or a dentist. So right after we graduated, he enlisted in the Air Force."

"I'm sure he'll look devastatingly handsome in his uniform," said Connie, adjusting the driver's seat of my car to accommodate her greater girth.

"Charlotte, I thought you were going to New York to start a theater company," I said.

"The best laid plans of mice and men, Nick. Hunter gave up on that idea after he starred as Torvald Helmer in our college's winter production of 'A Doll's House.' The stage fright nearly killed him."

"And he'll do better piloting a jet fighter?"

"He seems to think so. He loves it so far."

Like me Hunter is at a crossroads in his life. But I very much doubt I'll be enlisting in the military any time soon. I bet that dude played way more video games as a kid than I did.

Things I learned playing poker today with Charlotte:

She has changed her name (again) to Charlotte Simonov, that being her mother's maiden name. She's Russian on the maternal side, hence her Slavic cheekbones. Her father's notoriety has made the name Caxton socially unacceptable, not that the war in Ukraine has made being Russian all that popular.

She thinks my changing my name to Davidson is a "dumb idea." Welcome to the club.

Her father's trophy wife divorced him, but was unable to overturn their prenup. He may or may not be having an affair with his physical therapist.

She's looking for a place to rent, most likely a condo in

Culver City. (That burg is rife with condos.) Snooty Bel-Air dweller Connie thinks Culver City is a "pit."

She was intrigued to learn I'm renting a house in Mar Vista and made a valiant effort to weasel out of me what I was paying. I declined repeatedly to divulge specifics.

She's looking for a job, so she can become financially independent from her family. For example, she's thinking it might be "fun" to work in an art gallery. I said on what she'd make in that job she could afford to live in a cardboard box on the Venice boardwalk, but would have a grand ocean view.

She's eager to see the finished version of our Christmas movie.

She's not saying if Hunter is gone for good, but I can't really see her as an Air Force wife.

Today I surprised everyone by not losing ignominiously. I was up over $400 when we broke for lunch. (Everyone started with $1,000 in chips.) This was mostly because I was dealt decent hands for a change. I finished the day with $210, which I declined to convert to actual cash. As usual, Charlotte cleaned up, and Connie wrote her a check for her losses.

Charlotte could turn out to be the world's most expensive house guest. Instead of getting a job and an apartment, she could just live with Connie and fleece her daily at the card table.

FRIDAY, July 8 – A guy named Ramon knocked on my door today. He said he was Gary and Keith's gardener and asked if I wanted his services. The price seemed reasonable, so I said sure. He mowed the grass and switched the watering system back on. I switched it *off* after he left. If my grass craves water it will have to make do with the dew it collects from our morning ocean fogs.

I got a packet of fan mail today from Zach my agent. He

forwards these periodically and always deducts his postage costs from my checks. Fan mail is mostly a welcome ego boost, but the people expecting signed photos in return are a pain. Also unnerving are letters from strange women saying they're expecting my baby and we need to get married a.s.a.p. Scott gets those too.

This letter I found especially intriguing:

Dear Mr. Twisp,

I know you're not with Amalda Preston anymore, but I'm hoping you have a way of contacting her. I'm a counselor at the Francis Lake Music Camp. I think she should know that her boyfriend is having an affair with a fellow counselor named Marcie Florin. Every night they row across the lake to an island where there's an abandoned summer cabin. They think they're being discreet, but everyone knows about it, and it's the talk of the whole camp. I think those two are setting a poor example for the younger kids, especially considering the publicity Everest has received from his association with Ms. Preston.

Marcie is a cellist from the Eastman School of Music, so I guess she's used to spreading her legs. I find her to be an extremely loathsome and manipulative person.

Sincerely,

A Concerned Friend

A dilemma for me. Did I want to ruin Almy's triumphant week by forwarding that noxious letter?

Not being a very nice person, I did exactly that. I made a few copies of the letter and mailed the original to Almy in care of her grandfather's address. I'm hoping she gets it tomorrow. I appended a note saying she could call me to discuss this if she wished.

Later, Carli and I grabbed some burgers on S. Sepulveda Blvd. and hiked across the street to a small park for dining. Carli likes to do this because planes landing at LAX hurtle by a few hundred feet overhead. Your whole body shakes from the vibrations, which may be helpful for digestion. Probably not so great for your hearing. There's also a possibility that the pilot will come in low and you'll be decapitated while you dine.

SATURDAY, July 9 – I returned home at 2:01 this morning. I wanted to return last night after we concluded our activities, but Carli said being abandoned after sex makes her feel like "a tool."

So how does being jarred awake and expelled into the chilly darkness make me feel? Sort of like "a tool."

Then Dad phoned early and demanded my presence at breakfast. I asked him what Lefty was making.

"He's baking something sugary and the bacon is frying."

Good enough for me. I bombed over in my new car. Call me a shallow materialist, but I love having a garage for both of my cars. I think secure enclosed parking ranks right up there with sex, love, and good cell-phone service as a basic human need.

I thought Dad had talked to Connie and was going to give me grief about my new car. Instead, he had something else on his mind.

"Have you seen this?" he asked, handing me a *Hollywood Reporter*. "I've marked the page."

It was in their "Real Estate" section. It read: "Sold to actor Nick Davidson (formerly Nick Twisp II) a Mar Vista mid-century fixer for $2.2 million."

There was even a photo of my very modest-looking house.

"Oh . . . right," I muttered.

"So you're not *renting* that house," said Dad, peeved.

"You're *buying* it. And how do you expect to make the payments?"

That scary vein was throbbing again on his forehead.

"I have no payments, Dad. I paid cash. And I don't see why they're calling it a fixer. It was move-in ready."

"And where did you get $2.2 million?" he asked, shocked.

"I got a bit more than a Caddy from my great-aunt. That's why I'm changing my name. I had to go back to Nick Davidson to get the inheritance. It was a requirement in her will."

"So why didn't you tell us any of this?" he asked. "Why did you make up all that bullshit about drowning in a sea of Twisps?"

"I was trying to avoid interrogations like this. I figured it was my own business."

"I thought that woman was a nurse," said Dad. "How could she leave you so much money?"

"She was a thrifty gal, Dad. She skipped the spouses, the divorces, the lavish lifestyle, and the kids."

"Obviously, a smart lady," Dad conceded.

"I resent that," said Teejay. "They say my TV series will be sweeping the Emmy Awards this year. It's super popular. I am so famous!"

"Not now, Teejay," said his mother.

"So how much did that woman leave you?" Dad demanded.

"All I can say is you don't have to worry about me not being able to pay my bills. You can clear that off your worry list. You can forget about real-estate school for me."

"Congratulations, Nick," said Treez. "We're very happy for you. I don't think we need to pry any further into your affairs."

"I may not be done prying here," said Dad.

"I'm surprised the *Hollywood Reporter* heard about this," I said.

"They probably have some intern combing through the real estate transactions," said Dad. "Or your agent phoned in a tip."

Stabbed in the back by nice Ginny Koven? I hope not.

Dad continued to weasel, but I wasn't 'fessing up to my actual net worth. I don't see him "opening the kimono" on how much he's worth.

"If you'd told us you were changing your name to collect an inheritance," said Dad, "I would have understood. I'd change my name too if somebody paid me."

"I'll pay you $10,000 to change it to Dog Face Poopy Head," said Teejay. "Cash money from my bank account."

"You, shut up," commanded his dad.

"Nick, I'm going to tell Lucia that you're rich," said Teejay. "Boy, will she be sorry that she dumped you."

"You do that, 'bro," I said. "Let me know how she takes it."

After breakfast, they all trooped down to look at my new car. Yeah, I think I saw my ex-wife peeking out the front window of Cliff's house.

No call today from Almy. Has the shit hit the fan or not?

SUNDAY, July 10 – Cal phoned early.

"Nickie, are you in bed with someone?" she asked.

"Let me check, dear,"

I counted off three beats. "Nope. I don't seem to be."

"Can I come over?"

"Sure."

"How much time do you need?"

"I need to shower, shave, and dress. Give me 10 minutes."

"You guys have it so easy."

I was fumbling with the espresso machine when she arrived. Twenty minutes later we sat down to a breakfast of scrambled eggs, sausage, and toast. Being an EOC (Enemy of Carbs), Cal skipped the toast.

"Nickie, according to the *Hollywood Reporter*, you're a big, fat liar."

"Yeah, I bought this place. I also traded in my Matrix on a new Mustang. My great-aunt was wealthier than we thought. Her will required me to change my name. I didn't have a choice if I wanted the bucks."

"I figured that out already. So how rich are you?"

"Very low eight figures."

"Are you counting the two numbers on the other side of the decimal point?"

"No, nobody counts those puny numbers."

"Jesus. . . .Or are you lying to impress me?"

I told her the full story on Aunt Grace's investment savvy as related by Murchison.

"Wow, you had an intelligent relative—except you're not actually related to her."

"I am biologically related to Teejay Twisp, and he's a genius. Did you watch his show?"

"Naturally. Your ex-girlfriend was sickeningly sweet."

"It's not her fault the screenwriters are piling on the hardships for her to endure with plucky resolve like the second coming of Mary Pickford. Heck, it was the Depression."

"If you ask me, her biggest burden was having given birth to that little monster. I told Liam if he went sailing this weekend, it was over between us."

"I take it he went sailing."

"He did. Why is it that men don't want to be with me?"

"That's not true, dear. Ninian was with you for over a year."

"And then he dumped me for Dior and married that slag in a flash."

"Guys do crazy things on the rebound from you, darling. That's a well-established fact. And I've loved you since the first day we met. That's going on seven years."

"So you say, but I know why you bought such a modest house."

"Why's that, darling?"

"You deliberately chose a place with inadequate closet space so I could never move in with you."

"I can assure you that was *not* a consideration at all."

"So why didn't you get some place bigger and nicer?"

"I didn't want everyone to go weird on me because I'm rich. This house is plenty big enough for me."

"How crusty are your sheets?"

"I'll go change them, darling. I did splurge like a maniac on linens."

So we spent the rest of the morning in my bedroom. Still the pinnacle of the act for me. No one is as loving in bed as Cal. It's the rest of the time that she can be a trial.

Limp and drained, I hopped out of bed and retrieved a copy of the letter from "A Concerned Friend." Cal looked it over.

"Backstabbing at the music camp," she said. "Those musicians can be vicious. If Almy was smart, she'd just ignore this extraneous gossip."

"How can you say that, darling? Her fiancé is cheating on her!"

"They're out there in the woods running around in the fresh air, Nickie. They're experiencing nature, playing chamber music, and eating campfire meals. Wild strawberries are being dunked in rich, thick cream. Society's constraints have fallen away. So of course they're pairing off. It's only natural. If I were Almy, I'd be worried if my guy wasn't off in the woods shagging some chick. I'd wonder what was wrong with his sex drive."

"I very much doubt that she's so enlightened."

"You're just trying to wreck her happiness because you want her back."

"That's not true at all," I lied.

"You just proved my point."

"What point is that, darling?"

"You just had me, but obviously you want someone else. I just don't rate with men."

Since Cal was feeling insecure, we spent the whole day together. Somehow I wound up buying her a ruby pin to match the ring I gave her a few years back. As I put down my credit card I stressed I was purchasing her the bauble only out of friendship.

Left unsaid was the fact that I had tried marriage with someone a whole lot easier to get along with than Cal. Since I had failed with Luco, there was no way I was going to turn around and try it with her.

I may not be a genius like Teejay, but even I had the smarts to figure that out.

While we were in BH, I picked up some stunning sunglasses for me and a card and gift for the lil' genius. Teejay turns four tomorrow. At an upscale sporting goods store I bought him a genuine Rodney "Butch" Bolicweigski first baseman's glove, always an inappropriate gift for a klutzy Twisp.

MONDAY, July 11 – Teejay's party started at two. For some reason all the Twisps were there, even the Tyler Twisps. Otilia had arrived and was assisting Lefty with the eats. She remembered my name and gave me a hug.

I was dodging Uma, Aunt Lillian, and Aunt Joanie, when Trent Preston arrived with his wife and granddaughter. I slithered over to say hello to Almy. No hugs from her.

"Everest assured me it was not true," she said, skipping the salutations. "Did you write that ugly letter yourself?"

"Not my handwriting, dear. I'm glad to hear you're so trusting. Did you Google Francis Lake?"

"Why would I do that?"

"If there are no islands in the lake, then you know Ms. Anonymous is lying. Do you ever talk to Everest at night?"

"They have poor cell-phone reception there. He calls me when he goes into town."

"Right. I imagine the camp has a land line. You could call him some night that way. But there's no need since you trust him."

"That's right, Nick."

"I'm enjoying your show so far. You're excellent in the part."

"Thanks. I hear you bought a house and a ruby pin for Valerie Haseltine."

"Who told you that?"

"The *Hollywood Reporter* and Cooper Tucker's wife."

"Jackie Tucker still talks to you?"

"I'm still on her radar for some reason. Have you two set a date?"

"I'm not marrying anyone, dear. Although I'm willing to make an exception for you."

"What I said before still stands. Excuse me."

She walked away and joined the crowd around Teejay. I think that kid would be happiest if he could have 365 birthdays a year. Then to make my day complete, Luco entered with her BF. Eventually, she wound up standing next to me.

"Teejay says you're now rich," she commented, spooning in lemon cake and ice cream. I went for the chocolate alternative.

"Yeah, I inherited a rather enormous pile from my great-aunt. I was trying to keep it a secret, but I got outed by the *Hollywood Reporter*. They felt the need to snoop into my personal life."

"I also hear you may be engaged to Valerie Haseltine."

"Not true, dear. I bought her a jeweled pin because she got dumped by her latest beau. I know how much that can hurt."

"I don't see why you don't marry her. Everyone thinks you're an ideal match. Did you have sex with her while we were married?"

"Only after you walked out the door. I know you didn't believe me, but I was totally faithful to you. I thought I would be spending my whole life with you."

That statement brought only an awkward silence. So I turned away and had a pleasant conversation with Cliff Swandon. We agreed that Teejay was over the top and out of control.

"A lot of child prodigies go on to lead fairly mediocre lives," he observed.

"Yeah, Teejay's life may be peaking right now at age four," I said.

"I hardly remember anything from when I was four."

"Me neither, Cliff. But I don't think I was being adored by the entire world."

I left before Teejay got around to opening my gift. Probably an anticlimax to what his grateful network gave him: the fanciest of the high-end Mac laptops. I jokingly suggested he could use it to write his memoirs. He replied, quite seriously, "That's just what I was thinking."

TUESDAY, July 12 – Carli showed up at my door this morning. She had baked a coffee cake, so I invited her in. I made cappuccinos, and we sat at my kitchen table.

"This cake is excellent," I said. "What's the spice besides cinnamon?"

"Strychnine. Just kidding. I added a dash of nutmeg. Do you know the rumor site hollywooddirt.com?"

"Is that the one with the slogan 'All the Sleaze that's Fit To Sling'?"

"It could be, Nick. Anyway, they're reporting that you gave a $3,900 ruby pin to Valerie Haseltine."

"Yeah, I did. It came to more than that with tax."

"And why did you do that?"

"Valerie is one of my oldest friends. She felt the pin would go nicely with the ruby and diamond ring I had given her previously. I'm told the same designer created both."

"So you're now engaged?"

"No, I tried marriage. Been there, done that. Marriage is off the table for me."

"How about monogamy?"

"Not seeing much point to that either."

"You intend to have sex with multiple girls?"

"I certainly hope so."

"And what if I want to have sex with multiple guys?"

"Not a problem, dear. I do suggest you always use a condom like I do. No one needs a nasty disease or inconvenient baby."

"How many girls do you think you'll be sleeping with?"

"I suppose if I really worked at it, I might reach ten by the end of the summer."

Probably an exaggeration, but Carli felt motivated to leave in a huff. She took the rest of her cake with her.

I'm not usually that mean to girlfriends, but something about her attitude ticks me off.

I was Googling Francis Lake when Charlotte arrived. Yep, there was the camp and there was an island a few hundred yards offshore. At least geographically, the veracity of that note was confirmed.

I shared the note with Charlotte as part of her house tour.

"It looks legit to me, Nick," she said. "I see you're still hung up on poor Almy Preston."

"Just trying to save her from inappropriate men."

"I expect in your world all of her suitors are inappropriate. What's this framed letter?"

"The wise words of my new guru."

Charlotte leaned over my desk to read Samuel F.

Broughton's letter. While she did so, I embraced her from behind and nuzzled the back of her neck. She smelled divinely enticing. She turned around and kissed me on the tip of my nose.

"You're friendlier, Nick, than you used to be."

"I'm now unconstrained by the vows of marriage."

"Too bad I'm constrained by the need to inspect rental condos. So this dead Iowan failed at being an actor, and now you're giving up your career?"

"I have no career, Charlotte. I had a few lucky breaks. That's all. Why don't we take the day off and look at condos tomorrow?"

"Sorry, Nick. Some of us need to get our lives in order."

We went in Charlotte's Audi. It was the same sporty model as last year, but a different car in a different color (red). Now Charlotte was doing the driving, and no hulking bodyguards would be handing me $350 in cash for my time.

Since it was a warm day and she was wearing a sleeveless top, I inquired about the scar visible on her shoulder.

"Did you have your fox tattoo removed?" I asked.

"Yeah, I did, Nick."

"Did that hurt?"

"It hurt like fucking hell. And now I have that ugly blotch on my skin."

More proof that tattoos on chicks are a bad idea.

We looked at seven condos, mostly in Culver City and a couple in Santa Monica. None in your budget category. Landlords are really into gouging these days. No wonder the city is awash with homeless people.

We stopped for a late lunch at a salad/soup place in West L.A. Hard to fill up on that grub, so I supplemented my order with three desserts. Charlotte said she was leaning toward the condo one block from the beach in Santa Monica.

"The one you liked in Culver City is better," I said, crunching into my salad like John Wayne wading ashore at Guadalcanal.

"And why is it better?" she asked.

"OK, it's on the top floor, so you won't hear people tromping around above you. Also the soundproofing in general seemed better. It's a newer building, so you'll have less chance of being invaded by roaches. If you have people over, they can park on your street, which is always iffy close to the beach in Santa Monica. Plus, it's $800 a month cheaper."

"All true, Nick, but there's no ocean view in Culver City."

"You want an ocean view, Charlotte, come hang out in my bedroom. I've got a clear shot at the blue Pacific."

"I expect your view would be obscured by horny bachelors crawling all over me."

"We can take breaks to gaze out the window."

No sex with Charlotte today. She dropped me off, saying she was due back at Connie's. At least she had forked over for lunch. Exiting the Audi, I waved at Carli, who was watering her flower bed. That girl did not wave back.

I was doing the dishes when Kinsley arrived. Oh right, it was TV streaming night. Another installment of Almy and Teejay struggling to survive Hard Times.

"Your house is just as neat as it was last week," observed Kinsley, settling back in her chair with her popcorn.

"Yeah, I'm not a slob. So sue me."

"I hear you've been buying Valerie Haseltine expensive jewelry."

"I love how my life is an open book to the world. Was that the lead story on the evening news?"

"I heard about it on hollywooddirt.com."

"FYI, Kinsley: Valerie and I are *not* engaged. We're just friends."

"How soon do I qualify as a friend of yours? There's a diamond necklace I need for when I'm nominated for an Academy Award. I'll be wearing a low-cut gown and will need something to distract the world from my lack of tits."

"You appear to have plenty of those to me."

"Not compared to your ex-wife."

"There's more to life than large breasts."

"I'm sure I wouldn't know."

"To answer your question, Kinsley, we may be friends soon. You're doing fine so far. How's your script outline coming?"

"Not well, Nick. And it's not like there's any pressure. It's just that our entire future in the industry depends on it. I don't see why they expect us to be screenwriters. Steven Spielberg *directed* 'Indiana Jones.' He didn't write it!"

"Now you see why I skipped college entirely, dear."

Tonight's episodes featured Almy submitting to being kissed and pawed by the radio station owner to get her son air time. Very galling to watch. I looked the guy up on my phone. There's an actor I'll never be hiring if I become a big-shot producer.

Kinsley exited promptly when the show was over.

Is it my breath?

WEDNESDAY, July 13 – The weather is heating up. Temps may hit 100 at the beach today. I went to switch on my A/C and to my horror discovered that I didn't have any. No telltale units mounted outside on pads or on the roof. Up there I have only two small vents. My roof cooks in the sun, my attic becomes a fiery inferno, and heat blasts down through my ceiling like a giant toaster oven.

I phoned around to local A/C companies. They're all busy and booked up solid. The best I could do was an appointment in mid-September. So I went to Lowes and bought a medium-size window unit. They sell larger ones, but I wouldn't have been able to hoist them out of my trunk.

I think these things work best in windows that slide UP to open. All of mine slide *sideways*. So I got the A/C in place and had a large open area above it freely admitting hot breezes and bugs. Plus, the dinky cord wouldn't reach a wall outlet. So I went to a hardware store and bought a heavy-duty extension cord and a large piece of cardboard. I cut the cardboard to fill the gap. As I was taping it in place, my new A/C unit slipped out the back, tumbled about ten feet, and smashed into the concrete walkway below.

Fuck!

As I went outside to view the dented, cracked, and mangled remains, Carli strolled out to see what had caused the loud crash.

"I don't think your warranty is going to cover that damage," she remarked.

"What did Gary and Keith do on hot days?" I asked.

"They had fans. And if it got really hot like today, they came over and hung out in my place."

"You have A/C, huh?"

"It was a minimum requirement when I was looking to buy."

"Those guys should have disclosed that their house had no air conditioning!"

"I guess they just assumed their prospective buyers weren't blind. Good luck with your project, Nick."

She turned and walked away.

Damn.

I dumped the carcass in my trash bin and returned to the hardware store to buy a fan. Then I went and mooched dinner off Dad. Their place is fully air conditioned. After that I went and hung out beside Harvey and Tiara's lap pool. They didn't seem to mind. Harvey's sister strolled over in a striped bikini to join me. I was intimately familiar with all her goods, but it's always nice to view them attractively showcased.

"I reached a compromise with Liam," Cal announced, spreading her towel on the grass beside mine.

"What sort of compromise, darling?"

"He's selling his sailboat. In return, I have to take up golf or skiing."

"And which delightful sport are you choosing?" I asked.

"Skiing, naturally, because that can't happen until winter, which is a long way off. The guy could be history by then. Jealous Liam wasn't happy about your buying me that pin."

"Are you returning it?"

"I hardly think so. After he sells his sailboat, he's going to send you a check to cover the full price of my pin."

Somehow I won't be holding my breath for that to happen.

I tried to get in a kiss and a furtive grope, but she said it was too hot for human contact.

"Nickie, do you have any interest in buying the matching earrings?"

"I don't have pierced ears, sweetheart."

"I mean for me, you idiot."

"Not if you're getting back together with Liam. Such largesse would seem a bit misplaced."

"I'm thinking I should attempt to shoplift them. You know, to prepare for my movie role."

"I'd start much smaller than that, darling. Try pilfering a candy bar from 7-Eleven. You'll probably only get probation for that offense."

THURSDAY, July 14 – My final name-change ad comes out in that Glendale paper today. I assume the court will be acting fairly soon after that. Then I can get my hands on the rest of Aunt Grace's loot.

I slept last night in the utility room on a mattress I dragged out of my sofa bed. Only semi-stifling down there.

After breakfast I phoned the A/C company again and this time I asked to speak to the owner. Eventually, he came on the line. I asked what it would take to get central air installed in a 1,400 square foot house today in Mar Vista. He said he couldn't jump on it for anything less than $15,000. I said I would be waiting here with the check when his truck and crew showed up. They arrived about 45 minutes later and are now beavering away.

Do I feel sorry for the hot but patient person whose appointment got cancelled because I jumped the line? Uh, not really. I figure in this era of rapid climate change, it's every man for himself.

While waiting for the crew to finish, I phoned the jewelry store in BH and asked to speak to the manager. I said Valerie Haseltine might come in to look at ruby earrings. While preparing for an upcoming movie role, she might attempt to shoplift them. In which case, they should let her have them and I would cover the cost. The manager agreed reluctantly after I assured her that Ms. Haseltine would not be making a habit of swiping stuff from their store.

My house is now the temperature of Fairbanks in late fall. In a spirit of goodwill I tipped each sweaty tech guy a Benjamin.

Charlotte phoned. She talked it over with her gimpy dad and is renting the inappropriate ocean-view condo in Santa Monica. Since she was not appalled by my furniture, we made a date for tomorrow to inspect the offerings at my pal Jim's big store in the Valley. She also said she has a business proposal to discuss with me then.

I'm hoping this involves some casual nudity in my bedroom.

FRIDAY, July 15 – The cooling ocean breezes returned

today. Those hot desert winds once again are confined to Barstow and Needles where they desiccate retired Boomers. Oh well, at least I'm now prepared for the next sirocco that blows in. I grossly overpaid, but that seems to be a theme in my life these days.

Charlotte came here and we drove to the Valley in my boss Mustang. On the way there on the 405 she outlined her business proposal. She wants me to hire her as my personal assistant. At a starting salary of $2,000 a week!

"And why exactly do I need a personal assistant?" I asked.

"All movie producers have personal assistants, Nick. You'll need me to find appropriate office space, acquire furnishings, arrange for the phone system, hire a secretary and web designer, and so forth. Then we can start reading scripts together and developing projects."

"Er, why do I need an office and a secretary?"

"You can't operate without business premises, Nick. And no one in this town answers their own phone. Or initiates their own calls. It's just not done if you want to be taken seriously as a player. So a secretary is a must, although I supposed you could try to get by with an intern."

"And why am I paying you $2,000 a week?"

"You can't get a decent assistant for less than that. Besides, I need at least that much to pay my rent and the lease on my car."

"Your father's not helping you?"

"You know as well as I do, Nick, that I can't be associated with him. My father is tainted in the eyes of the world. That's why I had to change my name. Anyway, you know I'm the deal of the century at that modest salary."

I did some math in my head. Her dad had been paying me the equivalent of $1,750 a week for tour guide duties, so I guess two grand was not that outrageous. And it's true that Charlotte is a forceful go-getter. Napoleon might have conquered the world with her arranging his schedule. I told her I would have to think it over.

Unlike me, Charlotte actually wanted to choose the furniture she was buying. She wasn't leaving matters to Jim's discretion. We trooped through his vast, jammed store and she made her selections. Then she negotiated brutally over the final price. Jim had to eat all the sale tax and toss in the mattress set for free. Charlotte said the delivery men would be receiving minimal tips and *she alone* would decide on furniture placement.

Jim appealed to me on that point. "Did you move anything, Nick, after my guys left?"

"Not even a quarter inch, Jim. Everything was arranged perfectly. Your men are artists."

"Hey, I'm the person living there," said Charlotte. "If I want to have my bed set on a diagonal in the center of the room, I'll do that."

An involuntary shudder shot through both Jim and me.

Since it was Friday, we didn't dawdle in the Valley. We bombed back over the hill and lunched at a Japanese restaurant in Santa Monica. This time I paid. Charlotte likes Japanese food, but doesn't touch rice. She ordered sake, which is the worst of the worst: like armpit-temperature distilled dirty socks. I stuck to green tea, which is not much better.

Since Charlotte bought the same pillow-top mattress as I did, I suggested we go back to my place to sample its comforts. She declined.

Here's the question: Would she be more willing if I were paying her $2,000 a week?

Does she genuinely find me repulsive, or is she being coy as a ploy? Or is she only attracted to unavailable married guys? Or some folks find sex during daylight hours disgusting. Is that her problem?

Charlotte warned me that I have to make up my mind

soon on hiring her. She said Connie is proposing they open a school to teach poker-playing skills. Does the world need more gambling addicts?

SATURDAY, July 16 – I spotted a strange car parked in Carli's driveway this morning. Then I noticed some dude leaving in it. Not that I care, but did he spend the night just so that girl could get back at me? If so, I find that highly manipulative and tacky. Should I become a successful movie producer, I very much doubt my neighbor will be featured in any of my output.

Later I got a call from the manager of Cal's favorite jewelry store. She had been in to inspect the ruby earrings.

"Did she swipe them?" I asked, dreading the answer.

"No, but as you'll recall when we remove items from a case, we display them on a black suede pad for customers to view. She slipped one of our leather pads into her purse."

"OK, you can charge that to my credit card."

"We have those custom made. They are Spanish calfskin embossed with the logo of our shop. We will have to charge you $1,250 plus tax."

"Uh, I'll retrieve the pad from Ms. Haseltine and return it to you."

"If it is damaged in any way, you will be charged the full amount."

"Right. Not a problem."

Damn.

I phoned Cal and explained the situation.

"Oh, dear, Nickie. I got cold feet driving down Wilshire and flung it out of my car. It sailed off like a Frisbee."

"And where on Wilshire did you do that?"

"I don't really recall. I was too pent up with dread, fear, and exhilaration. I feel I have gained some valuable insights into the mind of a shoplifter."

"Good for you, dear. But you owe that store $1,250 for their missing item."

"No, I believe that expense is on you, darling. Had you not interfered, they would have stopped me at the door to retrieve their stinking suede pad."

"Right. And had you arrested."

"No, I would have explained my purpose and everyone would have had a good laugh. After all, I had no use for their pad. I could not have used that argument had I taken the earrings. I am not an idiot. Or a criminal. So the fault here is entirely yours."

I phoned the store and told them to charge my credit card.

It's a good thing I'm rich, although I'm feeling less wealthy by the minute.

Cal phoned back 15 minutes later.

"I see now, Nickie, I should have just summoned the courage to steal those earrings, since you intended to pay for them."

"Yeah, well that impulse has expired, dear. The next thing you steal will be earning you quality jail time like your pal Desmond."

"Damn, Nickie, that is so unfair."

"Crime doesn't pay, darling. I'm out big bucks and neither of us has anything to show for it."

"I bet that overpriced pad is now gracing the shopping cart of some homeless person on Wilshire."

"Yeah, at least you made their day."

I was streaming a movie this evening when Almy Preston called. She asked if she could come over!

"Uh, you mean to my house?" I asked, stunned.

"Yes, Nick. I know you live in a $2.2 million house in Mar Vista, but I don't know your address."

I told her my address. She asked what I had on hand to drink. I said nothing alcoholic. She said she would pick up something on the way there. She arrived in due course with a bottle of tequila. Apparently, college students in NYC drink that stuff straight. She retrieved some small glasses from my hutch and poured us some shots. She chugged hers; I sipped mine. Pretty rank stuff minus the lime juice, crushed ice, Triple Sec, and salty rim. We took our glasses and the bottle into the living room. She settled in next to me on the sofa.

"Since when do you read *GQ* magazine?" she asked, downing another shot.

"Uh, pretty much never. What's up with you, Almy dear?"

"I took your advice and called that music camp. Last night about 10:30 their time. Some girl answered."

"You asked to speak to Everest?"

"I did. The girl giggled and said he was unavailable until morning. I said why's that? She giggles and says he's away on Borodino Island. So I ask to speak to Marcie Florin. Turns out she's unavailable too. More giggling. I ask how many people are away on Borodino Island? She says only those two as far as she knows."

"Yeah, anonymous notes can be credible in some cases."

"He called me this morning. Apologizing all over the place. I'd heard it all before. Why am I only attracted to scumbags, liars, and dirtballs?"

"Uh, that's a hard one to answer, dear."

"The thing is, Nick, I always knew you were untrustworthy. Right from the beginning. But I really thought Everest was different. He seemed to exude sincerity from every pore."

"I didn't get that feeling about him."

"Everest Weeden has six 'E's in his name. No other vowels at all. How suspicious is that? Yet somehow I overlooked them. The 'E's, of course, stand for ego. It turns out musicians have even bigger egos than actors."

"I'd go easy on the tequila, dear. It can sneak up on you."

Almy looked around the room, then poured herself another shot. "$2.2 million, huh? I could sort of see $1.2 million, but $2.2 million seems like a stretch."

"Yeah, I overpaid. How's your rape movie coming along, darling?"

"Very well, Nick. I play a girl abused by men, while in real life I'm a girl abused and abased by dirtballs."

I slid the tequila bottle away from her on the coffee table, embraced her, and kissed her. She sort of kissed me back.

"You were a cheat and a liar, Nick, but I always sensed you loved me."

"I do, darling. I was just immature. We met too soon, before I'd had a chance to grow up."

"And now you're a grown-up divorced homeowner with a giant TV."

"It's only 56 inches, dear. That's considered fairly small these days."

"I hear you bought a new Mustang. That doesn't sound very mature."

"I got the sensible and economical four-cylinder model."

"And you're still buying expensive jewelry for Valerie Haseltine."

"Only to console her for breaking up with her boyfriend, but they just reconciled."

"I hope all your future wives are aware that you come as a package deal with that girl."

"You're the only girl I ever loved, Almy dear. I know I have no credibility with you, but it's true."

"I should thank you for sending Stuart Dunham after Everest."

"I only wish your first boyfriend wasn't a total incompetent in all matters."

"You forget, Nickie, that Stuart successfully knocked up Sue Ellen Pingleton. He stuck it inside my best friend and blasted away."

"OK, darling. I will give him credit for that betrayal."

"At least you never knocked up anyone, Nick. Not even your legally wedded wife. You score some brownie points for that."

"Glad to hear it, darling."

"So when's the last time you had sex with Cal?"

"Uh, I'm not lying to you anymore, darling. I've resolved to be truthful at all times. I'm just declining to answer that question."

"It's none of my business anyway. Pass me that bottle, will you?"

I did so reluctantly. While we chatted, Almy gulped down a bit more than half the contents of her tequila bottle. Then I put her to bed as the inaugural occupant of my guestroom. She woozily read my framed letter and said that Samuel F. Broughton was a very, very wise man.

SUNDAY, July 17 – No stirrings in the guestroom until 9:45. Almy emerged at last, gulped two aspirins, and declined an offer of breakfast. She sat at my kitchen table while I made her an extra-large tall grande super-sized latte.

"That's a pretty fancy machine," she commented, leaning her head on her hand.

"It took me a while to get the hang of it. The technology is Italian."

"Like your ex-wife."

I passed her the steaming beverage and took a seat at the table.

"I don't usually drink like that, Nick."

"You had a good reason to. I hope, dear, you won't go back to treating me like a non-person. I hope we can be friends again. I hope you won't have to borrow someone's phone to call me."

"I called you last night, Nick, on my very own phone."

"That's progress."

"But enough about me. What are you up to these days, Nickie?"

I told her about Charlotte's business proposal.

"She sounds like an enterprising person, Nick. Too bad her father is such a scumbag. I can see why she changed her name. So are you going to hire her?"

"I don't know. I sort of like the idea of being a movie mogul, but the thought of all that work and struggle just makes me tired."

"Frankly, Nick, I don't see much overlap in your personality with someone like Ed Bedrossian."

"I'm thinking I should take some time off to sort out my life."

"You don't enjoy acting?"

"I like some aspects. I like hanging out on set, going on location, and meeting new people. I even enjoy memorizing scripts. But I'm getting burned out on all the rejection."

"I know, Nick. I've had it easy because my grandfather is so famous."

"Plus, you're beautiful and talented. That helps a lot. The best I can hope for are character roles, and I'm too young for most of those."

"How about doing more YouTube videos, Nick? Those were fun."

"That's a thought."

Someone knocked on my back door. It was my neighbor.

"I think there's something wrong with your sprinklers, Nick," said Carli, peering into my kitchen. "Your grass is turning brown."

"Thanks for the alert," I replied. "Carli, this is Almy Preston. Almy, this is a neighbor, Carli Eryngilli."

"I've admired your work, Ms. Preston," said Carli.

"Thank you," she replied. "It's nice to meet you."

Neither comment was registering high on the Sincere-O-Meter. Eventually, I managed to shut the door on the intruder.

"I take it you've had sex with that girl," said Almy.

"I don't lie to you anymore, darling. I was kind of seduced, but it was over quickly. Now she's at the stage of spying on me. I'm thinking of erecting a very tall fence."

"A chastity belt—locked onto you—might be cheaper."

"That's a thought, dear. And you can have the only key."

"I'm sure there'd be extra copies concealed about your person."

"I was totally faithful to my wife, Almy. Unfortunately, due to my past excesses, I had no credibility with her. So she felt free to cheat on me."

"Speaking of which, Nick, did we do anything along those lines last night?"

"Just a kiss on the sofa, darling."

"I remember that part. Well, I should be going. I'm sorry for what I said about your not measuring up to what's his name. That was uncalled for."

"Yeah, it was kind of the ultimate don't exist message."

"And yet you persisted in looking after me. I think you're crazy to do that."

"Sanity has never been a notable Twisp character trait."

"Now you're going to be Nick Davidson. Perhaps I can get along better with him."

"He certainly hopes so."

I gave her another kiss on the lips. She didn't scream or fight like a tiger. She even made the ultimate sacrifice and gave me her current email address.

Later I texted Almy that if rumor sites reported she spent the night with me, the source was my neighbor not me.

MONDAY, July 18 – Lucia DeFalco's 21st birthday. I hope Cliff Swandon does something nice for her in celebration. For her birthday last year I gave her a shaggy rug that soon got sold for cheap in our end-of-marriage yard sale. Also cleared out was that nuisance I.D. bracelet she had given me.

As usual, I met Cal for coffee in Venice.

"Did Liam go sailing this weekend?" I asked as we sat down on the patio.

"No, he just cleared out his stuff and polished his teak for the sale. Jackie Tucker passed me some news that I'm having a hard time crediting."

"What's that, darling?"

"She claims Almy Preston spent all of Saturday night in your house."

"Why is that surprising, dear? Almy Preston is one of my oldest friends."

"I was under the impression that girl regarded you as the lowest form of ectoplasm on the planet."

"You are so behind the times, dearest."

I told her how and why Almy came to visit.

"And how soon will she be making a drunken leap from your guestroom to your bed?"

"Probably not that soon," I admitted. "So far you're the only girl who's ever taken me back after a breakup."

"Remind me why I do that."

"Because we love each other and always will."

"So you keep insisting. We're doing more wardrobe fittings this week. Très chic!"

"I expect you'll be the best-dressed shoplifter in the paddy wagon. Who's playing your unfortunate husband?"

"They're trying to get Clive McGregor. He's completed principal shooting for Almy's lousy rape movie."

"So Almy told me. She says he's a total doll."

"I wouldn't mind doing a nude love scene with him."

"You have those in your script?"

"No, but we could improvise something in my dressing room."

"That guy is old! Plus, he's married and has kids."

"I'm willing to overlook his flaws."

I told Cal about Charlotte's proposal to become my $2,000 per week personal assistant.

"So how much of that fee would cover sexual favors?" she asked, picking at my muffin.

"I have *not* slept with that woman. Nor do I expect to. She would be assisting on my climb to the top as a big-time movie producer."

"I'll make you a better offer, Nick. You pay me $2,000 a week, and all I'll do is have sex with you. I won't bother you otherwise."

"How many times?"

"Oh, interested, huh? Two grand lands me two nights a week."

"You don't think Liam would mind?"

"We won't be telling darling Liam."

"We'd be trying to keep our liaisons secret in the same town in which Jackie Tucker has spies everywhere."

"That's true. Fuck!"

"I'll think it over, darling. Perhaps you could park around the corner when it's dark and wear a disguise. And don't worry, I wouldn't regard it as prostitution."

"I would, kiddo, but delude yourself however you like. I'd want cash under the table, of course."

"I think I should get one time for free because of your expensive shoplifting fiasco."

"Spoken like an actual movie producer. You may not be a complete incompetent at business."

I'm not sure Cal was serious. Sometimes her sarcasm can be way too subtle for the likes of me.

When I returned home, there was a black footlocker on my front porch. Taped to it was this note:

Dear Nick,

I hope you're loving your desk and credenza. Here's the last item from that estate. It's my gift for bringing in that new customer. Sorry no key. You could drill out the lock or pop it with a crowbar.
Thanks again,
Jim

I dragged the heavy footlocker into my living room. Stenciled on the front were the initials S.F.B. Could it contain actual personal belongings of my guru Samuel F. Broughton? I went at the lock with a screwdriver, but got nowhere. My ex-wife always had a selection of wrecking bars in her closet, but I was lacking that useful tool. So I went to Venice Hardware and bought their largest size. I pried away, and eventually the mangled lock popped free.

OK, inside were some books. These I put aside for inspection later. Then there was a tiny gray typewriter called a Hermes Baby. Made in Switzerland and possibly worth something. Next were two Denison High School yearbooks, one for Samuel's year (1951) and one from 1939. The latter opened to a page featuring a photo of lovely Donna Belle Mullenger. Looks like 'ol Donna later changed her name. Under that were numerous scrapbooks featuring clippings on the life and career of Donna Reed. Also a pile of loose glossies signed "to Sammy with best regards, Donna." Looks like my guru had a serious case for Donna. Not unlike my devotion to Almy? Among the photos were several of her grave. These I could have done without.

Under all that was a shoebox containing canceled checks going all the way back to 1953. In that year he was writing checks to Bel Aire Apartments for $23.50 and to Southern California Edison for $4.12. Prices have gone up some since then.

Another shoebox contained personal items such as cuff links, tie clasps, a high school ring, wallet-size photos of miscellaneous Iowans, nail clippers, old car keys, expired driver's licenses, etc.

I checked out his photo. Definitely not leading man material. A prominent nose and weak chin get you nowhere in Hollywood.

Another shoebox contained more old black-and-white photos. Probably friends and relatives, and some I guessed were Samuel as a kid. Looks like he grew up on a farm, but dreamed of fame in Hollywood. We all know how that turned out.

Under assorted clothes smelling of mothballs was a heavy metal box that rattled. Secured with a dime-store hasp and padlock. Like soft cheese under my wrecking bar. The box was filled with Mexico 50 peso coins that appeared to be gold. All were dated from the 1940s.

So I Googled that coin. These days they're going for about $2,800 each. I counted my stash. My guru had left me 121 of the gleaming coins. The math came out to $338,000. Enough to purchase Cal's sexual favors for three years and three months. That's a lot of activity between the sheets. I'll have to find out if she's willing to do it for Mexican currency. I don't suppose she'd accept hard-to-find Donna Reed scrapbooks.

The books I arranged in my bookcase. The little Swiss typewriter I displayed on a corner of my desk. The metal box of pesos I stashed temporarily behind my clothes dryer.

The rest of Samuel's life I returned to the footlocker, which I then stowed in the back of my bedroom closet.

All in all, not a bad day!

TUESDAY, July 19 – Seka (Mrs. Frank C. Wyatt) phoned early.

"So, Nick," she said, "when are you hosting your house-warming party?"

"I don't know, dear. When should I host it?"

"I'm thinking next Sunday."

"OK, what time would be good?"

"Noon is easy for everyone to remember."

"Noon it is then. I'll email the invitations today."

"Good. We'll see you then. Little Nick loves seeing his favorite uncle."

"And I love seeing him," I lied.

That girl probably has some ulterior motive, but I'd been thinking it was time to introduce my new home to my curious relatives. So I emailed invites to all branches of the Twisps, plus the usual suspects. I even sent one to my ex-wife. I specified "no gifts" because I don't need a lot of useless junk.

Then I rode my bike to Santa Monica to visit Charlotte in her newly furnished condo. Just as I expected, there were no empty parking spaces on her street. I hope she enjoys social isolation.

Her newly furnished place was looking pretty good, as was she. Quite the view from her balcony, but who even looks at the view after a few days? Meanwhile, you still have to pay the extra premium for the supposed eyeball enhancements.

"What have you decided, Nick?" she said, pouring me a cup of coffee. "Am I to be your budget-priced personal assistant?"

"A thoughtful P.A. would be accessorizing this coffee with a donut or two," I pointed out. "However, I'm willing to overlook your misstep. I've decided to give you a trial. I'm hosting a house-warming party at noon on Sunday. I need you to arrange drinks and eats catering for 100 or so guests."

"This coming Sunday?" she asked, alarmed.

"That's correct. Is there a problem?"

"Uh, we'll see. You want munchies and an open bar?"

"Munchies yes, open bar no. I don't need a bunch of drunken Twisps on my hands. We can serve coffee, juices, and a rationed quantity of sparkling white wine. Nothing fancy or expensive."

"OK, Nick. I take it this shindig will be happening in your back yard."

"Correct. I turned my sprinklers back on so the grass should be slightly greener by then."

"And what is your budget?"

"Whatever it takes, within reason."

"OK, I'll give it my best shot. So drink up your coffee and get the hell out of here. I'm going to be busy for a while."

I did as she said. I think the key to success in life is mastering the art of delegating all work to other people.

Later, Cal phoned. "Nickie, can I bring Liam to your party on Sunday?"

"Oh, why not? Assuming the twit wants to come. That business we discussed yesterday. Were you serious?"

"I'm always serious about financial matters, Nick."

"Good. I've got some gold coins that are worth about $3,000 each. I'm thinking after six, uh, events I could give you two coins."

"No, darling. First you give me two coins and then you get six events. You got these from your dead aunt?"

"Very possibly. I think you should keep them and not spend them. In bad times the value of gold always go up. They could serve as a financial cushion for you."

"I may do that, Nickie. I've always been deeply enthralled by the lustrous sheen and satisfying weight of gold."

"I know you'll cherish these coins, darling. Almost as much as you'll cherish our times together."

"Or vice versa," she replied.

Since it was Tuesday, I popped the popcorn and made the ice tea. Kinsley arrived on time, but was not looking happy.

"What's wrong, dear?" I said. "I hope your father has not been indicted for tax fraud."

"My father is fine, Nick. My problem is you. I see you once a week. You never call or text. All we do is sit here and watch your ex-girlfriend do her thing."

"Sorry, Kinsley. I've been rather busy."

"Busy doing what? Aren't you unemployed?"

"It takes a lot of work buying a house and making it comfortable. Last week I had to face a sudden air-conditioning emergency. Plus, I'm swamped with a million details in getting ready for my party. Are you coming?"

"How many of your ex-girlfriends and/or wives will be there?"

"I expect most of them will turn up. I try to maintain cordial relations with them all."

"From what I hear you try to maintain sexual relations as well."

"People like to gossip about actors. Most of it is made up."

"Do your ex-girlfriends mind that you're still stuck on Almy Preston? I hear she broke up with her fiancé and spent the weekend with you."

"First part true, last part false. She had too much to drink and spent Saturday night sleeping it off in my guestroom. Nothing happened between us."

"I don't see where I fit in your life, Nick."

"We're taking it slow, Kinsley. I'm on the rebound from a

traumatic divorce. I'm not rushing into things these days."

"So how many other girls are you not rushing into things with at present?"

"You're the only one, dear. How's your script outline going?"

"That's the other disaster in my life. Let's turn on your TV and escape reality."

We did so. A shocking incident in tonight's episodes. The village grocer, hoping to work off Almy's tab through other means, invited her to a bar. Playing piano in a dim corner was Everest Weeden. Nobody told me that twit had been hired. Then I had to watch the amorous grocer putting the moves on Almy—all the while maintaining a look of disinterest because Kinsley kept glancing over at me.

This time Kinsley stuck around after the show for some nuzzling on the sofa. I don't see why she's complaining about her breasts. They felt quite nice to me.

WEDNESDAY, July 20 – Got a progress report from my P.A. She's contracted for a caterer. A wedding got cancelled due to infidelities issues, so a well-respected firm had an opening. I had to phone the gal in charge and give her my credit card info. She said she admired my work and was looking forward to making my party a great success. Always nice to hear. She wanted to discuss the eats menu, but I told her to take that up with Charlotte. I did tell her that nobody minded Italian Prosecco, even obscure off brands. I also told her that a decent percentage of the guests would be kids, who were not heavy drinkers.

I went back to the hardware store. The clerks there are beginning to greet me by name. This time I bought a shovel and a rake. There's a hatch off my utility room into the crawl space. In a corner where one could still stand mostly upright I dug a hole. I extracted ten gold coins from the metal box, pocketed them, then buried the box in the hole.

I smoothed over the dirt with my rake. I think it would take a very enterprising burglar to locate that buried treasure. The ten coins I stashed in a box of oatmeal in my kitchen cupboard.

I phoned Cal to work out the details. She will wait around the corner from her house. I will pick her up and she will ride very low in the seat. When we get to my house, I will pause by the side door and she will dart quickly through the unlocked door. Then I will park in the garage and saunter back to my house. Our first event is set for tomorrow night.

Major news: Today's mail brought five copies of my court-approved name-change petition. Looks like Nick Davidson is back officially. I went to the post office and sent off two copies to Murchison by Express Mail. I think I'll put Charlotte in charge of dealing with all the places I have to shed my Nick Twisp identity. I hope the officious DMV doesn't make me take another driver's test. Naturally, I've forgotten who has to back up if two cars meet on a one-lane road on a hill. And I haven't a clue what that white curb signifies.

Charlotte checked in by phone again. "Nick, we need entertainment for the kids. Do you want a clown, a juggler, or a jump house?"

"Clowns are scary and no Twisp wants to see more juggling. Jump houses are tacky and invite loud screaming. How about a puppet show?"

"OK, I'll see what I can scrounge up. It's too bad you don't have a pool."

"At least no kid will be drowning on my premises."

"Well, they might work at it in a bathtub. I think a few die every year in toilets and buckets. Are you thinking of names for your company?"

"Like what?"

"Like something catchy and prestigious-sounding."

"How about Metro-Goldwyn-Davidson?"

"I think you might have copyright issues with that brand."

I said I would think about it. Armpit Films works for me, but I doubt Charlotte would approve.

Later I phoned Almy. She actually picked up and sounded semi-pleased to hear from me. I asked if she was interested in dinner sometime.

"I can't right now, Nick. Everest showed up today."

"What does that cad want?"

"He's begging me to take him back."

"I trust you recall you showed no mercy when Stuart and I transgressed. We both got the boot, and you remained quite firm."

"I'm not sure that worked out so well for any of us."

"Musicians have giant egos, dear. You told me that yourself. Plus, he sounds like a complete narcissist. Being involved with a narcissist always ends badly. Ask any psychologist."

"I happen to be in therapy now. I'll discuss that at my next session."

"Please do, darling. Send that dude back to New York. Don't delay! I'm sure Marcie misses him!"

Almy laughed. "Yeah, I bet she does."

If Almy marries that guy, I will be so pissed. Why should he be forgiven when I got banished from her life for all those years?

So I phoned Kinsley and made a date for dinner on Friday. I'll surprise her by taking her to Providence, that super-expensive place on Melrose.

THURSDAY, July 21 – My elusive agent Zach phoned. He said my Catholic seminary series will be shown on the BritBox streaming service starting next month. For some reason I don't get paid anything extra for that. This wallet-bite I'm attributing to poor agent negotiating. Nevertheless, I invited him to my house-warming party. I also told him my name change had come through and Nick Twisp II was kaput.

He grumbled about that and had the nerve to ask how I could afford a $2.2 million house in Mar Vista. He suspected I was paying for it with YouTube earnings I wasn't sharing with him. I assured him that was not the case.

No, I didn't tell him I'm now rich. Agents work hardest if they think their clients are starving.

Later Arthur K. Murchison phoned. He received my court-approved petition and will be sending me "all matters and documents" related to the rest of Aunt Grace's accounts.

"That's great," I said.

"You realize, Nick," he said, "that you must maintain use of the name Davidson in every and all contexts. You can never change it. Were you to do so, you would forfeit your great-aunt's entire estate and all of its incomes."

I decided to tease the guy. "What if I figure out that I'm gay and opt to take my new husband's name?"

Long pause before he replied. "Your great-aunt made no provision in her will for sexual deviance. Such a circumstance might have to be litigated in the courts."

"That sounds complicated. I think I'll stick with girls."

"That, of course, would be my advice, Nick. I hope you have retained her Cadillac."

"It's parked right here in my garage. Aunt Grace must have pulled some strings with God because it passed its smog test."

"That's wonderful news, Nick. Your great-aunt would be so pleased."

I know that sounds like sarcasm, but I really think the old guy was sincere. It's a known fact that people in the Midwest are less cynical than us jaded Californians.

My stealthy retrieval of Cal worked as planned, but my next house is going to have an *attached* garage. All window blinds were closed; all doors were securely locked. The sheets on my bed were freshly laundered. I had taken a shower and smelled halfway decent. I handed her two of my precious coins. She bit into one of them like those skeptical pirates and banditos in old-time movies.

"These appear to be genuine gold," she said.

"You had doubts?" I asked, embracing her.

"I half expected foil-wrapped chocolate coins pilfered during some Hanukkah dinner. Where do you want me?"

"How about the bed?"

"Oh, a traditionalist. How quaint."

We stripped and went at it. Extremely satisfying as usual. Cal also appeared to be having a good time. Our passions spent, we lay together in blissful repose.

"Did you get your money's worth?" she asked.

"You know I did, darling."

"I hope you'll give me a good Yelp review. So do you mind sharing me with Liam?"

"I mind immensely, dear. Guys really hate the thought of other dudes drawing from the same well."

"You could marry me. And have me all to yourself."

"I tried marriage, darling. Too much heartache. Marriage is agony on a stick."

"So you never intend to get married again?"

"Let's just say the institution offers no appeal at present."

"What if Liam asks me to marry him?"

"Just tell him to drop dead and keep on collecting the gold from me. Everyone will be better off."

"I might say yes to him. I haven't tried marriage yet."

"Take my word for it, dearest. It sucks."

FRIDAY, July 22 – Cal didn't spend the night. I returned her to that Venice corner just as stealthily. In a small notebook I keep in my night-stand drawer I wrote down yester-days date, noted 2c (for two coins), and made one mark. Above the mark I wrote a small "f" (for freebie). I intend to continue with this bookkeeping system to avoid any dis-putes with Cal over what is owed to whom.

I don't consider this arrangement paying for sex. Cal and I are just continuing our long-term relationship while supplementing her income. I could marry her (she sounds willing), but who wants to be married for their money? Not me.

Only two days until my party. For some reason everyone seems intent on coming. No turndowns yet. There's no ac-counting for my sudden popularity.

Charlotte phoned. She has found some puppeteers: three people who travel around in their van giving shows. I hope the kiddies like 'em, 'cause those dudes don't work cheap. I told her to hire them, but to work on chiseling down their fee.

Ramon came and mowed my parched grass. He also blew some unsightly leaves over into Carli's yard. And sprinkled some fertilizer on my reviving grass.

Later, workmen arrived and erected two canopies for the drinks station and for a shaded sitting area. Folding chairs got arrayed here and there. Also some tiny tables. I'm told all edibles will be served by waiters circulating from my kitchen. The puppet van will be stationed in the driveway in front of the garage.

Damn, it occurred to me I could save money by turn-ing this gala event into a wedding reception and marrying someone. Too bad I'm not further along on my reconcilia-tion with Almy or courtship of Kinsley.

Then it was time to pick up Kinsley in Holmby Hills. Both parents were there, but not yet overtly hostile. I told her dad I would be giving him the final package from Mur-chison when it arrived.

"I look forward to untangling your complicated affairs," he replied.

"And who is your designated driver?" asked Kinsley's slim and fashion-forward mother. The woman reeked of old money and expensive perfume.

"I am," I replied. "I'm not much of a drinker."

"Nick doesn't like the taste," her daughter explained.

As we were driving down Melrose, Kinsley said, "I hope you're not taking me to Providence, Nick."

"Er, why not?" I asked.

"It's a great restaurant, but I go there all the time with my parents. Let's try this new Bolivian place that just opened on San Vicente."

So we went there instead, and had anticuchos and chaj-chu with cuñapés and humintas. All very tasty and light on the wallet. Kinsley told me about growing up as a rich kid in Holmby Hills. I told her about growing up in a family of marginal dry-cleaners in Terre Haute, and my abrupt transformation into a Twisp at age 15.

It turns out Kinsley went to the same snooty private school as Lauren Bedrossian, who was one grade ahead of her. I asked her what kids at the school thought of Lauren.

"She was pretty popular because she was smart, in the business, and friends with Cooper Tucker, who has to be the cutest blind guy on the planet."

"He's coming to my party on Sunday. You'll get to meet him."

"I'm looking forward to it, Nick. I'm counting on him to distract me from all your old girlfriends prowling around."

Since I was taking it slow with Kinsley, we went back to her place and necked down by the pool. I was all for taking a nude midnight swim, but she said there were too many security cameras trained on the pool area.

SATURDAY, July 23 – Party day minus one. Almy phoned

early and asked if I wanted to meet for breakfast at the diner on Pico. I said OK, but we couldn't dawdle 'cause the place got busy fast on weekends. I bombed there in the Mustang and grabbed the last table. She showed up 10 minutes later, setting off a noticeable tremor in a place filled with blasé L.A. types. Starring with my genius brother clearly has upped her profile. Also she tends to cause a stir because she's achingly beautiful. To stake out my territory, I leaned over and kissed her when she sat down. Once again, no scream or slap. Progress is being made.

Also entering with her was a stocky older guy, who took a seat at the counter. She confirmed that he was Mr. Clancy, her bodyguard. He glanced our way throughout his meal; I don't think he liked my looks.

We ordered and then got caught up. I told her my party was coming together and that there would be puppeteers. She kept her excitement in check. She said Everest had returned to New York yesterday.

"A positive development, dear. And did you resolve your issues?"

"Not entirely, Nick. Things are a big mess between us. And I'll be in school with the guy all next year. I had an emergency session with my therapist."

"Oh?"

"She had me do this test. I answered a series of questions about Everest. According to the test, he scored a high probability of being a grandiose narcissist."

"I knew it! Didn't I tell you that?"

"So we did the same test referencing you."

"Oh . . . so how did I do?"

"Not that bad. Muriel says it's unlikely you're a narcissist; she thinks you're trending more toward B.P.D."

"What's that? Bold, Personable, and Debonair?"

"No, Borderline Personality Disorder. They have a major fear of abandonment."

"So normal people are fine with being abandoned?"

"I think it's a matter of degrees, Nick."

It's true I was abandoned emotionally by my stepfather, and then abandoned for real when my mother dumped me on that stranger Nick Twisp. So I may have some sensitivities around that issue.

"I think I'm better these days, dear," I said. "I've matured and gained a great deal of self-awareness."

"That sounds positive. Also some self-control might be helpful. So when's the last time you had sex with Cal?"

"I really don't wish to discuss that with you, darling."

"Didn't she get back together with her boyfriend?"

"Yes, she did. She's thinking Liam might pop the question soon."

"So she's not having sex with you?"

"Uh, why don't we change the subject? How are your eggs?"

"Oh, so she *is* having sex with you. So she's doing it with two guys?"

"Not simultaneously. There's nothing kinky about it."

"So what? She's taking pity on you because you don't have a girlfriend?"

"That could be one interpretation. People do need sex. It's kind of a basic human need. Were I married, I wouldn't be touching that girl."

No way would I ever be stupid enough to confess to Almy that I'm paying Cal to sleep with me.

"And what if you grew tired of your wife?" she asked.

"I don't expect I'll be doing that, dear. I take marriage very seriously—unlike certain pianists I could name."

"So you really do come as a package deal with Valerie Haseltine."

"Not at all, darling. I've only ever loved one person, and I'm watching her eat a cheese omelet right now."

"You didn't love your wife?"

"I was fond of her until she got a tattoo and moved in with a neighbor."

"You don't like tattoos?"

"On chicks they make me physically sick. If you want to get rid of me for good, get a tattoo."

"That could be a useful piece of information."

She laughed, so I think she was joking.

I paid the tab because I'm rich and also a guy. Mr. Clancy paid his own bill.

I went back home and vacuumed and did other stuff to prepare for the party. For example, I put this note on the front door: "Door is locked. Come around to back." Then I went inside, locked the door, and taped over the lock. Under it I put a sign that read: KEEP DOOR LOCKED ON PAIN OF DEATH!!!

Nevertheless, I expect some moron will exit out the front, thus leaving the door unlocked and allowing uninvited strangers to saunter in and swipe my valuables.

SUNDAY, July 24 – Party Day! For some reason these occasions always fill me with anticipatory dread. At least this party is during the day. People will come, inspect my house, sneer at my furniture, eat some pricey snacks, and leave. I don't have to worry about keeping them entertained all night like at my infamous Bel-Air party.

Charlotte arrived around 8:30. She brought donuts, but from the less-preferred shop. She also said donuts were "the single worst food" the human body could ingest. Could be, but I ate three and am still alive to write this journal.

She reports her upstairs neighbors are noisy, and she smashed a cockroach in her kitchen this morning. I said if she saw one, there are 10,000 more waiting in the wings.

"Roaches are the Rockettes of the insect world," I added.

Various catering folks arrived and also the puppeteers:

two guys and a gal, all in their mid to late twenties. The gal told me that Bronson Flange was "profoundly subversive to the prevailing Zeitgeist." I took that as a compliment.

Since my driveway slopes a bit, they took the trouble of leveling their van on blocks. It's one of those newer models with a high roof. A long compartment door had been installed horizontally on one side up near the top. When unlocked from inside, the door sprang up and was held open by struts. This revealed the extra-wide puppet theater. I guess this troupe is offering puppet shows in CinemaScope and VistaVision. That side of the van was covered in colorful and elaborate graphics highlighting the name ZANZIBAR TRAVELING THEATRE OF ARTISTES AND GROTESQUES. Smaller lettering underneath read, WORLD HEADQUARTERS: DEEP WITHIN YOUR MIND.

I'm keeping my garage door open to show off my secure parking and growing automotive fleet. I also moved some of the tiny tables to lessen the tripping hazard. Lawsuits I don't need, plus I don't recall ever signing up for house insurance. I may have to have my P.A. look into that while she's changing my name everywhere.

The drinks station opened at 11:30 and was descended upon by the puppeteers. A smiling waiter offered me cheesy snacks from a tray. I sampled one and said, "Very good."

All too soon, guests were thronging about. Twisps as far as the eye could see, and smaller ones right underfoot. My ex-wife arrived with Cliff, plus Sligger and Richie Shapcott. Sligger commented, "Jesus, Nick, your house is huge!" His wife added, "I do color consulting, Nick. Call me if you want to update your exterior. Tan stucco is so last century."

Uncle Jake shook my hand and said, "$2.2 million, huh? Now I know prices have gone insane. At least your air conditioner looks new. That should save you some bucks down the road."

"Right, Uncle Jake," I replied. "That was my thinking too."

Then Cal arrived with Liam, Harvey, and Tiara. I hate it when guys turn out to be even better-looking than their photos. Handsome Liam shook my hand and said he hoped I would be "steering clear of jewelry shops." I said I "hoped so too." Naturally, Cal was wearing her new ruby pin. Matching blood-red gems sparkled at her ears. "A gift from darling Liam," she whispered as her warm lips lightly brushed my cheek.

Aunt Joanie came over, munching snacks. "I hear you're rich, Nick. You better save some for your old age. It will be here before you know it. So what happened with you and your wife?"

I spotted an incident developing across the way and excused myself. I intercepted Teejay as he was heading down the driveway with my Hermes Baby typewriter.

"Where are you going with that?" I demanded, grabbing him by his shirt.

"This is an amazing machine, Nick. It prints letters on paper without batteries or electricity! It's powered by your fingers!"

Somehow the kid had reached the age of four without hearing about typewriters. I removed it from his sticky little fingers.

"It's called a typewriter, Teejay, and it's a very valuable antique. It's not for little kids to play with—or steal."

"I'll give you a thousand bucks for it," he said.

I considered the offer. "OK, you get your mother's permission to buy it, and I'll sell it for that price. Cash only. Meanwhile, keep your grubby paws off my stuff."

I returned the typewriter to my study, where Zach my agent was reading my framed letter. "Hi, Nick," he said. "What this guy lacked was decent representation."

"Yeah, I know the feeling."

I hurried into the living room, where my front door was standing ajar. I closed it, locked it, taped over the lock, found my sign discarded on the floor, and taped it again to the door. I was considering blocking it with the sofa, when Seka walked up sipping from a plastic glass of bubbly Prosecco.

"Oh, there you are, Nick. Your house is very nice. You know my husband, your brother, is an artist. He will never be wealthy like you."

"He's a talented guy. I expect he will do very well."

"We're starting a college fund for little Nick Twisp Wyatt. He is named after you, of course."

"I thought he was named after his grandfather."

"Well, it's true you both have the same name. Or at least you used to. We're thinking a contribution of $100,000 to our fund would be appropriate for you. And you should buy some of Frank's paintings for your walls."

"Most Twisps don't go to college," I pointed out. "For example, all the preceding Nick Twisps."

"College is essential, Nick. We can't all count on inheriting fortunes from unknown relatives."

I told her I would think about it.

Then Almy arrived with her glam grandparents and paunchy bodyguard. The tone of a party always ascends stratospherically with Prestons on the scene. I welcomed Almy warmly but refrained from kissing her so as not to inflame her grandfather. Trent shook my clammy hand and said he was happy I had "landed on my feet." I'm not sure what he meant by that. I got kissed by his wife Apurva. Every party needs at least one exotic guest dressed in a colorful silk sari.

Later, I caught a waiter trying to hand his screenplay to Trent. I told him to desist and get back to work. I also noticed Zach deep in conversation with Carli, who I don't recall having invited to my party. Another neighbor from across the street was seen poking around in my garage.

Things were hopping in the back yard, but I mostly

hung out in the dining room so I could keep an eye on my front door. Twice I had to yell at idiots trying to exit that way, including Uma. She said, "Oh, excuse me," then read my sign. "Under pain of death," she said. "That seems a bit extreme, even for you."

As I was chatting with Lefty and his girlfriend Candy, we heard waves of laughter and applause from the back yard. Then Kinsley came in. "Oh, there you are, Nick," she said. "You should go see your puppeteers. They're amazing."

I said I would check them out later and introduced her to Lefty and Candy.

"Is everyone watching the puppet show?" I asked.

"Almy Preston and Valerie Haseltine are talking to your ex-wife and Cooper Tucker," she replied. "Not being insanely glamorous I slunk away unseen."

"I'll introduce you to Cooper before he leaves."

"Who are the two dreamboats with Ms. Haseltine?" she asked.

"That would be Harvey her brother and Liam her boyfriend."

Charlotte came in looking upset. I asked her what was wrong.

"Your father's being an ass, Nick. He's been berating me for my dad getting shot on his premises. How is that my fault?"

"Just ignore him, dear," I said. "That's what I do. Twisps can be trouble. I caught his youngest son trying to steal my vintage typewriter. Fortunately, I'm now a Davidson."

Kinsley excused herself to go watch more of the puppet show as Tiara Diamond strolled in.

"Nice party, Nick," she said. "Your puppet artists are fabulous."

"Are they doing some commedia dell'arte-type show?"

"Hardly. The part I saw had a Japanese pearl diver falling in love with a dragon and being rescued by Oscar Wilde disguised as Madonna."

"Great, I guess. I hope it's not too mature for little kids."

"The kids are loving it, Nick. And Trent Preston is enthralled."

A sudden commotion of loud shouting drew us all to the back yard. Mr. Clancy had Stuart Dunham face-down on the ground and was handcuffing his fat wrists behind his back.

Yeah, the big oaf and committed stalker was back from New York state. I thought that guy was in jail for assault.

Post-party roundup:

Frank C. Wyatt apologized for his wife "putting the bite" on me. I said I would contribute $50,000 to his fund. This is the equivalent of 50 nights in the sack with Cal, which is my new way of thinking about money. Frank said that was "extremely generous" of me. In gratitude he said I could take my pick of any of his paintings. But I have a different plan for using his talents.

My brother Scott said I should have consulted him. He said there are better houses for less money in Encino. I said I didn't want to live in the Valley and battle the 405 daily to have a life.

Treez said she would find Teejay a "sturdier typewriter for less money." That's fine with me. I have no wish to part with my guru's much-loved machine.

Carli reported that Zach has signed her as a client. He has also promised to take her to lunch soon. I wished her luck on both endeavors.

Tiara Diamond handed me a crisp $100 bill. She said it fell out of a book she had removed from my bookcase. I said I'd been using the Benjamin as a bookmark. She said she was impressed by my choice of reading matter as the book was titled *How Donna Reed's Character in 'It's a Wonderful Life' Proves the Existence of a Just God*. I made a mental note to take a closer look at S.F.B.'s books.

Kinsley decided to make the Zanzibar Traveling Theatre the subject of her student film. She thinks it will be a documentary, but needs to discuss this with her team of fellow students. She said she talked it over with my ex-wife and they've agreed that Marant Tucker (Cooper's son) is the "cutest and sweetest" kid ever. She added that having Cooper, Liam, and Harvey all in the same room was "almost more than any girl could stand."

Speaking of which, Almy said she didn't understand why Liam C. Collier "wasn't enough for one girl, even one with an ego like Cal's." I reminded her not to judge a book by its cover, and said even tall, handsome, and hearty Princeton grads can be duds in bed. She seemed perplexed and doubtful.

The party wound up costing me a hair under $9,700. Kind of pricey, but people appeared to have a good time. Unknown persons walked out with my hair dryer, two throw pillows, my sharpest kitchen knife, and Jordyn Michaels's hand-woven napkins. I'm not ruling out the possibility that she sneaked in unseen and confiscated them herself. Also, someone left a screenplay in my kitchen towel drawer. I read the first two pages, gagged convulsively, and tossed it in the recycle bin.

MONDAY, July 25 – Almy phoned with some news. Stuart's mother is in town and is dragging him back home to Kansas. If he doesn't settle down and get a job, his parents are threatening to stop making his child-support payments. If that happens, 'ol Stuart could wind up in alimony jail.

"I hear you were having a conversation with my ex-wife," I said.

"Lucia told me that she misjudged you. Now she doesn't think you'd been cheating on her."

"I wasn't."

"But she says she's much happier with Clifford Swandon. He seems nice."

"Yeah, Cliff's a great guy. I'd go out with him myself if he wasn't taken."

"Was that sarcasm?"

"Do you have to ask, darling?"

"Who was that cute blond girl talking to the puppet people?"

"You may mean Kinsley Vanoxit. Her dad is my tax accountant. She's in her final year at USC. I may be auditioning for her upcoming student film."

"And what other role are you auditioning for with her?"

"We've had a couple of dates, dear. Should you agree to marry me, I'll never speak to her again."

"Does she know about you and Cal?"

"No, but I'll tell her if she asks. I'm an open book these days. My kimono is always open."

"That's a rather disturbing image."

"Sorry. So when can I see you?"

"My grandfather isn't happy that we're talking again."

"Even more reason to get together. I never let my relatives control my love life. I've commissioned Frank C. Wyatt to paint your portrait. You'll have to come here to pose."

"I suppose you want me fully undraped."

"That would be ideal, but I'll leave it up to you. When would you like to start?"

"We'll see, Nick. I'll call you."

Amalda Preston has one E in her name. That letter stands for *elusive*.

I put Charlotte to work converting all my identities everywhere to Nick Davidson. She says if my dad gets in her face again, she'll quit working as my P.A. and open a poker-training school with Connie. Also she bugged me again to start thinking of names for our production company. How about Extremely Reluctant Films?

I searched through S.F.B.'s books and shook out eight more Benjamins. Almost enough to buy another session with Cal. Two bills fell out of a book titled *Travels with Charley*, which I took as a sign from my guru. I put that book in my bathroom for casual reading on the throne.

Later, I picked up Cal on the corner for another stealth event. On the drive to my place I told her that Liam was too handsome to fall for as he will always be the target of man-hungry girls.

"You're just jealous, Nickie, because he bought those lovely earrings for me."

"I expect my ruby pin refund will be even more delayed."

"Very possibly. I'm surprised Almy Preston came to your party."

"Girls love to see me and spend time in my company. It's a well-known fact."

"Well-known in your mind at least. Her actual motivation for attending remains obscure."

"She loves me, darling. I've commissioned my brother to paint her portrait."

"No doubt while you lurk about trying to curry favor with a girl who's been rejecting you for years."

"You've mostly been rejecting me for twice as long and here we are together again."

"Together in a commercial capacity. I predict you'll wind up with the painting, but not the girl."

"We'll just have to see, darling."

It's probably not wise to discuss Almy before hopping into bed with Cal. She didn't seem quite as loving this time. I kissed her as we lay in the afterglow, but she told me to "knock off the mushy stuff."

So we discussed her movie instead. They hired Clive McGregor to costar as the distressed husband. Shooting starts in August. Once filming begins she may be too busy and/or fatigued for events with me. I said I would treasure any time we could spend together.

She seemed subdued on the drive back. Paying for sex may be more complicated than it first appeared.

TUESDAY, July 26 – I've been reading the Steinbeck book. It turns out Charley is an aging French poodle that he dragged along on a cross-country trip in a truck camper in 1962. Not very posh compared to today's RVs. Not even a bathroom to hide an illegal in. Later investigators determined that Steinbeck mostly stayed in deluxe motels or with his ritzy friends. Plus, most of the travel encounters he made up. Still, it makes for an OK bathroom read. I'm wondering if Donna Reed will show up at some point. It's true that his departure was delayed for two weeks by Hurricane Donna. 1962 was back before even my ancient dad was alive. The Beatles were around, but hardly anyone had heard of them. Also Marilyn Monroe died that year.

A big package of financial stuff arrived from Murchison. I guess it wasn't a scam after all. I hauled it all over to Kinsley's dad's office in Century City.

As requested, Kinsley arrived here for dinner. Being a bachelor, I served takeout from a Chinese restaurant on Venice Boulevard. She had a glass of my party-surplus Prosecco, but I stuck with water.

First surprise of the evening: she told me the puppeteers have been camping out for the past few days on their property in Holmby Hills.

"They live in that van?" I asked, rolling mu shu pork in a skinny pancake.

"Most of the time, Nick. It's all set up for cozy living. They're hot to be in my movie."

"Does it have a bathroom?"

"Just a pull-out portable potty. Lots of truck stops offer shower facilities these days."

"Sounds extremely primitive. How do they accommodate two sexes in one small space?"

"That's where it gets interesting. They're a trio."

"What's that mean?"

"It's like a couple, but with one more person. All three of them are in love with each other."

"So they're all sleeping in one big naked heap?"

"Pretty much. Cyril and Brian do it with Elsa, but also do it with each other."

"Have they invited you to join in the fun?"

"Certainly not. They're committed to each other and to their art. They're very happy and love what they're doing. Elsa told me she likes to accommodate both Cyril and Brian at the same time."

"How so, dear?"

"Apparently, if you're nimble, you can get two penises in one vagina."

"OK, if you say so."

"It's apparently extremely pleasurable for all three of them. Frequently, they can all achieve orgasm at the same time."

"That should make an interesting subject for a student film."

"I hope to mention that in my film, but I won't be showing it, of course."

"Damn, and I was going to buy the first ticket."

"I'd need their permission to go into that subject, but naturally viewers of the film would wonder."

"People have extremely dirty minds," I confirmed.

Second surprise of the evening: Kinsley was willing to accommodate my penis in her vagina. I'm no expert, but it didn't seem to me that she had a whole lot of room to spare. We did this after slogging through two more hours of Hard Times with Almy and Teejay.

I was all for taking it slow, but she decided it was time to cut the mustard. Fortunately, I had changed my sheets since last night's event with Cal. We employed two condoms as the gods of love decreed, and she spent the night in a naked heap with me.

WEDNESDAY, July 27 – Kinsley left after breakfast. I kissed her good-bye and said I hope her parents hadn't filed a missing person report with the cops. She said they know she's an adult and don't expect to be tucking her into bed every night at eight p.m.

Thankfully, it did not appear I was the first guy to have trespassed on her divine portal. I have given up on virgins, and will be advising everyone I meet to do the same.

Charlotte reported in. She downloaded the passport form and will be dropping it by for me to fill out. She said there's a place near the Post Office that does passport photos while you wait. Then I need to take the form and photo plus the court petition to the Post Office. Also she made an appointment for me at the DMV to get a new driver's license. All too soon, Nick Twisp II will be a fading memory, lingering only in the hearts of certain select girls.

Or will he? Today's mail brought a small box. Inside were two Mexico 50-peso gold coins. No note. Damn, I wish I could remember what I said that offended Cal. I phoned her, but she wasn't picking up. So I left a contrite message. I did remind her that the event business had been her idea. I said I was fine if she wished to cancel, no hard feelings.

The whole thing seemed like a win-win situation for both of us, but I guess not. If in doubt, keep it in your pants. That's a lesson guys have been learning the hard way for eons.

Treez phoned to invite me to Dad's birthday party on Saturday, July 30. That, of course, is not his birthday. We usually celebrate his birthday on August 1 even though he was born on August 2. He changed the date years ago because the first of the month is "easier to remember." God forbid anyone should forget his special day. On Sunday they leave for Nova Scotia, so Dad will be turning the big 6-0 in Canada next Tuesday. On that day he officially becomes a Dead Albeit Still Breathing Old Fossil.

Treez also said she found a Smith-Corona typewriter for Teejay in a thrift store for 30 bucks plus tax. I said I very much doubt it's as nice as my classic Swiss-made model. I went on Ebay to see what huge sums my version were commanding. Only a couple hundred bucks at best. I should have nailed down Teejay's offer on the spot.

Later, when Charlotte dropped off the passport form, I asked her to shop for a birthday card and gift for my father.

"You realize I heartily dislike your father," she pointed out.

"In which case I'm sure you'll find something appropriate for him. He's turning 60. The party's on Saturday."

"What's your budget?"

"Niggardly at best."

"OK, I'll see what I can do."

THURSDAY, July 28 – No call back from Cal. That girl may be back to hating my guts.

Guess who I noticed leaving Carli's place this morning. Zach my agent. I hope she's not trying to undermine my career by seducing my agent and turning him against me.

I read some more of the Steinbeck book. He left in the fall and headed north toward Maine. Most people would have headed south toward Florida. These days nobody would be writing a tedious book about their RV trip. They'd be documenting their travels on YouTube and earning hefty ad money. Jack Kerouac and Neal Cassady would be bombing back and forth across the continent and recording it all on their iPhones.

Steinbeck won the Nobel Prize, but that was back when they were mostly handing them out to old white guys. I doubt this travelogue book was wowing the dudes in Stockholm. So far I'm not figuring out why S.F.B. stashed $200 of his own money in this book. Why did my guru want me to read it? Is he telling me to adopt a large and smelly poodle?

Almy phoned to say she had been talking to my brother.

"Which brother is that?" I asked. "I've got lots."

"I spoke with Frank about your so-called portrait project. We worked together on the show for four seasons. He's happy doing my portrait from memory or with the aid of a few photos."

"Not at all an ideal way to capture your vital essence, dear."

"Too bad because my essence soon will be departing for New York. We have a bit more ADR work, and then I'm out of here."

"What's the rush, darling?"

"You forget, Nick, I don't live here anymore. I live in New York. That's my home now. I've been camping at my grandparents' place, and now my grandfather is twisting my arm to do a follow-up season."

"Your show is a tremendous success, dear. And your short co-star is champing at the bit to be reunited with you."

"That seems to be a feature of you Twisps. Wouldn't you be happier with a painting of Masked Girl in one of Frank's fanciful masks?"

"No way, darling. Here's an idea: let's take a few days off and go back to that ritzy resort in Montecito. I'll pay. I can take some photos of you on the beach with my phone for Frank. We had a fun and relaxing time there before."

"I remember that trip. It was right before you eloped to Las Vegas with another girl."

"Only because you refused me. You could have spared

everyone a lot of grief by running off to Vegas with me instead."

"I'm not so sure about that. OK, let me think about it."

"Running off to Vegas?" I asked hopefully.

"No, your original plan. A return trip to Montecito."

She's still the most elusive girl I know. I hope she's not eager to return to NYC so she can hook up again with that cheat and liar Everest Weeden.

Charlotte showed up with Dad's card and gift: a boxed DVD set of Jeanette MacDonald and Nelson Eddy movie musicals.

"Has it occurred to you that he might actually enjoy these?" I asked.

"Could be, Nick. But you're still conveying the meta-message that he's a superannuated geezer."

Thoughtfully, she'd also gotten me a replacement for my stolen hair dryer.

She harangued me for failing to take my passport form to the post office, then departed.

Having a P.A. shares many aspects with being married.

FRIDAY, July 29 – Cal texted that she would be at the Venice coffee place at 8:45. So I arrived there promptly. She refused my kiss, announcing that she was "done with men." I apologized again and asked what I could do to make it better.

"You could assassinate Liam C. Collier," she replied.

"Oh, having trouble with Liam?" I asked, taking a seat beside her. Better that dude than me.

"I'm going to order *The Joy of Lesbian Sex* with one click and live the rest of my life across the aisle."

"That's certainly, uh, a plan, dear. What did Liam do?"

"He'd been acting suspiciously—as long as I've known him. Getting all these calls. He said they were clients. But who calls their financial advisor at 10:30 at night?"

"Not me," I agreed.

"And he had these suspicious foods in his refrigerator—like wheat grass juice and nutritional yeast. What guy eats stuff like that?"

"Certainly not me, dear."

"And then I found a box of tampons in his bathroom cupboard. Do you keep tampons in your bathroom?"

"No, but I've been thinking of putting in one of those dispensers for extra income."

"Yeah, you would. So I'm over at his place the other night. Liam is a very sound sleeper. Hearty guys tend to sleep like cadavers. Their rippling muscles need time to recuperate.So I get up and start poking around."

"Snooping and spying. Probably a wise idea, dear. Did you check his phone?"

"Protected by a fingerprint reader. I considered holding his finger against the phone, but I figured that might wake him. So I checked his wallet."

"Was it loaded with photos of his wife and kids?"

"No, but I found a suspicious note. It read: 'Sherry. R.S. 8.'"

"Sounds like maybe some wine he likes."

"Guess again, buddy. So I shake Liam awake and I ask him why he needs to know that Sherry's ring size is 8. It all tumbles out before he's fully awake. It turns out he's been engaged to this Sherry person for 15 months."

"Jesus, what a cad."

"It gets worse. He never even bought a sailboat. He only told me that so he could spend weekends with Sherry. She was getting pissed because he was always busy."

"But didn't you go see his boat?"

"I saw a boat. It turns out it was his buddy's. So that was the last straw. Now I'm only into chicks. Do you think I should phone Maya Chan and ask her out?"

"I'd hold off on that, dear. Maya never seemed that into you."

"I need to start hanging out in lesbian bars. How do I find out where they are?"

"Probably on Yelp. Or just Google it. I've never really explored that topic. Don't you ever check out these guys first on social media?"

"Liam's not on social media. He says he values his privacy."

"Yeah, so he can deceive unsuspecting chicks. At least he bought you those ruby earrings. He wasn't a total waste of your time."

"I wasn't completely truthful about that, Nick. I bought them myself, thinking Liam might reimburse me."

"And I don't suppose he did."

"No, the guy is much too cheap. He's only interested in money."

"I suppose that's why he became a financial advisor."

"So what do chicks do in bed?" she asked, picking at my muffin.

"I think at times their activities can involve double-ended dildos."

Cal recoiled. "Well . . . I'm sure I could learn to enjoy that over time."

I told her what Kinsley had said about the sexual quirks of the Zanzibar Traveling Puppeteers.

"Two at once, huh?" she said. "That sounds very, uh, fulfilling. Perhaps that's the secret. Hook up with two guys. And then you always have one in reserve when the other one breaks your heart."

"At least now you won't have to take up skiing," I pointed out. "You won't be crashing into a tree like Sonny Bono."

"I'll probably wind up with a muscle-bound dyke who's into bowling and motorcycles."

"Just be selective, dear. You have a lot to offer to the right person."

"I suppose you've slept with that Kinsley girl by now."

"Only once."

"And how does she compare to me?"

Not being an idiot, I refused to go down that road. When pressed, I did concede that Kinsley was doing it for free.

Cal happened to have the receipt for the earrings in her purse. I said I would send her a check for that amount. She smiled wanly and acknowledged there was at least one guy in L.A. who wasn't "a total waste of planetary resources."

"Dig up some other guy, Nick, and I'll try stuffing you both in at once. I'll only charge him. You I'll do for free."

"I think not, dear. I leave kinky sex to the acrobatically inclined."

Later, I had a long conversation with Kinsley's dad. No, he wasn't demanding a shotgun wedding. We discussed my financial situation. I'll be engaging in some obscure gyrations on my tax forms as rich people tend to do.

"I thought those nice Republicans got rid of soaking the rich," I said.

"They've been very helpful over the years for people in your income bracket. Don't worry, we'll be minimizing your hit from Uncle Sam."

Poverty may suck, but at least you're not writing giant checks to the government. And I wish I'd had this conversation before I volunteered to pay for Cal's pricey earrings.

FRIDAY, July 29, Dad's party day – Dad lucked out today. His birthday is being celebrated, yet he avoids turning 60. If his plane crashes on the way to Canada, he'll never have to face that wrenching milestone.

The guest list was better than I expected. Almy was there (with her grandparents). Always the essence of tact, Teejay announced in a loud voice that he liked his TV mom better than his real mom. He got a time-out in his room for that slander. The short dude is working up a musical encomium to typewriters for his YouTube channel. He asked to borrow my machine for Edy to use in the video, but I refused. He turned very red in the face and silently mouthed the F-word. Being a Twisp, the kid doesn't handle rejection well.

While munching on the tiniest sliver of cake, Almy mentioned that she had heard that Cal broke up with her boyfriend yet again.

"Who told you that?" I asked.

"Your brother."

"Teejay is up on the latest gossip now?"

"Your brother Frank told me. He already started in on the painting. He's doing me as I looked in the series with Teejay."

"I may not want a painting of you looking down and out in the Great Depression."

"Well, that may be what you're getting. I asked him to paint me looking away from the artist, but he refused."

"I definitely don't need a painting of the back of your head, dear. I've seen too much of that already."

"You are speaking metaphorically here?"

"Yeah, you're always walking away from me. Are we going to Montecito tomorrow?"

"We could—assuming you can get reservations."

"I'll have no trouble with that; I'll just mention your illustrious name."

"And we need separate rooms."

"We did fine in one room the last time."

"That depends on your definition of fine."

"I totally respected your insane refusal to have sex with me."

"I have to be back on Monday. Can you handle that?"

"I suppose, dear."

Dad received a lot of useless gifts, but Lefty's cake was excellent. Treez invited my ex-wife, but she declined to put in an appearance. Just as well. I'm still resenting her comment that she greatly prefers life with Clifford. I can understand why that might be, but I didn't need to hear it.

When I got home, I phoned for reservations. The resort was thrilled that Almy Preston would be gracing their premises. Even though it was the weekend, they were able to dredge up two pricey rooms for us. What a tragedy if they'd only had one.

I confirmed our plans with Almy. She didn't want me to pick her up. She'll be coming here instead. I told her to make sure Mr. Clancy, the ex-cop, got left behind.

Then I phoned Kinsley to broach the delicate subject of why I was unavailable this weekend. It turns out she and her fellow students are busy filming the puppeteers. They had to jump on the project right away because the Zanzibarians are leaving for Santa Fe in a few days.

"I'm sorry I have no time to see you, Nick," she said. "I hope you'll forgive me."

"Not a problem, dear. Call me when you're free, and we'll make a date."

"Thanks for being so understanding, Nick. Some guys would be pitching a fit right now."

"Not me, darling. I love that you're so dedicated to your work."

At some point, she'll likely hear I was up in Montecito cavorting with Almy. I'll cross that rickety bridge when I come to it.

SATURDAY, July 30 – I got up early to haul assorted Twisps to the airport (LAX). I took the Caddy because it has a six-body trunk. With two little kids and a baby, those dudes don't travel light. They even lugged along Teejay's bulky Smith-Corona. Treez said they would have brought Otilia too if she had proper documentation for crossing borders.

I dropped the whole crew off at the curb and "laid a

patch" when exiting. Stopped at my preferred donut shop on the way back, and waved at my agent as he was leaving my neighbor's house. Looks like it's more than a one-night stand with those two. Better him than me!

Almy was right on time. It's scary how dependable that girl is. How did I ever imagine I could get away with cheating on her?

She had brought one modest bag for two nights; perhaps this time she's skipping the bulky, undiaphanous nightgown. I placed her bag next to mine in the trunk of the Mustang.

"Do you need to make a pit stop before we leave?" I asked.

"I probably should, Nick."

We did our business in separate bathrooms and hit the road.

"I'm surprised you didn't get an electric car," she said, adjusting her seat.

"Jack Kerouac never drove an electric car," I pointed out.

"Right, Nick. And neither did Attila the Hun. I see you have the movie star's sunglasses."

"Timothée Chalamet begged me to tell him where I bought them, but I refused to say."

Skipping the 405, we went via the Pacific Coast Highway through Malibu. No movie stars in convertibles were seen. Not much of the ocean was seen either because the beachfront is packed solid with houses for miles.

"I guess you got rid of your Matrix," said Almy.

"Yeah, traded in that sucker."

"Too bad, Nick. I liked your little car."

"Me too. I was driving that car up at Clear Lake when I had the greatest day of my life."

"So you've said. I'm surprised you haven't had at least a few days since then that topped it."

"Not likely, dear, since you disappeared from my life."

"Did I tell you I got a call from Cal?"

"No. What did she want?"

"She was giving me all these reasons why I should forgive Everest."

"What business is that of hers?"

"She said music camps are like film sets. She says people always pair off, but it doesn't mean anything."

"So what did you say?"

"I said she's probably right. I know our genes always want us to have the greatest reproductive success. They want to get passed on to the next generation as much as possible. So guys are programmed to cheat. They see an attractive girl, and boom, they want to get it on."

"I don't think we're quite that primitive, Almy."

"I'm not so sure, Nick. You Twisps especially. Your father has *eight* children. Do you think he consciously wanted to have that many?"

"I know he didn't."

"And here you are sharing many of his genes. And here I am going away with you again. I must be crazy."

"I thought we were discussing Everest's case."

"Right. So there's my fiancé rowing out to an island every night to get it on with some horny cellist. And I'm supposed to overlook that?"

"His transgressions are worse than mine, darling. We were never engaged when I was seeing other girls."

"And Everest was simulating sincerity even more deceptively than you. I actually believed his lies for a time."

"Doris Day married a horn player, dear. He was always knocking her around. And other singers and actors who married musicians almost always came to regret it."

"My parents and grandfather really like Everest, Nick. That's another major strike against him."

"So you're done with that turkey?"

"Don't ask me. I'm at sea, as usual."

I had to ask. "Are you done with me?"

"I sure used to think I was."

We stopped for lunch at an Italian restaurant a couple blocks from the beach in Carpinteria. We sat on their pleasant garden patio in back where masks were not required. My phone rang while Almy was away powdering her nose.

"Hello, Cal," I said, "I don't appreciate your trying to sabotage my reunion with Almy."

"If she sleeps with you, Nickie, it's only to get back at Everest. It doesn't mean anything."

"I'm not having this conversation with you," I said, hanging up on her.

Now I wish I hadn't mailed her that check for $2,700. I think she should return those earrings. Most lesbians I've met aren't into flashy jewelry.

Over lunch I tried to get Almy to talk about her life in NYC. She's such a private person, her life for the past few years is mostly a blank to me. She said she was anxious to get back to Manhattan in case she has to find a new apartment.

"What's wrong with your old one?" I asked.

"I'm sharing it with Everest, Nick."

"Oh, I didn't know that. Why doesn't he move? He's the cheat and liar."

"We're on the third floor and his piano doesn't fit in the elevator. It has to go down the stairs. Piano movers charge by the step. It would cost a fortune to move it."

"Most musicians carry their instruments in a case, dear. Only the extreme narcissists require something that weighs half a ton."

"Everest wants to be a composer of film scores. He needs a piano for that."

"So he hooks up with a promising young actor with a famous name. That was a smart career move."

"I hope we're not going to be spending our weekend discussing him. Guess who my landlord is?"

"I have no idea."

"New York's second most famous landlord."

"Oh, you mean the son-in-law? The dude whose daddy bought him into Harvard?"

"That's the guy."

"So do you have bugs?"

"The building's over a hundred years old, so bugs are not unheard of. They tend to wax and wane depending on when the exterminator shows up. You get used to them."

"Not me. I'd be grossed out. I hear New York has a bad rat problem too."

"It's mostly a great place to live. It was scary when Covid first arrived and there was no vaccine yet. People who could get out were leaving in droves."

"So how was college by video meetings?"

"Kind of a joke, especially my acting classes. I think I learned more about the craft while making this last movie than in three years at Juilliard."

"That bug came along just in time to sabotage everyone's college years."

"Are you having second thoughts about dropping out?"

"Not at all. I was never a fan of school."

"You're fortunate you don't have to worry about making a living."

"I know. It's a gift."

"I never heard you mention that great aunt."

"I almost never thought about her. My step dad and his family I was eager to put behind me."

"And now you're a Davidson again, Nick."

"That's true. Bought and paid for."

After lunch we strolled around Carpinteria's small downtown, then zipped up 101 to the resort. Very gracious and welcoming staff when you arrive with Amalda Preston.

Our rooms were opposite each other at the end of the hall on the second floor. Almy was assigned the one with the sweeping ocean view; I got the view of the parking lot. We changed into swim wear and went down to the pool. Many heads turned when we arrived, but Almy was used to that. We sat in lounge chairs and opened our books.

"I'm surprised you're reading that," Almy commented. "I found it rather preachy and judgmental."

"It belonged to my guru Samuel F. Broughton."

"I'm not sure why you've selected a guru who failed completely in life."

"I'm learning from his mistakes."

"And what are you learning, Nick?"

"Don't get swept up in impossible dreams. Be realistic about your abilities and prospects."

"Some people work hard at impossible dreams and make them come true."

"Right. That's the myth we've been sold, darling. I'm not buying it anymore."

Almy sighed and returned to her book. It was a thick novel by a woman with a long foreign-sounding name.

"Are they going to make a movie of that book?" I asked.

"I doubt it, Nick. It has no plot and almost nothing happens."

"Then why are you reading it?"

"It's quite engrossing and beautifully written."

Could be, but I returned to Steinbeck walking his poodle in Sauk Centre, Minnesota. We read our books and chatted until chilling clouds rolled in from the ocean. We returned to our rooms, layered up, and walked to the end of the beach and back. Along the way I snapped a few candids of Almy for Frank.

Almy said she was still full from lunch, so we skipped dinner. I ordered a sandwich from room service. My BLT was unexceptional except for its price (highest on the planet?). Almy ate two of my French fries and a major part of my brownie. Next time I'll order two desserts.

She expressed little enthusiasm for listening to the jazz combo in the bar, so we watched a movie in my room. Eventually, she gave me a hug, a peck on the cheek, and retired for the night across the hall. Twenty minutes later my phone buzzed.

"Are you in bed?" asked Almy.

"I am, dear."

"Can I sleep in your bed, but with no sex?"

"Sure."

"What are you wearing?"

"Not much, but I could put on my tighty-whities."

"OK. And don't turn on the light."

She arrived wearing the resort's deluxe loaner robe. She discarded it on a chair and slipped into bed. I joined her there. We embraced and I kissed her lightly on the lips. She appeared to be clad only in panties. I liked the feel of her warm body against mine.

"You seem to have an erection," she commented.

"It's nature's gauge of beauty, darling. And you're scoring extremely high."

"I doubt beauty has much to do with it. Your Twisp genes are anxious to perpetuate themselves."

"That could be the case, darling. I'm surprised genes haven't figured out a way to prevent guys from donning condoms. You know, causing a temporary paralysis of the hands or such."

"They have other ways. For example, Everest is allergic to latex. Condoms give him a rash down there."

"I hope it gets severely infected and falls off."

"That's interesting, Nick. The mention of a rival's name wilts an erection."

"Only partially, dear. I expect its awesome magnificence will be returning soon."

"You've grown some hair on your chest. I like that."

"And you haven't, dear. I like that also."

She laughed and slipped off her panties. It was evident to my touch that her genes had been preparing for reproductive work as well.

"Speaking of condoms, Nick. Did you bring any?"

"I placed a modest stash under my pillow. Here, let me fight crippling hand paralysis and slip one on."

I did so and we joined together as luxury resort guests often tend to do.

"Do you like that?" I asked, slowly stroking in and out.

"Shut up," she gasped. "And don't stop."

Thinking of my bad reviews, I got past the triggering phase, and was primed to go all night. Eventually, Almy climaxed and I followed a moment later.

"That was fairly stupendous," she said, kissing me. "All that practice with other girls is paying off."

"I did it all for you, darling. I felt driven to practice and get better."

"You were pursuing an impossible dream?"

"I was, dearest. You were the inspiration that every guy needs to excel in every way possible."

SUNDAY, July 31 – We did it twice more this morning. Always a pleasant way to start your day. I familiarized myself again with Almy's delectable body by kissing it all over. Then we took a bubble bath together in my room's oversized tub. Then we went down to the resort's sunny restaurant and had a lavish but leisurely breakfast. I mentioned that there was a place in Santa Barbara that rented snorkels and wetsuits.

"You're trying too hard, Nick. I'm here to relax. You could probably afford to buy me a 20-minute ride into space on Jeff Bezos's rocket, but I don't want to do that either."

"Keep me posted if you change your mind on either of

those activities. Or, if you're up for a hot-air balloon ride across Antarctica, just say the word."

"Shall we cancel my room for tonight, Nick? It would save you a bundle."

"OK, but you'll have no place to retreat to if I say something stupid like I love you."

"Wasn't that a song by your father's favorite singer?"

"Could be, dear. I try to blot out those details."

For some reason, the desk clerk seemed thrilled to hear we were cancelling one room. She was even happy to take the charge ($1,385) off my growing tab. Even though Almy hardly used her room, she left a Benjamin on the dresser as a tip for the maid.

Later we drove to Santa Barbara and checked out an arts and crafts fair along the waterfront near downtown. Almy attempted to buy me a set of hand-crafted wind chimes as a house-warming gift, but I refused the offer. There's enough noise pollution in L.A. without my adding to the din. I bought her a tiny (3x5 inch) framed watercolor of a hillside view of Santa Barbara. She agreed it could fit in even the smallest NYC apartment.

We strolled along and had an early dinner at a seafood restaurant. For some reason, all the diners in the place burst into applause as we were led to our table. I don't think they were clapping for Bronson Flange. I think Almy was more embarrassed than flattered; people don't understand that actors want to be famous but crave anonymity. While waiting for our fish, I broached a new subject.

"So, this rape scene with Clive McGregor," I said. "How graphic was it?"

"I wondered when you were going to get around to that. It wasn't very graphic, Nick. It was the 1950s. Celebrity rapists were in a hurry back then. He just pushed up my dress and went at it. I struggled a bit then went limp. That was the way it was written in the script. I showed a bit of upper leg, that's all."

"And what was Clive showing?"

"His bare posterior. It appeared to be quite cute in the playbacks I saw."

"So 'ol Clive was grinding his package against you while simulating sex. How many takes did you do of that?"

"Too many. We were both getting a bit sore."

"Why so many takes?"

"My underwear kept showing. So finally I had to remove my panties."

"Wow, so you both were bare. And was 'ol Clive having any anatomical reactions to that?"

"He may have at some point. We were trying to be professional in a demanding situation. How would you have done grinding your privates against Maya Chan?"

"Like a grave, dear. Like a cold, dead grave."

"Yeah, you weren't one of her favorites either. I'm sure if Maya were speaking to me, she'd be giving me grief now for associating with you. Can you keep a secret, Nickie?"

"Always."

"I took a morning-after pill the next day in case there was any leakage. Clive wasn't wearing a condom because he was supposed to be limp and faking it. You can get pregnant just from the lubricating fluids that guys emit."

"I know. Genes are smart. There are unwed mothers out there who are technically still virgins."

"What was your wife doing to forestall Twisps?"

"She was on the pill."

"So you were sharing fluids. No wonder she got upset when she thought you were cheating."

"So what were you and that incredibly inappropriate pianist using?"

"Lambskin condoms on him."

"That was risky. Celibacy would have worked so much better. Or castration by a rusty knife."

"I don't doubt you'd think so."

My phone buzzed; I looked at the screen.

"A call from Teejay," I said. "Do you mind if I answer this?"

"Go for it," said Almy.

I asked Teejay how they were doing in Canada.

"Awful," he replied. "I got four mosquito bites already. Stinky Marilyn got some too. Guess what, Nick?"

"What?"

"The house we're renting has an old typewriter that types in French. Real accent marks and everything. I showed it to Daddy and he started blubbering."

"Really? That's weird."

"Yeah, and then Mommy saw him and got mad."

"Parents can be strange, kid. Did Edy see her friend Marie?"

"Yeah, they just *looove* each other. Don't ask me why. So what the hell are you're doing with Almy?"

"Got to go, kid. Thanks for calling."

I can only hope that in 40 years, when I hear the tinkle of wind chimes, I'm not brushing back tears.

AUGUST

MONDAY, August 1 – Even the greatest weekend of a guy's life has to come to an end. All too soon in my case. At breakfast I got a call from Charlotte reminding me that my DMV appointment is at 2:15 today. I growled and said I would be there.

We packed our bags, Almy peeled off another Benjamin for the maid, I paid the scary bill, and we hit the road.

On the drive south I laid the L-word on her. She said her feelings about me were "evolving." She said she was "inching toward feeling" that she could trust me.

"Anything in a positive direction is good news for me," I said. "I realize I was starting from a low position."

"The lowest," she said, smiling. "If I agree to do the sequel series with Teejay, do you want to be in it?"

"You know I do, dear—assuming my part is decent."

"Spoken like an actor. OK, I'll see what I can do."

"Here's a thought, darling. You could skip returning to New York."

"What do you mean?"

"Do you really think any director or producer ever will care that you only had three years at Juilliard instead of four?"

"I can't drop out of college, Nick. My parents would have a fit."

"OK, live your life for your parents instead of for yourself."

"I finish the things I start, Nick. I'm going to graduate next year."

"Or you could graduate from UCLA or USC. They'd love to grab you as a transfer student."

"Nobody transfers in their last year of college, Nick. It's just not done."

"Oh. I never heard that rule."

I was reminded anew that Almy's character tends toward cast-iron inflexibility. Generally with My Love, it's her way or the highway.

"Here's another thought, dear. You kick out Everest, I pay for moving his lousy, stinking piano, and I'm your roommate for your senior year."

"And what will you be doing in New York?"

"Looking for stage work, going to museums, getting to know the city—the usual stuff actors do in New York."

"Didn't you just buy a house in L.A.?"

"So I'll sublet it. No big deal."

"You're serious?"

"Do I look like I'm joking?"

"I thought you hated bugs and rats."

"We'll hire our own private exterminator."

"I don't know, Nick. This is moving way too fast for me. I'll have to think about it."

"OK, dear, we have plenty of time."

"And what about your new girlfriend Kinsley, the sexy film student?"

"Say the word, dear, and she's out of the picture."

"But in the meantime, you'll continue sleeping with her?"

"No, darling. That's finished. Kaput."

"Should I send Mr. Clancy over to check on you? When's her next visit scheduled?"

"We usually get together Tuesday nights."

"That's tomorrow. So tomorrow are you taking me out to dinner?"

"I am, dear. I'm phoning Kinsley today and breaking our date."

"My grandfather is not going to be happy about all this socializing with you."

"We've borne that cross before, Almy. Very few people conduct their lives to please their grandfather. It's just not done."

"Very few people have a grandfather like mine."

Yeah, Trent Preston is super famous, but never won an Oscar. And now Teejay put him on the map as a producer. You'd think he'd be more tolerant of us Twisps.

Almy didn't say much on the rest of the drive. I suspect her mind was churning. I may have overloaded her circuits. But then she's been overloading mine for years.

Did I want to move to Manhattan and freeze my ass off next winter? I just endured the full arctic experience in England and said never again. But the alternative (saying goodbye to Almy for nine months or possibly forever) was even more unbearable.

When we got to my place, I lugged her bag to her car, then embraced and kissed her. I also said the L-word again in case she thought the first time was an aberration.

"You know, Nick, my parents live in Hoboken. We have dinner with them nearly every Sunday. They love Everest and his entire family."

Such inappropriate fraternizing with the extended Weeden clan had to stop!

"I thought your folks lived in Brooklyn."

"They were renting in Brooklyn. To buy a place they had to resort to Hoboken, which is cheaper."

Could be, but something inexpensive in West Virginia or Kentucky would have worked so much better.

"I'm not a struggling musician, darling. I'm worth eight figures. That should improve your mother's opinion of me."

After Almy clarified where I was setting the decimal point, she admitted that it might.

I phoned Kinsley from the DMV waiting room. I asked her how the filming was going.

"Very well, Nick. It's been hectic, but I'll be free to see you tomorrow."

"I think we should hold off on that, dear. I think I'm coming down with something. I don't feel at all well."

"Perhaps you got too much sun in Santa Barbara."

"Oh, you heard about that, huh?"

"Amalda Preston has a very high profile these days from her TV series."

"We've been friends for years."

"When and if you get over your sickness, Nick, give me a call."

Yeah, that was awkward.

Through some miracle, I had all the documentation necessary to get a new driver's license. I stood in front of their camera and tried to look like a confident, reliable Davidson instead of a shifty, conniving Twisp.

I stopped at a drugstore on the way home to stock up on condoms. I also got a toothbrush for Almy should she want to sleep over. I love her, but she'll have to purchase her own tampons.

TUESDAY, August 2 – Dad turns 60 today. That must suck the hairy mop. No doubt he'll be getting a second celebration in Canada to help ease him into old age. Does he get fitted for a coffin now or do they wait on that?

Cal texted that she would be getting coffee in Venice. I considered skipping it this time, but I showed up like Pavlov's dog. When the bell rings for me, there I am salivating for abuse. I drove the Caddy as a reminder not to wimp out.

"I take it she slept with you," said Cal, sipping her decaf soy latte.

"What makes you say that, dear?"

"You have that look of having triumphed over a superior rival."

"I do not consider Everest Weeden to be superior to me in any respect."

"You're certainly scoring higher than him in delusional thinking. So what's the plan?"

"Almy's not quitting school or transferring here. I may be spending the winter in New York."

"Doing what? Starring in a revival of 'A Streetcar Named Desire' on Broadway?"

"Probably getting mugged in the subway and freezing my ass off."

"And all the while Almy is busy with college and her friends."

"So what would you suggest I do?"

"Stay here, fix up your house, and date that USC girl, Ms. Kinsey Report. It ain't ever gonna work out with you and Almy. That's broke for all time."

"We just had a rocky patch. Now we're back together. What's happening with Liam?"

"I fired him as my financial advisor. I turned the page on that guy. Unlike you, I don't look back."

I didn't point out that she had looked back at me plenty of times.

"Now you can make a play for poor Clive McGregor," I said.

"Nigel, our director, likes to rehearse. We start tomorrow. What did Almy say about Clive?"

"He was grinding his privates into her for quite a few takes for the rape scene. She says he has a cute ass."

"You'd need to gain 30 pounds to even acquire one. Was it only simulated or was penetration achieved?"

"Just simulated, dear. You'll have to try to do better."

"You only say that because you think you're done with me. You think you're in tight with Almy, so I can be discarded."

"I shall always love you, darling. Until the day I die."

"If you marry Almy, she won't tolerate your seeing me."

"That remains to be seen, dear. Your future husband won't want me hanging around either."

"I may marry a major mob figure, who will have you snuffed just to adhere to his code."

"I hope not, dear. Such notoriety could put a serious dent in your acting career."

Later, Charlotte dropped by and resigned as my personal assistant. Everyone seems to be abandoning me today, greatly exacerbating my B.P.D. She said I wasn't serious about getting anything accomplished in the film world. She also may have heard about my weekend at the beach with Almy and got pissed about that for some reason.

I wrote her a check for $8,000 for her time and as severance. She had me sign it as Nick Davidson. I need to work on my new signature. The letters composing "Davidson" are not as flamboyant as the ones in "Twisp." If you aim for a spectacular "D", no one can tell what letter it is.

As usual Almy didn't want me to pick her up. Nor did she want to go to Providence, since it's her grandparents' favorite restaurant. So we went to Musso & Frank, the oldest eatery in Hollywood. Naturally, I took the Caddy and had the traditional $56 filet. Almy went with their economical sandabs.

"How do you pack all that away and never gain an ounce?" she asked.

"I burn a lot of calories pining for you."

"Everest has to eat like a girl or he gets a pianist's paunch."

"More bad genetic traits you should skip passing on

to your children, dear. I've decided that guy and his piano should stay put. I've been checking out New York rentals. There are plenty to choose from. It's only hard to find a rental if you're looking for some place cheap. There are some nice apartments in newer buildings with river views in our price range."

"And what's our price range, Nick?"

"Under $10,000 a month. Plus, they offer parking for my Mustang."

"You're planning on having a car in Manhattan? That's insane."

"A car is useful for getting out of the city. I hear they have nice beaches in a place called Montauk."

"Yeah, mostly owned by rich people and not that clement in January. I haven't committed to any of this yet."

"I know, darling. I'm just checking out the possibilities. Would you like to live in one of those tall, pencil-like towers?"

"All New Yorkers hate those monstrosities. It's just developers ruining the skyline to get rich. So we won't be renting there."

"Right, I didn't think so. So in winter with millions of people crowded onto one small island does it stay fairly comfortable?"

"Like from what, body heat? No, it's more like the tall buildings funnel icy winds down to the sidewalks. Big snowstorms are kind of fun. It's like the whole city turns into this wintry dreamland. Just buy a warm coat, a scarf or two, a hat and gloves, and you'll be fine. Also some thick wool socks and maybe some boots."

How about a snowmobile while I'm at it? None of that stuff you need in balmy L.A., I thought but didn't say.

Almy used her new toothbrush and spent the night. I have to hold her in my arms to believe she's really back.

WEDNESDAY, August 3 – Zach, baller of my neighbor, phoned early while Almy was in the shower. For all I know, he may have been phoning from next door.

"How's your passport, Nick?" he asked.

"It's resting comfortably in my desk drawer. Thanks for asking."

"Those Brits in Leeds are hot to do another season."

"Since when? I heard it didn't do so well."

"Some archbishop condemned it in the strongest terms and turned the whole thing around. Viewership doubled overnight. So they want you back next month. I'm getting you 20 percent more than before, plus improved prospects for U.S. earnings."

"I'll have to think about it, Zach."

"What's to think about, Nick? Working in British TV is a coup for American actors. It wins you plenty of prestige and respect with producers here."

"Who I notice aren't falling all over themselves to hire me."

"That will come, Nick. I need an answer from you by next week at the latest."

"OK, Zach. I'll give it some thought."

Fuck!

No, I didn't tell Almy about the call. That would just give her more ammunition for refusing to live with me. After breakfast I kissed her goodbye, this time skipping the L-word. I think she interprets that word as too intrusive and pressuring.

At least my linens were scoring points with her. She said my towel was the thickest and most absorbent she had ever used. In these small ways I endeavor to crawl back into her heart.

Dazed and confused, I went to the photo place and the post office. For better or worse, I filed to get a replacement passport under my new name.

When I returned, there was a low-riding 1960s Chevy parked in front of my house. Dark tinted windows and super skinny tires. A Latino-looking fellow exited as I was retrieving my mail. He was dressed sharply in a pink sharkskin suit, cantaloupe-colored shirt, magenta tie, and matching cantaloupe/magenta lizard-skin saddle shoes that tapered to a needle-sharp point. His long black hair was combed straight back in a very tall wave. His sunglasses looked even more expensive than mine.

"Hey, if it isn't Nick Twisp II," he said jovially.

"I used to be. Now I'm Nick Davidson."

"I have a message for you from a friend."

"What's that?"

"Watch your back."

Still smiling, he socked me hard in the stomach. I dropped my mail and doubled over as he strolled back to his car. The guy wasn't big (except for his hair), but he delivers a powerful punch.

The back of his car hopped up and down energetically as he drove slowly away.

THURSDAY, August 4 – I have a nasty-looking bruise on my stomach in shades of purple and green. Any torso movements produce twinges of pain. Not acutely crippling, so I don't think anything internal got busted.

I assume the message came from imprisoned criminal Desmond Orton, but who knows? Other possible candidates include Everest, Stuart Dunham, my ex-wife, Liam C. Collier, Trent Preston, Almy's mother, Carli next door, or my tax accountant. I can't entirely exclude a bitter and vengeful Valerie Haseltine. Or even Almy's prior NYC boyfriend, the vile Joe Sipper. (She refuses to tell me anything about that cad.) Nor am I ruling out Teejay, who informed me by text that he is calling dibs on Almy. I texted back that no state in the union permits a four-year-old to marry.

Recuperating on my sofa, I phoned Connie Saunders and asked if she knew why Charlotte quit.

"She thought you were partners in a film enterprise, but you were treating her like a lowly secretary, right down to the sexual harassment."

"I was only flirting a bit."

"Flirting can be taboo these days, Nick. The Golden Age of male chauvinism appears to be over. It went out with panty raids, wife-swapping, and tangoing in smoky night-clubs. I can't talk long, we're leaving for Vegas today."

"To do what?"

"We need to improve our street cred for attracting clients to our poker school. So Charlotte's competing in a big tournament this weekend."

"What does it cost to enter that?"

"The buy-in is thirty grand. I'm backing her. You want a piece of that?"

"OK, put me down for ten."

"I heard about you and that Preston girl. You know, Nick, when a girl is done with a guy, she's done with him. Girls don't go back."

"I thought Liz married Dick Burton twice. And what about Jennifer Lopez and Ben Affleck?"

"OK, sometimes they go back, but it's only temporary."

"I was Almy Preston's first lover and remain number one in her heart."

At least the first part of that statement was true.

That enchanting girl herself checked in by phone.

"Guess what I was doing last night, Nick."

"Wishing you were here in bed with me?"

"That's true. I was watching the first two episodes of 'Over the Monastery Wall' with my grandparents."

"Oh, right. It's available for streaming now. Did the old folks stay awake?"

"They did. My grandfather was even grudgingly complimentary about you. I thought you were excellent."

"Thanks, dear. That means a lot coming from you."

"It turns out while we were having our relaxing weekend at the beach a blizzard of phone calls were going back and forth across the continent, including to Nova Scotia."

"Your grandfather was bitching to my dad, huh?"

"Your father stuck up for you. He said you were a responsible adult and everyone should back off and leave us alone."

"Good for Dad."

"It would have been better for us if you had skipped those lipstick commercials. They were very antagonizing to my parents."

"I needed the money, dear. We were trying to remodel our shackette."

"I'm afraid they are seared forever into my mother's brain. She gave me hell for seeing you again."

"She never liked me anyway. For some reason Twisps never score high with mothers. We'll give her a cute grandchild, and that will appease her."

"I hope this theoretical kid doesn't turn out like Teejay."

"All his quirks came from the maternal side, dear. He's one-quarter Romanian, you know."

"We watched some new Romanian films at school last year. They were sort of zany, but all well done."

"Did you tell your grandfather you want me in the sequel?"

"Not yet. I'm waiting until he's in a better mood. I don't want him to have a heart attack and keel over dead from shock."

Here's today's plan: she will watch two more episodes tonight, then bail and spend the night here. Now I need to think of an excuse for why I'm moving stiffly, wearing a

T-shirt to bed, and requiring the female-superior position for sex.

Taking it easy, I watched the remaining episodes of "The Beauty and the Little Genius." Kind of heart-warming as my little brother and his brave TV mother brought better times to their hard-pressed fishing village. The ending sort of implied that love would be blossoming between Almy and this Canadian Mountie dude named Hugh. That chiseled guy and his flashy red uniform definitely need to disappear from the sequel.

Something weird is happening to the reinvigorated grass in my front yard. It seems to be dying in places. Almost as if it had been sprayed with a herbicide.

FRIDAY, August 5 – Almy dragged my T-shirt off last night. She also dragged out the story of my mystery assault.

"Jesus, Nick, instead of punching you, he might have shot you. You could have been lying dead and bleeding in the street!"

"He was just delivering a warning, dear. It would have been helpful if he said who it was from."

"What did they say at the hospital, Nick? Are you OK?"

"Uh, I didn't feel the need to get medical attention. It was only one punch."

So instead of having cautious but rewarding sex with Almy, we spent three hours in a Santa Monica hospital waiting to have my torso examined. The harassed emergency room doc palpated my midriff and asked if I had blood in my urine. Since I didn't, he told me to "avoid strenuous exercise" until I felt better. He offered to tape me up, but I declined. He also said the bruising pattern suggested the assailant had augmented his punch with a weapon such as brass knuckles. He recommended I file a report with the police, but I'm resisting that. Cops and Twisps are not a happy mix.

At breakfast Almy was still trying to figure out who sent the guy to hit me.

"It really doesn't sound like Everest," she said, buttering her toast. "It was more likely some poor girl you wronged."

"I have not had any ugly breakups, dear."

"You mean not since me?"

"That was more excruciating than ugly. And I get along OK with my ex-wife. I suspect it's one of your boyfriends lashing out in despair. You can drive guys to extremes."

"Everest just sent me a nine-page letter of contrition. It's in my purse, Nick. Would you like to read it?"

"How's his spelling and grammar?"

"Faultless. He's an excellent writer. And parts of it are in French."

"He probably thinks he sounds more sincere in that language. I suggest you burn that letter and dismiss it from your mind."

"It's hard to give up on someone you expected to spend the rest of your life with."

"You're preaching to the choir, darling. I went through three agonizing years of doing just that with you."

"Two years of which you were married to someone else."

"I still felt terrible. You were always on my mind."

I'm forever speaking to that girl in lyrics from songs, but I just can't stop loving her.

Since neither of us had appointments today, we sat on my sofa and checked our email and messages. I texted Almy, "Baby, I say u look so fine that I really wanna make u mine." She texted back, "Don't call me baby," then leaned over and kissed me.

She excused herself and went in the guestroom to return some calls. I hoped she wasn't talking to anyone back east with the initials E.W. Let's face it: he and I are in a fight to the finish and the stakes couldn't be higher. Both of us have experienced that enchanting glimpse of paradise. We've had that captivating peek at radiant and blissful heaven. I don't expect him to back off or give up any time soon. So I chose not to torture myself by reading his lousy letter.

When Almy returned she was leafing through my book on narcissism.

"Can I borrow your book, Nickie?"

"Please do, darling. You'll find whole chapters in it just on Everest."

"Oh, is he mentioned by name?"

"He should have been."

"I just talked to Clive McGregor."

"That aging Scottish actor? Was he inquiring if you were pregnant?"

"He was asking about your girlfriend Cal. They've been rehearsing this week and she's been coming onto him strong."

"What advice did you give him, darling?"

"I told him to resist her by all means necessary."

My doorbell rang. It was Carli from next door.

"I know it's none of my business, Nick, but have you checked out your front yard lately?"

All three of us trooped out to inspect my landscaping. Large brown letters of dead grass spelled out the message DIE YUPPIE SCUM!

"Did you do this, Carli?" I demanded.

"Not me, Nick. I'm not into toxic poisons, just toxic relationships. But I've turned the page on that."

"Who calls anyone a yuppie these days?" asked Almy. "Have you offended some Baby Boomer?"

"They did it with weed killer," I pointed out. "And who do we know with the word 'weed' in their name?"

"Everest is 3,000 miles away, Nick," she replied. "You're just being paranoid."

Graffiti you can paint over, but what do you do with a massive curse writ in poisoned soil? Feeling helpless, I shrugged and returned to the house with Almy. We locked the doors, closed the blinds, and went back to bed. Minimizing extraneous movements, I managed to have a very good time.

Later, my doorbell rang again. Resenting the intrusion, I yanked open the door in the buff. It was my agent Zach, looking shocked.

"My God, Nick," he said. "What happened to you? Were you in an accident?"

"Punched in the stomach by an anonymous low-rider. Probably the same fiend who defaced my yard."

Always business-minded, agents are undeterred by nudity. Zach asked if I had decided on the English offer.

"Sorry, I'm still thinking it over."

"I need an answer very soon. Since I was in the neighborhood, I brought you your mail."

He handed me some envelopes.

"Are you getting enough to eat?" he asked, surveying my bony frame.

"I'd eat more regularly if I had more work," I replied, closing the door.

Almy, still lounging in bed, was excited to read my fan mail. Of course, she herself receives far too much for any one mortal to cope with. Her impressive influx, though, pales in comparison to Teejay's daily stacks—each missive of praise ratcheting up the kid's gigantic self-regard.

By comparison, my take was only paltry. No one seemed eager to marry me or have my children. One letter wasn't even intended for me. I read it and then handed it to Almy. It read:

Dear Mr. Twisp (or Davidson),

I understand this is the way to reach Amalda Preston. I hope you will be able to forward this letter to her. I'm Marcie Florin, who she may have decided is a horrible seducer. Contrary to what everyone may think, I am a sincere and honorable person. I did NOT enter into a liaison with Everest lightly or to ruin anyone's happiness. I love him sincerely and I believe he cares for me as well.

Everest and I bonded over our mutual love of music. We have this immensity of interest in common. I understand that Amalda plays no instrument and knows little about music.

If you marry a musician, you will be surrounded by musicians who will talk about little else. They will have rehearsals and meetings and performances from which you will be excluded. Most musicians I know are constantly busy. Their private life does NOT come first.

Therefore, it is my belief that musicians are happier in the long run with fellow musicians.

I hope you can believe that I did not set out to entrap Everest. Our shared interests brought us together. Our sleeping together on the island was a happy consequence of our love for each other. I take delight in his company, admire his talents, and very much hope to see him again.

Yours sincerely,
Marcie Florin

P.S. Congratulations on the success of your TV show.

"I hope you didn't write this yourself, Nick."

"Again, dear, it's not my handwriting."

"So what do you think, Nick?"

"I'm not at all impartial. It doesn't matter what I think."

"Do you think musicians are better off with musicians?"

"I can see how that might be true. It depends on the people involved."

"I would never have the nerve to write to someone whose fiancé I slept with."

"It's pretty ballsy, but she sounds sincere."

Almy was all for discussing that point endlessly, but she had an appointment with Muriel, her therapist. After she left, I dressed, straightened up the house, and made another trip to Venice Hardware. I bought their largest blue tarp and some U-shaped metal clips used to fasten down weed barrier. I spread the tarp over the offensive message in my grass and secured it with the clips. The look is trailer-park tacky. Now my house looks even less like it's worth what I paid for it.

SATURDAY, August 6 – I felt a bit less stiff this morning, but my bruise was even ghastlier. Urine-hued tans were creeping in amid the deathly greens and purples.

For some reason Cal felt the need to invite herself over for coffee. I'd have been happier to see her had she brought along something sweet in a grease-stained bag. I made do with toast as we sat with our coffees at my kitchen table.

"Is Almy still sleeping?" whispered Cal.

"Almy did not spend the night, dear."

"Oh? Tired of you already?"

"She was planning on watching more of my English TV series with her grandparents last night. We spent most of yesterday in bed together."

"That's gross and more than a bit disgusting. Where's your show streaming?"

"As I told you before, on BritBox."

"Who the hell subscribes to that?"

"Anglophiles would be my guess."

"So who did you bury under that unsightly tarp in your front yard?"

Swiping through my phone, I showed her the photo I had snapped of my grass defacement.

"Die yuppie scum," read Cal. "I don't see how you qualify, Nick. College dropouts are *not* yuppies."

"I never claimed to be one."

"I would have scrawled Die Low-brow Scum."

"Thanks for clarifying that point."

She reached over and pulled up my shirt.

"I heard about your interface with Latino culture, Nick. That's one gnarly bruise. Did it hurt?"

"Of course it hurt. The dude hit me with brass knuckles. I think your pal Desmond sent him."

"Probably getting you prepared for his exit from prison. If I were you, I'd be pricing guns and bodyguards."

"I may have to. How's Clive McGregor?"

"So sweet, so talented, and so good-looking. He has these wonderful crinkly lines around his dreamy blue eyes."

"That's because the dude is old. Like elderly! Way too old for you. So why does the script have you married to such a fossil?"

"I'm his second trophy wife. His first wife was this shrew, as no doubt Almy will prove to be for some unlucky victim of her fatal charms."

"So has Clive asked you out?"

"Not yet. But I'm sure he will. We're getting along marvelously."

"What does he say about Almy?"

"Not being desperate for conversational topics, I haven't broached that dreary subject."

I told Cal about the letter Almy received from Marcie Florin.

"That's bad for you, Nickie."

"And why's that?"

"With another girl making a desperate play for Everest,

it raises his perceived value while simultaneously goosing Almy's competitive instincts. The only way for her to defeat Marcie now is to take Everest back."

"Fuck! You may be right. So what should I do?"

"Congratulate yourself for another narrow escape."

Not at all helpful as usual.

When Cal was ready to leave, she wrapped her arms around me, kissed me, then slipped her hand down the front of my pants and grasped my unit. Instant response from my tool. Nevertheless, I removed her hand.

"None of that, dear," I said.

"I was just checking to see if it had been worn down to the nub. Or possibly sucked entirely off."

Later, Almy came over for another session in bed. Everest may be writing her pleading letters, but I'm putting it directly to her. If only I could skip that layer of latex as I used to do with Luco. Once you've done it bare, it's hard to go back to wearing an inner tube.

Relaxing in a naked heap, Almy told me she had spoken to Trent about my appearing in the sequel.

"Did he require CPR?" I asked.

"Fortunately not. He's more alarmed that I'm spending nights here. He said you could audition for the part of the crooked music promoter who tries to sign Teejay to an exploitative contract."

"Not what I was thinking, dear. I think Hugh the amorous Mountie should get transferred to northern Manitoba and then I get transferred in to replace him."

"Do they take Mounties as skinny as you?"

"Everyone was skinny in the 1930s, dear. It was the Depression. The dust storms were wrecking the wheat crop. Was your therapist any help about Marcie's letter?"

"Only in that she was trying to get me to explore my feelings about it."

"And how do you feel?"

"Mostly pissed off at the two of them. If they want to get together and discuss Beethoven's use of the twelfth minor chord, I say have fun and drop dead."

"Whereas we actors always will have plenty to talk about with our fellow actors."

"Except that most hookups between actors never last, Nick."

"I know, darling, you have to work at it. You have to check your ego at the door."

"Easier said than done," she sighed.

Later we had Chinese delivered and ate it in bed. John and Yoko spent some quality time in the sack, but we may be breaking their record.

SUNDAY, August 7 – A year ago Charlotte's dad, Wilcox T. Caxton, was getting his knees perforated in Dad's house. Almy was capering in Nova Scotia with her inappropriate fiancé. I was getting ready to celebrate my second wedding anniversary with my inappropriate but somewhat loving wife. Three years ago on this date I was trying to persuade Almy Preston to marry me. I'd still like her to do that, which is the one Great Constancy in my life. Now at least I may be edging a bit closer to that goal.

Since we went to bed early last night, we made it to the diner on Pico right as it opened. Almy studied the menu a long time and finally ordered the same omelet as on our previous visit. I tried something new called The Dutch Baby, described as "A German-style pancake with caramelized sugar, apples and a hint of nutmeg." I accessorized the kid with a side order of bacon.

"I've always wanted to eat a Dutch baby for breakfast," I joked to the waitress.

Not even a smile from the gal. She must have heard that jest way too many times. I told Almy about my experience with English breakfasts.

"Generally, they don't do potatoes with your eggs. They want to give you sliced tomatoes and weird little soggy mushrooms. And the bacon is always limp and fatty."

"What happens if you ask for it extra crispy?"

"Extra crispy in England means limp and fatty. As an experiment I once requested that the kitchen cook my bacon *twice* as long as they normally do. The waitress looked horrified, but agreed to pass on my request."

"How did it turn out?"

"It was limp and fatty, but a bit burned around the edges. They may have different pigs than we do here."

Having exhausted that topic, we returned to our phones.

"This is interesting," remarked Almy. "I got an email from Jackie Tucker."

"What's the latest gossip?" I asked.

"She says there's a rumor going around that you're paying Cal for sex."

No question who started that rumor. Cal was trying to sabotage my reunion with Almy!

"I can explain that, dear," I said.

"Please do."

I had a moment to collect my thoughts while our plates were delivered and our coffee cups refilled.

"OK, here's the story, Almy. As you may know I was paying Charlotte Caxton $2,000 a week to serve as my personal assistant, although she has since resigned."

"Were you paying her for sex as well?"

"Certainly not. So Cal heard about that and jokingly said she would have sex with me for the same amount. This was before you and I got back together. I inherited some gold coins from my guru Samuel F. Broughton and handed Cal a couple of them after . . . well, you know. She returned the coins a few days later and I haven't touched her since. So, no, I did not actually pay her for sex."

"Not strictly true, Nick. You paid, but got a refund."

"As a joke, dear. As a joke!"

"So did you buy her those gaudy ruby earrings?"

"She expected her boyfriend Liam to buy them, but he turned out to be a cad. So I did the gentlemanly thing and picked up the tab. From now on I will never *ever* buy jewelry for any girl except you."

"You haven't bought me any jewelry."

"Not true, dear. I bought you a lovely carved jade ring that you insisted on reimbursing me for. And then you gave it to Maya Chan."

"Oh, right. That's true. I think Maya may have misinterpreted my reason for giving her that ring."

"The next ring I buy you will be for a very clear and heartfelt reason."

"Muriel says B.P.D. types always push for very fast commitment from their love interests."

"I don't think wanting a hint of commitment after four years is pushing all that fast."

"Narcissists like Everest do the same thing. He asked me to marry him on our second date."

"He probably would have asked Marcie too, if he wasn't already engaged to you."

"I'm not sure that would have stopped him."

Kind of a tense conversation. Perhaps that's why the masticated Dutch Baby sat in my stomach like a lead weight for hours.

At least Almy kissed me as she was getting ready to return to her grandparents' place. We were back in my living room and spooning on the sofa. I told her I had plenty of closet space if she wanted to bring over a supply of clothing.

"No point to that, Nickie," she replied. "Since I'm leaving for New York on Friday."

"So soon! But why, darling?"

"I have a lot to do, Nick. I have to register for classes and find a new place to live."

"We can look for a place together, dear."

"That's silly, Nick. You can't move to New York."

"Why the hell not? I love you!"

"I had an email from my grandfather this morning. He talked to your agent. You're leaving for England next month, which I notice you haven't gotten around to mentioning to me."

"That's because I'm not taking that job."

"That's ridiculous, Nick. You can't pass up an opportunity like that."

"I'm passing. I'm passing."

"You take that job, Nick, and I'll finish my senior year. Then we can meet up again and see where we stand."

She may not have seen the fatal flaw in that plan, but I did. She spends nine months in close proximity with loutish Everest, while I'm stuck on the other side of the ocean. No way would that be happening.

Doing so would violate Nick Davidson's Primary Rule of Love: PROXIMITY IS ALL.

MONDAY, August 8 – Three years ago today I got married in Las Vegas. Too bad I was there with the wrong girl. Nick Davidson's Second Rule of Love: NEVER MARRY YOUR THIRD CHOICE IN WIVES.

Seems kind of obvious now, but my head was in a different place back then (as in right between Luco's ample breasts).

Charlotte phoned early from Vegas. She finished third in the tournament and won $90,000. Since she was splitting the prize money 50/50 with her backers, she said she would send me a check for $15,000. I told her to hold off on that.

"If they ever arrest Betty and Lois," I said, "you can donate that amount to their defense fund."

"I don't think my father would like that, Nick."

"So donate it in my name and he'll never know. Are you guys coming back today?"

"Nah, we're going to hang around a few days and see if we can fleece some tourists."

"Right. Well that's what that town is for. Have fun."

I made a donut run, then phoned my agent. I told Zach I was turning down the U.K. job. He did his best to change my mind, but I stuck to my guns. I said I was relocating to New York and would be open to offers in that town.

"I might be able to find you some commercial work," he grudgingly conceded.

"I'm fine with that as long as I'm not in drag. No more commercials with Bronson Flange pushing cosmetics. How are you digging having your office in faraway Glendale?"

"It's OK. Why do you ask?"

"Want to rent my house?"

"How much?"

"Fully furnished, but you pay the utilities, garbage, and gardener. You can have it for $2,000 a month."

"That's not a bad deal."

"It's a hell of a deal and you know it."

"Can I live there too? It would save me a ton of time and gas commuting to see Carli."

"OK, fine. But one space in the garage I'm reserving for my Caddy."

"I'll think about it, Nick. And I'll wait a few more days before I give those Brits a solid turndown. Please change your mind!"

"Please stop asking me to!" I replied.

I didn't tell him that he could expect to be strolling back home at 2:01 every morning.

Then I phoned Cal and gave her hell for trying to wreck things with Almy.

"I'm just looking out for your best interests, Nickie.

That girl has proven many times over that she's not right for you. Someday you'll thank me."

"I'll thank you right now to butt out. I mean it. I don't try to interfere with your disastrous choices in men."

"You were the biggest disaster of all my choices."

"No, I'm the one guy who actually loved you. Who cared for you. Who thought about your best interests."

"Should I consider that a proposal of marriage?"

"Please don't. And please stop gossiping with Jackie Tucker."

"Jackie Tucker exists on this planet to be gossiped with."

"Fine, gossip all you want, but leave my name out of it!"

Then I met up with Almy for lunch. As usual she came to my house. Her grandparents' house seems to be off limits to me. Mr. Clancy may have been instructed to shoot me on sight. After some negotiations, we decided on a Mexican diner in Culver City. We went in my Mustang. I had traveled a few blocks up Venice Boulevard when I got this text from Carli: "Yr lowridr is bak."

"Did I close my garage door, Almy?" I asked.

"I think you left it open."

"I better go back and check."

When I got back, the low-riding Chevy was parked in my driveway. I stopped in front of the drive, blocking it in. I could see that my Caddy was now sitting low as if all four tires had been flattened. The Latino dude was walking down the drive toward us with a knife in his hand. This time he was dressed in a green silk suit with yellow shirt, blue tie, and very shiny patent-leather blue shoes. Also he had grown (or penciled in) one of those skinny John Waters mustaches.

"Keep your door locked, Almy. I'm dialing 9-1-1."

"Wait, Nick," she said, opening her door and getting out.

I watched in disbelief as she walked toward the armed dude.

"Maya?" she called.

The dude stopped. I got out of the car.

"I can't believe you're back together with that douche bag," said Maya, pointing toward me. She had dropped her husky Latin accent, but retained her knife.

"I love him," said Almy. "I always have."

There was some surprising news that a guy can use.

"How can you love that creep, Almy?" asked Maya. "He's the lowest of the low."

"You were always running him down, Maya," said Almy. "I see now you were trying to poison me against him. So what are you doing here in those strange clothes?"

"She was slashing my tires!" I pointed out. "Those are expensive Michelins! Brand new last month!"

"Relax, asshole," Maya replied. "I'll write you a check for the damage. And I didn't slash them. I poked into your tender sidewalls with my blade. Be glad I wasn't poking it into your stinking guts."

"This violence is completely uncalled for, Maya," said Almy. "It's completely unacceptable."

"That depends very much on your point of view," she replied. "And the name's not Maya, it's Estaban."

Evidently, she had gone from being a meek Chinese girl to a flamboyant Latino guy. But something wasn't adding up.

"Hey, Estaban," I said, "are you wearing lifts in your shoes?"

"Suck my cock, dickhead," she replied.

"And why did you poison my grass?" I demanded.

"I didn't touch your lousy grass, Mr. Suburbia."

"Somebody wrote 'Die Yuppie Scum' in weed killer across my front lawn," I said.

"Wasn't me, snowflake. Besides, you're no yuppie."

At that moment an L.A. police car screeched to a halt in front of my house.

"Nick, I told you not to call the cops!" exclaimed Almy.

"I didn't, darling."

"I called them," said Carli, popping up from behind her hedge.

"Oh, fuck!" grunted Estaban, pocketing her blade.

Two cops approached with guns drawn.

"Jesus," said the older cop. "That looks like Amalda Preston."

"Yeah," said his partner, "and with Bronson Flange."

"Who's the pachuco in the fancy threads?" asked the first cop.

"Believe it or not," I replied, "that's Jade Ming."

"That guy has got a knife!" called Carli.

"Which guy?" asked the first cop, confused.

"The Mexican, uh, person," said Carli.

Estaban consented to be searched. They found his knife in one suit pocket and brass knuckles in another. They also noticed that my Cadillac was sitting flat on its wheels. Almy looked at me pleadingly, so I declined to press charges. Both cops grabbed selfies with Almy and me, but Estaban refused. Eventually, the cops left, taking Estaban's weapons with them. The dude retrieved his checkbook from his Chevy's glove box and wrote Nick Davidson a check for $3,000. (I asked for $2,000, but Almy made him add another grand for the gut bruising.)

Estaban declined Almy's invitation to join us at lunch to "hash things out." Thank God for that. He did more hydraulic-powered car hopping as he drove off. Too bad they didn't offer that feature as an option on my Mustang.

I think Carli may have been expecting a lunch invitation too, but I skipped that.

At our delayed lunch I asked Almy if she was surprised

that her best GF had morphed into a Hispanic lounge lizard in elevator shoes.

"She never seemed very happy being what she was. But I never expected her to go off the deep end like that. I hope she gets some help."

"Her family has lots of resources, dear. They can get her help if she wants it. She may only be this Estaban character when she's out terrorizing me."

"Let's hope so, although she seems to have invested in quite a wardrobe and that odd car. I hope she stops. I'll call her later and talk to her."

"Do you have her number?"

"Damn, I may not have her current one."

"Yeah, I used to have that problem with you. How did you figure out it was Maya? She sure fooled me."

"I recognized her walk. I'm surprised you didn't, since you two were TV intimates all those years."

"We worked together, dear, but we found it painful to look at each other. So I wonder who wrote that message in my grass?"

"You seem to be a person with many enemies."

"Or it could be some enemy of Gary and Keith who hadn't heard they moved. Or some disgruntled house bidder who couldn't top my exorbitant $2.2 million offer."

Since deceit was no longer my thing, I confessed to Almy that I had turned down the U.K. job, was renting my house to my agent, and was flying to New York on Friday.

"What are you going to do there?" she asked.

"Look for an apartment to rent. You, of course, are under no obligation to share it with me."

"I don't need a view of the river, Nickie. It would be good if it were within walking distance of Juilliard."

"I'll see what I can do."

"I'm having dinner with my parents on Sunday in Hoboken. Are you ready to run that gauntlet?"

"Bring it on, dear. I have no fear of your father."

"What about my mother?"

"That's a different story entirely."

Later, my Caddy got winched aboard a truck and hauled off to a tire store. I stayed behind and entertained Almy in my bedroom.

TUESDAY, August 9 – Almy requested oatmeal for breakfast. As I was pouring out the oats, a large gold coin clanked into the measuring cup.

"They're putting exceptionally deluxe premiums in cereal these days," she commented.

"I forgot I was hiding them in here."

Almy examined the coin.

"Is this thing real gold?"

"About $2,800 worth."

"And you gave two of these to Cal for having sex with you?"

"It was buying quite a few, uh, sessions. The joke was she required payment in advance."

"I would think two coins would buy many sessions with Cal. Like several thousand at least."

"Uh, let's not go there, darling."

"Since you're rich, why doesn't Cal want to marry you?"

"She probably would if I asked. But I'd rather not get married for my money."

"How many of these coins do you have?"

"Not many. Only 121."

"Jesus. And they all fit in that box?"

"No, there are just a few in here. The rest I buried in my crawl space."

I told her how I came to acquire $338,000 in Mexican gold peso coins. I explained how they were a gift to me from my guru.

"I bet it's because of him you turned down that job in England."

"He hasn't steered me wrong yet. What do you think of Donna Reed?"

"I always liked Donna Reed."

"Donna Reed was my guru's inspiration in life. I could never be with someone who didn't like Donna Reed."

"You are such a strange person, Nick."

"I believe I'm fairly normal compared to Teejay."

Spooning in her oatmeal, Almy said she had a thought about my violated grass.

"You know that guy Joe I was going out with?" she asked.

"The sociopath you refuse to tell me anything about?"

"So what do you want to know about him?"

"Is he an actor or a musician?"

"Sort of a combo. He's in the opera program."

"How was he in bed?"

"He was extremely attentive to satisfying his own selfish needs."

"I see why you dumped him."

"OK, Joe once stopped a rehearsal and told the conductor he was swinging the baton like a yuppie bond trader from Scarsdale."

"So where is this rude dude now?"

"I have no idea what he's doing this summer, but his parents live in Pacific Palisades."

"Oh, so he's rich. He can probably afford the price of a can of weed killer."

"He can get jealous. Joe came to our place uninvited when we were having a party and poured a can of beer down the inside of Everest's piano."

"That doesn't show much imagination. I would have tossed in a carton of eggs. And barfed up my lunch as a chaser. OK, we're blaming Joe for the vandalism until a better candidate comes along. I may have to deck him when I see him."

"He's very large and built like an opera singer."

"OK, I may have to chastise him severely."

Since Trent wasn't loaning us his private jet, we juggled Almy's flight reservation to get adjoining seats in first class. If you get really famous, you have to fly first class because otherwise your fellow passengers will wonder what you're doing back in coach. It's another toll you face as part of the Price of Fame.

Almy asked me what I wanted to do on our trip to New York.

"I want to go dancing at Studio 54 and take in the floor show at the Copacabana."

"OK, Nick. And we can visit Barnum's Museum, do some shopping at Lord & Taylor, spend a day at Coney Island's Luna Park, and tour the New York World's Fair. How about a ride on the *Hindenburg*?"

"Sounds good to me. And I want Andy Warhol to paint my portrait."

After Almy left I texted Dad, "Moving 2 NYC + living w/Almy. Agent Zach 2 rent MV house."

He texted back, "WTF. Serious?"

I replied, "Yes."

He replied, "OK. Thanx 4 update."

Texting can really streamline family life.

Then I called the New York rental agent that Almy had used before. I told her what we needed and our price range. She said she would line up some listings for us to view on Saturday.

I didn't have to go pick up my Caddy. I paid extra to have it delivered. The tire people also washed it, which was appreciated.

Then Ramon showed up and demanded to know what

was happening with my tarped front yard. He said it will have to be rototilled and reseeded. I told him to go for it.

Then I phoned Kinsley and told her I was blowing town with Almy Preston.

"What about your house, Nick?" she asked.

"I'm renting it to my agent. He's having an affair with the gal next door."

"The one you were dating?"

"All the complexities in my life are getting ironed out."

"Sounds like that means I'm getting kicked to the curb as well. Thanks for letting me know, Nick. Have a good time in New York."

She didn't sound bitter, which was a relief. I would have stuck it out with that girl if Almy hadn't reappeared. We only did it one time, but in no way was it a one-night stand.

WEDNESDAY, August 10 – Almy spent the night again. My B.P.D. fear of abandonment really kicks in when she sleeps elsewhere. Being a fast reader, she finished my book on narcissism. She said the insights gained would be helpful in "dealing with future boyfriends." I said I hoped to minimize her need for such diversions.

I'm not thrilled that she's done it with a variety of guys. I was her first (as she was mine), and we should have stuck with that program. But who am I to talk? We've both experienced a representative sample, which should satisfy our curiosity in that area. At least I hope so.

Almy won't be here tonight because her grandparents feel a sick need to monopolize her time. Also they want to finish watching "Over the Monastery Wall" with her. No, I'm not invited. I think we should have a kid fairly soon just to make Trent Preston a great-grandfather. That will teach him for slighting me as an unworthy Twisp.

I talked to Zach over my backyard fence. We were both sipping our morning coffees. He was yawning because he had to get up at 2:01 a.m. and relocate to Carli's guestroom. He will be moving into my place on September 1. Also, he's been talking to the Brits. They are so hot to have me back they're willing to consolidate all my shoots.

"So they'd only need you for two and a half weeks in November and three weeks in January," said Zach, stifling a yawn.

"That sounds doable," I admitted.

"Good, because I already gave them a yes."

"I'll need the scripts in advance so I can learn my lines."

"They said they'd send you the scenes well in advance. You're making a wise career move here, Nick."

"By going back to England?"

"Yes, and by hooking up with Almy Preston. Having her on your arm can only improve your profile in this town."

"We happen to love each other, Zach. We have for years."

"So much the better, Nick. Carli thinks you're a shit, but I can deal with her."

Almy was fine with my U.K compromise deal, although I'm not so sure that Samuel F. Broughton would approve.

Almy and I drove to Chatsworth for lunch with the Frank C. Wyatts. Her portrait was coming along nicely. Frank is depicting Almy dressed for the Depression with the fishing village in the background. The likeness so far was spot on.

"What's that murky shadow?" I asked, pointing.

"That's Teejay," replied Frank.

"Make sure he stays murky," I said.

Seka made pašticada, a kind of Croatian version of stew. Her bratty kid avoids ethnic dishes and had a hotdog instead.

Since we were discussing exotic cuisine, Almy said that she bought a book on Egyptian cuisine and had been experimenting on Everest. I very much hope he has downed his last Egyptian meal. Almy's Egyptian mother may be cooking up something special for us on Sunday. I plan to exchange my plate at the last second with another diner.

It was kind of an expensive lunch. I wrote a check to Seka for $50,000 and also gave her the ten gold coins from my oatmeal box. Would it be tacky of me to demand a refund at some future date if Nick Twisp Wyatt doesn't turn out to be college material? The fact that I'm funding his college education hasn't made my short nephew any friendlier.

THURSDAY, August 11 – I had a farewell coffee with Cal in Venice this morning. I decided to forgive her for trying to wreck things with Almy. In her own way that just proves she cares.

"So when are you leaving?" she asked, picking listlessly at my muffin.

"Tomorrow."

"For good?"

"No, I'm just going there to find an apartment. Then I have to return to pack up my stuff."

"Densely packed cities are horribly dangerous in pandemics, Nick. There's still plenty of Covid around."

"We'll be taking all the precautions."

"If you rent a place on the 19th floor, be sure never to take the elevator. Those claustrophobic boxes are hotbeds of contagion. It's like you're having sex with every passenger in the car."

"OK, that tip will save me having to join a gym."

"As if you ever would. So who am I supposed to have coffee with now?"

"You could make friends with your sister-in-law. And Desmond is getting out of jail soon. Or, there's your brother."

"You must really, really hate me."

"I think you know that's not true. How's Clive Mc-Gregor?"

"Kind of skittish around me lately. I think someone reminded him that he's married."

"Possibly it was his wife."

"So when are you lovebirds tying the knot?"

"I'm taking it day by day, dear. I've learned marriage is not something you rush into."

"Yeah, that's why my bridal gown is still gathering dust in my closet. I expect it will decay and fall to pieces on the hanger as I wither into a wrinkled old crone."

"You'll probably get married before I do," I assured her.

I told her about Maya's evolution into a tire-poking, gut-smashing Latino dude.

"She was semi-normal until she started sharing a house in Westwood with Almy. And now you're heading down the same road, Nickie. I hope you don't wind up dressed as a crazy woman and bugging tourists for spare change in Times Square."

"If I do, you have my permission now to stage an intervention."

"I very much doubt I will care about you at that point. What did Almy think about your paying me for sex?"

"She felt your services were a bit overpriced."

"I'm sure in her world two bucks would cover it all, with some change due to the customer."

"Let's not get catty, dear."

"Hey, buddy, she started it. Where does she get off stealing my boyfriend?"

"Meaning me?"

"I saw you years before she did."

"True, but you never got around to applying your brand to my hide."

"I may grab you again on the rebound. But then, I may not."

We left it at that. I gave her a farewell hug, but turned my head when her lips approached. You never know what can wind up on social media these days. And I was too far along with Almy to blow it all now.

I was nuking my lunch when my ex-wife phoned.

"I hear you're moving to New York," said Luco.

"Only for about a year."

"You want to rent us your house?"

"Sorry, dear, I already rented it to my agent."

"Oh. Can I ask what you're charging?"

"Two grand a month."

"That is so cheap. Are you marrying Almy?"

"I hope to someday. We'll see."

"She was always the love of your life, Nick."

"Uh . . . no comment."

"OK, I won't keep you. Have a nice trip."

"Thanks, dear."

Almy and her luggage got dropped off here by her granny. Trent was busy elsewhere. Probably off sulking in a Massive Snit. I was amazed when Apurva took me aside and confided that she prefers me to Everest. She said that pianist "is much too pleased with himself." She had spent some time with the cad last summer in Canada.

Generally, we Twisps (except for Teejay) avoid that syndrome. The world reminds us frequently that we have plenty of room for improvement.

My new driver's license arrived just in the nick of time. Now I can travel to New York as Nick Davidson, which matches the name on my new credit card. Too bad in my license photo I look like a criminal wanted in six states on child molestation charges. No sign of my replacement passport yet.

We walked to a nearby Peruvian restaurant for dinner. It's scary how convenient Mar Vista is to everything. Almy assured me that Manhattan also offers such amenities. She asked me how many times I'd been to NYC.

"Uh, approximately zero," I replied.

"You know, Nickie, you really won't be seeing New York at its best in August. Many people try to get out of town this month."

"I'm expecting urban hell at its most dystopian."

"It's not that bad. And autumn is really nice in New York."

"I hated fall in Indiana."

"Why's that?"

"It was followed inexorably by winter."

"Don't forget, Nick, you get to spend most of November and January in England."

"Yeah, right. A country on the same latitude as frosty Labrador. I'd rather spend them on the beach in Tasmania with you, darling," I sighed.

No final Mar Vistian sex tonight. Almy got her period. Apparently, there are no Twisps, Davidsons, McGregors, or Weedens on the way.

FRIDAY, August 12 – Travel day! An Uber car hauled us to LAX. The driver pretended he didn't know his passengers were famous, so I scrimped on his tip. I was afraid the TSA guards would take me aside for a strip search or swift trip to Guantanamo, but we made it through security fairly fast. Almy got noticed by our fellow passengers in the waiting area, but everyone was cool. No one yelled out, "Hey, Bronson! Where's Jade?"

You lose three hours flying to New York even if you're in First Class. The flight was fairly serene. I for one felt pampered. No stops were scheduled in weird places like Denver or Terre Haute. I finished my Steinbeck book. Donna Reed never showed. I'm assuming Samuel F. Broughton was signaling that I should be open to new travel experiences.

When we landed, it became apparent that New York had switched on the heat and humidity blasters. You'd think the gods of weather would save some of that heat to spread around in December. Our luggage arrived eventually and we took a cab to Almy's apartment. I was assured that Everest was still away at music camp (and likely balling Marcie Florin nightly).

The apartment was bigger and nicer than I expected. For example, the toilet was not next to the kitchen stove, but housed in a separate room with the other bathroom fixtures. Only one bedroom, but the living room was large and there was a separate dining room that a certain twit was using as a music studio. Thankfully, Almy went around first thing taking down photos of the happy couple. She also switched on the window A/C in the bedroom. If that thing ever lost its moorings, it would kill some unlucky pedestrian three flights below.

The piano was the largest upright I had ever seen. Extreme hernia-bait in carved ebony wood. I lifted its lid and sniffed. A definite beery aroma wafted out. Propped above the keyboard was a composition in progress. Fortunately, Everest—unlike Mozart—labors in pencil. While Almy was in the bedroom unpacking, I erased notes here and there, and sprinkled on quite a few at random. I'm sure I improved the score immensely.

Almy phoned out and had pizza and salad delivered. I paid.

"What do you think, Nick?" she said.

"About the pizza or your apartment?"

"Take your pick."

"The pizza is excellent. The lettuce got a little tired on its journey from Salinas. I think it went by Greyhound bus. The apartment is OK. We can do better. Did you change the sheets?"

"I did. All traces of Everest have been removed from sight."

"Good. Just don't expect me to get anything up in there."

"I had a life, Nick. And you were married."

"I know, darling. I'm just kidding. Everything is fine. What time do the gunshots start up?"

She laughed and kissed me. My first kiss ever in the Big Apple.

SATURDAY, August 13 – Scary thought: tomorrow I'm having dinner in Hoboken with Almy's parents. All in all I wish they'd stuck to their original plan and moved to Lisbon, Portugal. We could visit them once a decade or so.

To chip away at the urban heat, our bedroom A/C ran all night. The compressor chugged away, drowning out the sounds of the city. Sort of like the ocean sounds we hear in Mar Vista except here the tide is forever rolling in and never receding. You wake up knowing in your bones that the pace of life is relentless in New York.

I had kind of a restless night. I don't do well crossing time zones. Plus, I was expected to sleep in a bed where another guy had been boning the woman I love. Also, there was the ever-present fear that a roach would try to visit my brain via my ear canal. Hey, it happened to me before.

While I took a shower, Almy went down to the bodega on the corner to pick up supplies for breakfast. That's what you do here instead of driving to the supermarket. The only cereal in the cupboard was raisin bran.

"Who eats this stuff?" I asked, showing Almy the box.

"Everest."

"Does it make him fart?"

"Like standing next to a tugboat exhaust."

I returned the box to the cupboard and stuck with toasted bagels.

Our real estate agents were a mother/daughter team. Mom showed us the places, while the daughter drove the car and went off to "park" between apartment tours. Good luck on that task. Then her mother phoned for her to pick us up, and she would (usually) be waiting double-parked out front. We looked at five places, mostly in the west sixties. This appeared to be an area sandwiched between Central Park and the Hudson River. Possibly an affluent area, but New York is such a jumble it's hard to tell.

I told Almy the clear winner was the place on West 64th Street. It was big, came with two bedrooms, had a modern kitchen, the bathroom was tiled up the wazoo, there was a rooftop terrace with city views, and many floors below was secure inside parking for my Mustang. The location was a short three-block walk to Almy's snooty school. There was even a nifty little park across the street for walking our nonexistent dog.

"You really want to pay $11,500 a month in rent?" asked Almy.

"That's only $9,500 if you subtract the two grand a month I'm getting for renting my house," I pointed out.

"And you really think you need a car here?" she asked.

"New Yorkers may not need cars, dear, but I'm a Californian. We need to feel mobile. Like Neal Cassady, we have a constant itch to drive."

"Neal Cassady was from Utah," our agent pointed out. "From Salt Lake City. I was born there too."

While she and Almy discussed what had brought her to New York, I filled out the application form. The agent assured us that the management would be thrilled to have Amalda Preston residing in their building. How they would feel about me was left unsaid.

Mother and daughter were nice enough to drive us back to Almy's apartment, which I've deduced is more on the east side of town. No way she had been walking to school from here.

There was a surprise waiting for us when we entered. Everest was back and looking pissed.

"God dammit, Maldy!" he bellowed, very red in the face. "I can't believe you brought this fucking interloper into our home!"

The twit calls her Maldy?

"Why aren't you at your music camp?" demanded Almy. "It's supposed to run until next week."

"I wanted to see you, darling," he said, making a move to embrace her. Almy backed away.

"Don't touch me!" she commanded. "I'm going into the bedroom to pack. You stay here! Nick, if he follows me into the bedroom, call 9-1-1."

Everest stood by the bedroom door and glared at me. I glared back at him. He muttered curses under his breath. I made an effort to look blasé and unconcerned. He said something in French. Possibly unflattering to me, but I'm unable to note it here since I don't speak the language. Then he reverted to English.

"Maldy, I can't believe you went back to this excrescence," he yelled. "This guy is a nothing! He couldn't even handle college! He's a pantywaist! A void in the ether! A wind would blow him away! He looks like an Okie from Muskogee! I bet he's heavily tattooed in disgusting places!"

No reply from the bedroom.

OK, I'm fairly slim. I have zero tattoos. Also I had passed through Oklahoma a few times, but that was the extent of my experience with that state.

Everest ranted on. "I can't believe she could prefer such an obvious loser to me. I really don't see the attraction. Hey, buddy, what college did you flunk out of?"

"I dropped out of UCLA when Covid arrived. But I also got into Rutgers."

"God, I am *so fucking* impressed."

I felt a change of topics was called for.

"How's Marcie?" I inquired.

"None of your fucking business, asshole."

"Be-em-ef-es-you," I muttered.

"What did you say, you fucking loser?"

"You heard me."

That useful expression still stands for Both Middle Fingers Straight Up.

Everest sneered at me, strode over to his piano, sat down, and played an exceptionally loud and bombastic tune. OK, the guy can play the piano. Big deal. I can operate an Italian espresso machine.

In no time, Almy had packed her two rolling bags. Since I had barely unpacked, I was ready even faster.

"Don't go, Maldy," cried Everest from his piano bench. "Let's talk this over. It's not too late! We mean so much to each other. God dammit! I love you!"

"I'm moving out, Everest," Almy replied, coldly. "I'll call you to arrange a time to retrieve my things. I left your ring on the bathroom sink. I suggest you look into getting a roommate. You won't have my grandfather subsidizing your rent anymore."

We didn't travel that far. We walked down the block and around the corner to a boutique hotel. On the way I asked Almy how Everest found out she was back.

"We know most everyone in the building. Someone must have called him."

Another reason not to get overly friendly with your nosy neighbors.

The hotel was thrilled to have Almy Preston residing in one of their swanky suites. The desk clerk, being something of a T-DOG fan, even recognized me.

"Is it true that you're related to Teejay Twisp?" she asked.

"Yeah, he's my half-brother," I admitted.

"My boyfriend thinks Teejay is some kind of CGI cre-
ation. You know, all done with computers."

"No, he's an actual kid. He was precocious right from
day one."

I for one appreciated the change in venue. The A/C was
more effective and virtually silent, the décor was more upscale, room service was a phone call away, and no one (to
my knowledge) had been boffing Almy in the giant bed.

We embraced, kissed, and Almy asked if I planned to
drive my Mustang to New York.

"Only if you come with me," I said. "Otherwise, I'm
shipping it by truck."

"That might be fun," she replied. "I'll have to think
about it."

"All the greats take cross-country road trips," I pointed
out. "It's a rite of passage for us Americans."

"Stuart Dunham already has made two trips this summer, Nick. Does that make him great?"

"It makes him a nut case, and you know it."

The pristine bed was so inviting, we had a pleasant nap
with benefits. Later, we went down and had sushi in the
hotel's Japanese restaurant.

So far, except for boorish Everest and the humidity, I'm
not minding New York that much.

SUNDAY, August 14 – The hotel offers its guests a breakfast buffet on their rear garden terrace. The weather gods
had backed off on the thermostat, so it was pleasant sitting
there nibbling treats and drinking excellent coffee. Actual
birds were chirping in the modestly sized trees. Scruffy pi-
geons were loitering about and eyeing my plate.

Almy had some news.

"Nick, I've decided I love you too much to subject you
to my parents at this time. My father would be a trial by fire
and my mother would be worse. Everest really knew how to

suck up to those two. He had them completely charmed."

"I haven't always treated you right, darling. I'm sure I'm due some abuse by them."

"You went to France without your passport to get me back my life."

"That's another reason your parents despise me, but I was happy to do it. I'm ready to face your ever-formidable and snarling mother."

"Nevertheless, I'm cancelling dinner tonight."

More good news that a guy can use. Plus, I believe she laid the L-word on me.

"What religion are you?" she asked.

I gave it some thought. "I guess I'm a non-Catholic Christian."

"I think those are called Protestants, Nick. What is your denomination?"

"I'm not sure we had one. I think Aunt Grace was an Episcopalian."

"You know my friend Olivia?"

"I've heard you talk about her, dear. Is she an actor or a musician?"

"She plays the harp."

"Really? I didn't know anyone did that anymore."

"Yeah, she has to lug around a heavy instrument and hardly gets any gigs, but she loves it. She lives in Providence. Her father is a Unitarian minister. How would you feel about getting married by him?"

"That sounds like a great idea!"

"OK, I'll call her this afternoon."

"Why don't you call her now?"

Any delay could be problematic at this point.

"It's Sunday morning, Nick. I expect they're busy now."

Right. Being devout like that must really cut into your weekends.

"What have you got to be married in, Nick?"

"Not much, dear. I didn't really pack for formal occasions."

"Olivia's brother is about your size. We may be able to borrow something from him. And I expect she can dig up a dress for me."

"We'll need some rings, dear. Is Tiffany's open on Sunday?"

Almy looked it up on her phone.

"The one on East 57th Street opens at 11. But we could go someplace less expensive. I don't need anything too gaudy."

"Let's go there, dear. We don't need to scrimp."

I felt our ring-buying experience should be a step up from my previous one in a pawn shop in Barstow.

We returned to our suite, and Almy called her parents. Not a pleasant conversation from the sound of it. She said we were driving up to Rhode Island to visit friends and would see them when we got back. Marital plans were not mentioned.

Then we cabbed to Tiffany & Co. to look at rings. We got the full VIP treatment. Almy picked out a semi-modest diamond in a platinum setting and I got the non-sparkly groom's version. Under ten grand for both, which was better than I expected. They even threw in little plush boxes as a bonus. No breakfast items were served.

By then it was past noon, so Almy phoned Olivia. This conversation was much livelier than the one with her parents. Some exclamations and squealing transpired. A plan got hammered out. We're to drive to Providence today, stay with Olivia, and apply for the license tomorrow. Her dad knows everyone in the license department, so he'll go with us to expedite matters. If all goes as planned, the marriage will take place tomorrow afternoon in his church. No medical exam is required in that state. I guess Rhode Island doesn't care these days if folks are hollowed out from syphilis.

We cabbed back to our hotel, and I rented a car at the front desk. Fancy hotels provide services like that. From the choices offered I selected a Mustang, as I was already trained on its infotainment screen.

We packed our bags again and checked out, also making reservations for our return on Tuesday. Then our car got delivered, and we headed off in heavy New York weekend traffic.

Neither of us had been to Providence. Almy's phone said it was a bit less than 200 miles, and would take about three and a half hours to get there. We crossed some bridge and went through Brooklyn and Queens. Lots of dead people buried in vast cemeteries, reminding motorists that it's all over way too soon.

"You didn't really ask me, Nickie," said Almy.

"Ask you what, darling?"

"To marry you."

"Oh, right. Almy dearest, would you please do me the honor of becoming my wife?"

"I'll certainly think about it. Thanks for asking."

"Good. Try to make up your mind by the time we get to Rhode Island. And just for the record, I believe I've bugged you to marry me many times in the past."

"True, sweetheart, but you were doing that with lots of girls back then."

I realize Almy may be marrying me just to punish Everest for his treachery, but I'll take her anyway I can get her.

Note to self: Since I'm getting married, I should check with Kinsley's dad to see if we'll qualify for larger tax deductions by filing jointly. (Not that I care.)

Just past New Haven we stopped for snacks and a tinkle.

Cal had gone to college in that town briefly. It looked rather grim from what I could see from the freeway.

Almy's friend lives in East Providence, a burg across the Seekonk River from Providence. Their rambling clapboard house adjoins the old brick church where Rev. Britto is the dude in charge. I'd say his church is a century or two older than most any building in L.A.

We arrived and got descended upon by the whole family. Yeah, Olivia's mother showed me her tube of Gunslinger lipstick, but I'm used to that these days. Her shade was called Perjury in Divorce Court. Rather racy stuff for a minister's wife.

Dinner was grilled lobster on the church patio. I thought those critters always got boiled, but I guess not. Washed down with beer, which continues not to excite my taste buds. Olivia's brother Todd—soon to be a senior at East Providence High—aspires to be a pianist like that other twit. He plays the organ for his dad's church services. He's loaning me his black suit, which his sister says has been worn to countless funerals.

Kind of an intense kid, Todd was disappointed to learn that I wasn't nuts about Radiohead, his favorite band. I said I preferred Spark, which he characterized as "extremely progressive, albeit kinda fringe."

We're bunking in the guestroom in the basement of the church. Two twin beds and a compact bathroom across the hall. First time I ever slept in a house of God. Pleasantly cool down here. Visiting ministers often stay in this room. Also wives seeking refuge from violent husbands.

Needless to say, we'll be passing a celibate night.

MONDAY, August 15 – Nick Davidson's Third Rule of Love: NEVER GIVE UP.

At least I'm consistent. I always aim to get married in August. Makes it easier to remember one's anniversary.

We had a spot of trouble at city hall. The clerk wanted to see our birth certificates, which neither of us had brought. We both had our passports and driver's licenses, but mine featured two different names. I explained I was reverting to my birth name for family reasons. Fortunately, we had a respected local there as an advocate, plus Almy was famous. Nobody doubted who she was. We paid our $24 and got our license. Almy insisted on paying half the fee. She's investing some actual dollars in this marriage.

The wedding was at 2:00 p.m. The word had gotten around, so quite a few parishioners showed up. Olivia played the harp and her brother manned the organ. A retired parishioner named Omar snapped some wedding photos.

Olivia's uncle Fred escorted the bride to the altar. Then Todd trotted over to serve as my best man. Almy looked beautiful in a borrowed long dress. Sort of a faint rose color. In my black suit, I looked like an apprentice undertaker's assistant. Reverend Britto said the sober words and we repeated our vows. We were both pretty shaky, but we got through it OK. Getting married is a big deal, even if you've done it before.

The reception was on the church patio. Snacks, drinks, and even a multi-layer wedding cake materialized from somewhere. Quite a gala celebration compared to my first wedding. I drank many glasses of champagne and so did my bride. Many toasts were offered. Then Todd brought out a giant boombox and subjected everyone to his exotic mix tapes.

At one point Olivia sat beside me and remarked that I didn't seem at all like Bronson Flange.

"He was just a character I was playing," I replied. "Eyebrow shaving is not really my thing."

"I hope you don't hate me, Nick."

"Why would I hate you?"

"I'm the one who introduced Almy to Everest."

"That was a severe stab in the back, dear, but we may be able to get over that speed bump."

We heard some distant booms of thunder, but the rain held off until most everyone had left. Then it poured. The party continued in the house for several more hours, then we retired to our basement love nest.

"That was a pretty nice wedding," I said, removing my tie.

"The best one I ever had," Almy replied.

"Me too," I said, embracing her.

"It seems I have a husband now. I got a call from that agent when you were in the bathroom throwing up. We got that apartment."

"Great. And I wasn't throwing up, dear. I was just waiting for my stomach to settle. Too many champagne bubbles were fizzing in there. I hope in the morning I don't wake up and discover this has all been a dream."

"I hope not too, because I think news of our wedding has gone out on social media. I had to switch off my phone."

"Probably wise, dear. I've done the same. How pissed off will your parents be?"

"I doubt we made their day."

"Oops, and I neglected to clear my marriage plans ahead of time with my dad's wife. I told her I always would consult her first."

"So I guess we're both in trouble."

"Fortunately, we got married for ourselves and not for anyone else. You're the wife who has to live with me."

"And you're the husband who has to live with me. Good luck on that deal."

We kissed and retired to one narrow bed as the wind whistled through the old church above us.